RIVAL SECRETS
A Whispering Pines Mystery, Book Five

Shawn McGuire

OTHER BOOKS BY SHAWN MCGUIRE

WHISPERING PINES Series
Missing & Gone (prequel novella)
Family Secrets, book 1
Kept Secrets, book 2
Original Secrets, book 3
Hidden Secrets, book 4
Rival Secrets, book 5
Veiled Secrets, book 6
Silent Secrets, book 7
Merciful Secrets, book 8
Justified Secrets, book 9
Secret of Her Own (novella)
Protected Secrets, book 10
Burning Secrets, book 11
Secret of the Season (novella)
Blind Secrets, book 12
Secret of the Yuletide Crafter (novella)
Wayward Secrets, book 13

HEARTH & CAULDRON Series
Hearth & Cauldron, book 1

GEMI KITTREDGE Series
One of Her Own, book 1
Out of Her League, book 2

THE WISH MAKERS Series
Sticks and Stones, book 1
Break My Bones, book 2
Never Hurt Me, book 3
Had a Great Fall, book 4
Back Together Again, book 5

RIVAL SECRETS
A Whispering Pines Mystery, Book Five

Shawn McGuire

Brown Bag Books

This book is a work of fiction. Names, characters, places, and events are products of the author's imagination or are used fictitiously. Any resemblance to actual events, locales, or persons, living or dead, is entirely coincidental.

All rights reserved. In accordance with the U.S. Copyright Act of 1976, the scanning, uploading, and/or electronic sharing of any part of this book without the written permission of the publisher is unlawful piracy and theft of the author's intellectual property. Thank you for supporting the author's rights.

Copyright © 2018 Shawn McGuire
Published by Brown Bag Books
ISBN: 9781728859842

For information visit:
www.Shawn-McGuire.com

First Edition/First Printing October 2018

For my Villagers.
You all mean the world to me.
xoxox

Chapter 1

THE WOMAN'S BODY LAY FACE down on the Fairy Path, halfway between The Twisty Skein and Ivy's Boutique.

"You found her?" I asked Violet.

"No." Violet shook her head, staring at the woman with a deep frown. "Ruby stopped by the Bean Grinder to get a chai on her way to open the Skein."

"Open?" I asked. "That would've been before seven in the morning. Isn't that kind of early to open a craft store?"

Violet turned her attention from the deceased woman to me, one serious eyebrow arched. "You're very literal this morning, Sheriff Jayne. Ruby said she was on her way to work. I assume she planned to open at nine like always. By 'open,' I meant she would perform her opening procedures. I don't know her schedule. Maybe she does paperwork at seven in the morning."

I nodded, duly scolded. In the case of a death, especially one in Whispering Pines, anything out of the ordinary, no matter how minor, set off my instincts.

"I can't believe she's dead." Violet stared again at the body. "It's Gin, isn't it?"

Long, coppery-red hair covered the victim's face, but

there was no doubt in my mind of her identity. That hair made Ginger "Gin" Wakefield instantly recognizable.

Wakefield, head baker and owner of Wakefield's Treats and Sweets and former Whispering Pines villager, had come to the village to celebrate Mabon Fest. The villagers who had known her twenty years earlier were thrilled that she and her staff of celebrity bakers were coming for a visit. However, not everyone had been happy about her return. Sugar, the owner of the village sweet shop, had been childhood rivals with Wakefield. For Sugar, the woman's return was bad enough. When Wakefield entered the festival baking competition, the competition Sugar was determined to win this year, unhappy didn't begin to describe Sugar's reaction.

"I think we're safe to assume it's Gin," I told Violet. Other than to check for a pulse, I couldn't touch the body until the medical examiner got here, so assuming her identity was all we could do.

"It's going to be busy this weekend," Violet mused, gaze once again locked on the body. "Just like every year, we start relaxing after Labor Day and bam, Mabon Fest. Then we relax again and bam, Samhain."

"You were saying that Ruby found the body?" I asked, getting her back on topic.

"Right, sorry. Yes, Ruby knows we have a walkie-talkie at the Grinder, so she ran back over and asked me to contact you."

Because cell phone coverage was non-existent in the village, I had distributed walkie-talkie units to various businesses. That way my deputy and I could always be reached should an emergency happen. And they happened on a regular basis around here. Strange for a place so small.

"Where is Ruby now?"

Violet turned her back to the dead woman. "She was really upset, you know, shaken up over finding a body. I told her to go to her shop and that I'd watch over the woman until you got here." She indicated the short pine-green apron still around her waist. "I left the shop so fast I was halfway here when I realized I forgot to take this off."

"We need to keep people away from this area," I told Violet. "Deputy Reed is on his way, but until he gets here, I need to stay with the victim."

"What do you need me to do?" Violet asked, instantly ready to help.

My mind started formulating a to-do list as I glanced east along the Fairy Path toward Ruby's shop. Through dappled shadows cast by the early morning sun, I could just make out a small white blur a few yards past The Twisty Skein. The blur was Meeka, my West Highland White Terrier and K-9 deputy. She was standing like a security guard in the middle of the wood-plank pathway that wove through the grove of pine trees. As we'd walked this way from the sheriff's station, Meeka had become agitated by the scent of the corpse. Since the body was out in the open and I wouldn't need her help searching for it, I posted her there. Happy to have a job, my K-9 was ready to refuse passage to anyone who might try and come this direction.

"First," I told Violet, "I need people stationed at both ends of the path to make sure no one comes this way."

Violet flung a hand toward the commons. "My brother is covering that end."

"Who's manning the Grinder?" Ye Olde Bean Grinder, the village coffee shop, was always packed in the morning.

"It's not that busy yet. Villagers mostly. Lily Grace is keeping an eye on things until one of us gets back. She can't make specialty drinks, but there's a big carafe of regular blend she can use to refill cups. She also knows how to ring up a scone."

"Lily Grace?" The teenager was more talented than most

when it came to telling fortunes, but she wasn't always the most responsible with other aspects of daily life.

"She's been hanging out with us every day after school for the past week or ten days. Not sure why she came in so early today. Must've had a late night of studying and needed a caffeine hit. So, you want me to take over for Meeka?"

"Please. I also need to speak with Ruby."

"I'll stop in the craft shop first and tell her to come see you."

"Perfect. Thanks, Violet."

That was one complication out of the way. There was a bigger question before me now: Had a friendly baking competition really ended in murder? A possible killer came to mind immediately. It couldn't be her, though. Sugar wasn't a killer. Was she?

Chapter 2

THREE DAYS EARLIER

THE WHISPERING PINES WICCANS WERE positively giddy. Mabon Fest, or Harvest Fest as it might be called elsewhere, was about to start. For the village, the fest signaled the close of the summer tourist season. For the village's green witches—those who were skilled with plants—Mabon was the time to begin harvesting any fruits, vegetables, and herbs still in their gardens before the first heavy frost came and killed it all. Here in Wisconsin's Northwoods, frost could come at any time now. Mabon was also the time to complete any remaining business, reflect on the year that had passed, and prepare for the coming long, cold winter.

Whether referred to as Mabon, the Autumnal Equinox, the first day of fall, or simply September twenty-second, the thing I liked best about it was more scientific than reflective: it was one of two days of the year when sunlight and darkness were balanced. Twelve hours of each on equinox days.

When I'd come through earlier in the day, a team of green witches was busy transforming the commons area. They started by removing all plants past their prime in the pointed sections of the huge pentacle-shaped garden. In place of the waning plants, they set out bales of hay, cornstalks, and fifteen-foot-long cornucopias they had handwoven from pine branches. The cornucopias overflowed with pumpkins, squashes, apples, gourds, and anything else harvest related.

"That's what the cornucopias are for." I stood next to Morgan Barlow on the deck of her Wiccan/New Age store, Shoppe Mystique. "Anytime I asked about them, they told me to wait until Friday."

Morgan pointed vaguely to a spot off to her left in answer to someone's question and replied to me, "Sometimes it's more fun to discover something slowly and on your own."

"I'm the sheriff. I discover things on my own all the time. Believe it or not, I'm okay with people volunteering information sometimes." I scanned the crowd to make sure Meeka wasn't in anyone's way and spotted a small spunky woman supervising the troops from ground level. "Briar's here too?"

"Of course she's here. Despite Mama's reclusive tendencies during the rest of the year, you can barely keep her home during Mabon Fest. The crisp fall air invigorates her. There's no way she would miss out on the festivities this week."

"Everything looks amazing. Are you almost done?"

"I believe we are." Morgan pulled her black shawl embroidered with black moons and stars tighter around her shoulders. "Just a little more and our portion will be complete. Then Mr. Powell and his team will come in and set up picnic tables."

"And then we eat?"

Morgan smiled. "Yes, Jayne, then you can eat."

The Wiccans might treat the week-long fest as a time of reflection, but for visitors, it was a foodie paradise. What better way to celebrate a harvest than with a week of eating? Tourists could eat, drink, and take part in a variety of activities from seven in the morning until seven at night; sunrise to sunset.

I nudged Morgan's arm with my elbow. "This really is your favorite time of year, isn't it? You're absolutely glowing."

She exhaled a happy sigh. "Part of it, yes, is Mabon. The other thing is, at the conclusion of the fest we have the next eight months to live the other sides of our lives. Well, there are two days for Samhain, October thirty-first and November first, but that gathering will be half the size of this one." She took hold of my upper arm and squeezed. "I can hardly wait for you to experience Whispering Pines without tourists. Or with minimal tourists. We're seldom tourist-free."

Honestly, I was a little nervous about the minimal-tourist time. I lived my entire life in Madison, Wisconsin, which meant I'd always had plenty of people around me. Neither my boyfriend Tripp nor I were sure what to do with ourselves for those eight months. The villagers all had established lives outside the summer season while we had only been here four months. We'd been talking about renovating the attic of our house and turning it into an apartment for Tripp. Other than that, what would we do during the frozen-tundra winter? Hobbies. We both needed hobbies.

"You and Tripp will be fine," Morgan assured while straightening the silver rings on each of her fingers.

I narrowed my eyes at her. "What makes you think I'm thinking about Tripp?"

She just smiled in that witchy way of hers.

While the green witches were doing their thing with the Pentacle Garden, a few yards away a cluster of kitchen witches had gathered.

"They look just as excited as you all do," I noted.

"The other side of harvesting our crops," Morgan said, "is

using that bounty. As much as my sister green witches and I enjoy seeing the fruits of our labor come to completion at this time of year, the kitchen witches are just as excited to showcase their cooking and baking talents."

The aromas that had been wafting around the village for the last week or so had been making me crazy. Those villagers competing in the food competition had been practicing their recipes for baked goods and savory meals. As the village sheriff, I had a reputation for being impartial, therefore people had been coming up to me throughout the week to sample their creations. Good thing my cargo pants had elastic inserts at the waist because I was going to put on some weight before Mabon was over.

I put a hand to my stomach. "I can hardly wait. I'm going to go see what the mini-coven over there is up to."

"Blessed be," Morgan sang out after me.

Violet and her brother Basil were standing outside Ye Olde Bean Grinder with Honey and Sugar, owners of the village sweet shop, Treat Me Sweetly. Violet and Basil were not strictly kitchen witches. They both had incomparable talents when it came to brewing and blending coffee, but since coffee was technically a plant, that put them into the green witch category as well. Guess that made them green kitchen witches.

"Why do I feel like this gathering could be trouble?" I asked.

"Because you're the sheriff," Sugar replied, unamused with my attempt at a joke. "You're suspicious of everyone all the time."

Honey swatted her arm. "Sugar and I were getting Violet's and Basil's opinions on our entries for the baking contest this weekend."

I waited, breath held in anticipation. "Are you going to tell me what they'll be?"

No one responded.

"Can I at least get a hint?"

"You can wait like everyone else," Sugar snapped.

"Sorry." Honey gave me a look that was part stern schoolteacher, part mischievous schoolgirl. "As they say, loose lips sink ships."

"But Violet and Basil know," I objected.

Violet wiggled her fingers in front of her mouth; her version of locking her lips and throwing away the key. I'd get nothing out of her.

"Come on," Sugar barked at her sister and turned away, "let's get back to work. Competition is going to be tougher than ever this year, and I want to win."

We watched as the sisters walked toward their shop along the red brick pathway that circled the Pentacle Garden. When they were far enough away that they couldn't hear, I asked, "What's wrong with Sugar? She seems even crabbier than normal."

"And that's my cue to leave," Basil said. "Half an hour of that discussion was more than enough for me."

"What discussion?" I asked Violet. Not to say she was the town gossip, because she never repeated things with ill intent, but Violet had a way of knowing things before anyone else.

"Didn't you hear?" She looked side to side as though preparing to reveal state secrets to me. "Gin Wakefield and her crew are coming to town."

"As in Wakefield's Treats and Sweets?"

Wakefield's was one of the biggest commercial bakeries in the country. You name it, they made it, and they made it well. Cakes in every size from tiny cake pops to cupcakes to multi-tiered creations large enough for thousands. Any variety of cookie, pie, or candy. Last I heard, they were looking to break into the ice cream business as well. Gin Wakefield and her employees, each of them celebrity-status chefs, would surely cause a stir when they got here.

"Why are they coming here?" I asked.

"Didn't you know?"

"I probably wouldn't ask if I did."

Violet grabbed my arm and pulled me inside the Bean Grinder. "Come on in, sit for a spell, and I'll fill you in. Would you like to sample the Drink of the Fest?"

Like I had passed up a sample of anything even once this week. "Of course. What is it?"

"In honor of all things warm, cozy, and autumn-like," Violet announced, "I'm making chai lattes with your choice from a variety of different milks. Would you like soy milk, almond milk, coconut milk, or fat-free or full-fat cow milk?"

Took me half a second to bypass the healthier options. "Give me that fully fatted cow."

"Regularly spiced or with a hint of added chocolate?"

"Is that a legitimate question?"

She grinned and handed me a bag of dog biscuits for Meeka. "Chocolate it is."

We waited near the fireplace for Violet to come with my fat chocolate chai. I chuckled to myself, that was a pretty good name.

"How about a scone to go with it?" Violet called from behind the counter.

I just blinked at her this time.

"You have four options. Would you like a traditional Cranberry Orange, made with cranberries fresh from the bogs down in Warren? Cinnamon Apple Oat made with apples from our own orchard? Earl Grey and Honey, made with honey harvested by our resident beekeeper? Or Sweet Potato and Browned Butter?"

"Where did the sweet potatoes come from?"

"Sundry. We don't grow those here. Peyton orders bushels of them for Honey and Sugar this time of year. Sugar just dropped off dozens of each kind so she can pay attention to her competition creations. That means you've got to eat them while they're here because she won't be making more until after the fest."

"Well, I'd hate for anyone to accuse me of playing FAVORITES, so give me one of each."

A few minutes later, Violet set my beverage and plate of scones on the table in front of me and settled into a chair with her own drink. She cleared her throat importantly and in an announcer's voice said, "Ginger 'Gin' Wakefield grew up in Whispering Pines."

My jaw dropped. "Gin Wakefield was a villager? When did she leave? *Why* did she leave?" I sat straighter, feeling a bit of pride in knowing someone that famous grew up in our little village.

"Long story short, Gin is obviously a very strong kitchen witch. She and Sugar used to get together after school and on the weekends and come up with their own creations."

I held up a hand. "Hang on. You weren't here when Sugar was young. I assume this is what you've heard through the years?"

"It is, but you know I always do my best to ensure accuracy. Anyway, Gin and her mom moved here when Gin was twelve or thirteen, and she and Sugar became close friends. Everything was fine until Gin's mother decided she wanted to open a bakery. She went before the council with her proposal, but since Treat Me Sweetly was already up and running and doing really well, the council denied her."

"I can only imagine how well that must've gone over." I held my mug up to her. "This fat chocolate chai is amazing, by the way."

Violet bowed her head in thanks. "Cute name. And no, the decision did not sit well with Gin's mother. Especially because Honey and Sugar's parents were on the council and she had considered them to be friends." Violet sipped from her own drink. "After that, Gin wasn't allowed to associate with Honey or Sugar anymore."

"It's understandable there would be hard feelings, but that seems a little harsh."

"The way I heard it, the village was divided on the vote. Some thought another bakery was a great idea. Others were fine with what they had. Fast forward a few years and the girls are in high school. At the time, the rules of Mabon Fest stated that sixteen was the minimum age to participate in both baking and cooking. Now it's thirteen."

"Let me guess, a rivalry developed between Sugar and Gin."

"Rivalry is putting it very lightly. The two became fierce competitors. It got worse after they graduated high school and went to the same culinary school."

"No," I gasped. "Why would they do that to themselves?"

"Because they were determined to best each other, I guess." Violet perched on the edge of her chair. "My understanding is that Gin graduated two points higher than Sugar and took the top spot in their class. After they graduated from culinary school, Sugar obviously came back here to run Treat Me Sweetly. Gin traveled the world, working in the best restaurants and studying under world-class chefs. Fast-forward a little more, Gin's award-winning bakeries in Chicago not only led to a line of top-selling commercial desserts, she was offered a multi-million-dollar contract for a line of kitchen equipment as well."

I swallowed a sip of my chai. "I heard about the kitchenware. It looks like good stuff. Does Gin come back for Mabon fest every year?"

"No, if I'm remembering right, it's been a good ten years since she's been here."

I pondered that while choosing a scone to start with.

"Didn't that line of kitchen products just come out? Like right before Christmas?"

"Yep. They advertised it everywhere. Online, in magazines, on television. I think I even saw a billboard with her logo." Violet shook her head, amazed. "That was one massive campaign."

"If you're right about the rivalry, is it safe to assume this might be a rub-it-in-Sugar's-face visit?"

Violet frowned. "I hate to say it, but I think we should be prepared for some Whispering Pines drama."

I slumped back into my chair. Great. Just when I thought we'd hit the time of year when the drama would slow down.

Chapter 3

AFTER FINISHING HER BISCUITS, MEEKA took a power nap while I drank a second chai and nibbled my scones. Not sure I could pick a favorite. The cranberry-orange was tart and sweet. The tea-and-honey soothing. The sweet-potato-and-butter would be good with a pork chop dinner. The apple-cinnamon almost like a dessert. I put half of each one in a parchment bag to bring home for Tripp—I seriously had to get a handle on all this sampling—then we said goodbye to Violet and Basil and headed back to the station.

We'd only gone a few feet along the red brick path when we saw Honey and Sugar coming out of Treat Me Sweetly to meet with Reeva Long. Reeva was another highly talented kitchen witch. Wonder what she'd say about the Sugar/Gin situation?

Normally, I'd think nothing of three villagers standing and chatting. Wouldn't even notice it, in fact. But just as the three came together, roving reporter Lupe Gomez froze in her tracks and hovered near a bench at the edge of the Pentacle Garden with one ear turned toward them.

"There must be something juicy going on." I startled Lupe, making her jump. "You didn't even hear me coming up on you. What's the scoop?"

"Oh, Jayne, good. Stand here with me. I might look suspicious by myself."

"Spotting suspicious behavior is my job, and I can verify, you definitely look suspicious. What are you doing?"

She held a finger to her lips and whispered, "I'm not sure what's going on yet. All I heard was something about the baking competition."

"And you decided—"

"*Shhh.*"

"And you decided," I repeated in a whisper, "that meant there must be a story?"

She made a face at me. "If you spin it the right way, there's a story in everything." She turned an ear toward the trio and leaned closer.

Lupe had been in Whispering Pines since just after Memorial Day weekend, writing articles about the village and its villagers for the online magazine that sent her here. Originally, her assignment was only supposed to last until the end of Labor Day weekend, but since we had article-worthy events going on past the standard summer season, she got an extension until after Halloween. At the time, the extension had thrilled her. It meant she had more time in the village she'd become fond of, but more importantly, it gave her more time with my deputy, Martin Reed, the man she had become more than fond of. Now, the thought of leaving was even harder for her than it had been before.

Just then, Sugar demanded, "You too?" The question directed at Reeva. "There's no reason for me to even enter. I may as well just be a vendor. I'll go make more scones, set up a table, and sell to the tourists."

"Sugar, don't say that." Honey did her best to soothe her sister. "You know you can bake with the best of them."

"I certainly didn't intend to upset you," Reeva told Sugar.

"The best competitions happen when the entrants are equally matched. It's no fun for anyone when one person dominates. Besides, how can we measure our own skills if we don't go up against worthy opponents?"

Reeva stood, silent and expectant, waiting for Sugar's reply.

"Fine," Sugar responded after a long moment. "You better go warm up your spatula, then. I intend to win this."

"Game on." Reeva gave her a wink and a grin.

Lupe turned to me, eyes wide with excitement. "See what I mean? There's got to be a story there. What do you suppose that was all about?"

"If I had to guess, I'd say that Sugar is feeling threatened."

"Threatened? Why would she feel threatened?" She scribbled something in her pocket-size notebook as she walked with me along the Fairy Path.

I let Meeka's leash extend all the way, so she could explore as we headed to the station to get my SUV and go home. Lupe kept pushing for more, so I told her there was a history between Sugar and Gin Wakefield.

"So that's it." Lupe jotted down something else. "People have been buzzing about her coming to the village. Sounds like this could get juicy."

While her English was very good, every now and then, Lupe's accent amused me. Like now when "juicy" came out "*you-see.*"

"Where are you getting *you-see-ness*? All I said, literally, was that there's a history between them." In fact, knowing she might use my words in an article, I purposely said nothing more than that. Lupe quoting what I said Violet had heard from others who may or may not have been here at the time? What could possibly go wrong with that?

"Oh, come on." Lupe's black-brown eyes sparkled. "You heard Sugar. She wants to win this. Throw Reeva and now Gin

Wakefield into the mix? Sounds like there will be some serious competition in the baking division. I'll have to pay special attention to that side of the contest."

"Let's hope things don't get nasty. This is supposed to be a friendly competition."

"I'm okay with nasty. An article about a friendly baking contest isn't likely to make the front page. But a hometown showdown between an unknown villager and one of the country's most beloved bakers?"

"I've got to hand it to you, you do know how to spin things."

Meeka darted from one side of the Fairy Path's wooden walkway to the other to play with a squirrel running our way with a mouthful of pine boughs. But when the squirrel stood on its back legs, front legs held up in a wide V, Meeka yelped and jumped back on the walkway.

I turned to see Lupe with camera in hand. She showed me the image on the tiny digital screen, and we both laughed at the look on the little Westie's face.

"Jayne, there's something I wanted to ask you."

Sounded serious. "Sure. What is it?"

"It has to do with me staying in Whispering Pines."

"Staying? Did you get another extension? That's fantastic. How long is this one?"

"No, I didn't get an extension. I want to know, what do I need to do to become a resident?"

"Did you talk to Reed ... to Martin about this?"

"Not yet. I wanted to wait until it was a real possibility. You know how twitchy men can get about relationships moving forward."

True. Tripp, however, would be thrilled. I was the one holding back in our relationship.

"You can stay as long as you want as a tourist, you know."

"I know, but that means renting a guest cottage or hotel room. That would get very expensive very quickly. Fortunately, my articles have been popular, so it's been worth it for my employer to pay for me to stay. Once this assignment is over, I'm on my own."

"You really like it here that much?"

She blushed. "I like Martin that much." She gave me a shoulder bump. "And a few other people as well."

The first time I met Lupe, I thought she had an angle. To me, and Tripp too, she didn't appear to respect the villagers. She seemed excited to interview them and write stories about them because they were different. Some of the carnies, for example, were the stereotypical freakshow freaks on the outside, and I worried that she wouldn't see how beautiful they were inside. The more I got to know Lupe, though, the more I realized that wasn't true. I'd read all her articles. Never once was she anything but respectful. Honestly, I'd miss her if she left.

"Well," I began, "you'll have to come before the village council to get permission to stay. Having a job here is ninety percent of the battle. As in, you have to get someone here to hire you."

"That's it?" Confidence radiated off Lupe.

"That's it. That simple and that hard."

The council—comprised of business owners, Original villagers who'd been here since its inception, and me—was determined to not let the village become overpopulated. Since I had become a member in early June, no one had approached us about moving here. To my knowledge, Tripp was the last person to even ask. They denied him because he wasn't "odd" enough. He could, Morgan told me, fit in anywhere. The rule was simple, a person had to have a legitimate problem to live in Whispering Pines. That could mean something like being ostracized for religious beliefs or a physical disability. I had been the exception. My grandparents, and now my family, owned the village land. The council had no say in how long I stayed here. Tripp finally got to stay because I hired him to work for me.

"What about opening my own business?" Lupe asked. "Would that be considered a job?"

"It would, but that's an extra hurdle. You'll have to convince the council that your business will bring value to the villagers. We're having a meeting tomorrow morning. It's an early one. We're starting at five thirty." I groaned just thinking about it. "If you can have a presentation ready for us, I'll make sure you get on the agenda."

Her smile both warmed my heart and broke it a little at the same time.

"Put me on the agenda. I'll have a presentation for you. Thank you so much, Jayne."

I was about to tell her that just because I agreed to let her present, it wasn't a guarantee that even I would approve her proposal. But she had already scurried off.

Chapter 4

FINALLY HOME FOR THE NIGHT, I took a few minutes to run upstairs to my apartment over the boathouse, give Meeka some food and water, and change out of my uniform and into jeans and a T-shirt. Then I crossed the backyard to the main house where I found the great room empty but heard plenty of grumbling coming from the kitchen.

There, Tripp Bennett, my boyfriend and business partner, glowered at something on his laptop screen while scribbling in a notebook sitting next to it on the granite counter. He also had open cookbooks scattered across the kitchen island.

"What's going on here?" I asked. Tripp was the cook for Pine Time, our B&B, and always kept a tidy kitchen. To see it in disarray was surprising, to say the least.

He looked up at me with an expression of pure desperation. "Gluten-free."

"I'm sorry?"

"As if it wasn't stressful enough having to make breakfast for Gin Wakefield and her employees—"

"That's why the name was so familiar," I blurted and slapped my hand down on the counter. "Other than the obvious reason, of course. Everyone's been talking about them, and they're staying here. In our bed-and-breakfast."

Tripp blinked at me. "Right. I told you that a dozen times."

I shook my head. "You just called them the Wakefield party. You never said it was *Gin* Wakefield and her chefs." I stood a little taller. "Makes me feel kind of swanky to know we've got celebrities staying with us."

"Can we focus on my panic for a moment?"

"I'm sorry. Of course we can. What about gluten-free?"

"The other guests, the ones not here with the Wakefield party, are gluten-free. They never mentioned that when they made their reservations." He scrubbed his hands over his handsome face. "We have to make sure we cover dietary needs when booking people. Will you add that to the online reservation form?"

"Sure. You always put out plenty of fruit every morning. That's gluten-free, right?" I thought for half a second. "Eggs are too. You make good eggs."

He gave me the same look my mother used to give me when she felt I wasn't "cooperating."

I frowned at his scowl. "What's wrong with fruit and eggs? Add in coffee and juice and that's a fine meal. Oh, bacon is gluten-free. That's a very hearty breakfast."

"Will you be serious, please? We've discussed this before. Half of a bed-and-breakfast experience is the breakfast. I can't give our guests eggs, bacon, and fruit and expect that that will be enough."

I *was* being serious, but Tripp was trying to develop a reputation for serving upscale breakfasts, and my suggestion wasn't even close to upscale. I gestured to all the books laid out on the island in front of us. "You're looking for some gluten-free options? Is that what all this is? Can I help?"

His shoulders dropped with relief. "Yes to the first two questions, and please to the last. I need to come up with something for tomorrow morning."

"Don't bite my head off for this, but do you have to serve breakfast? I mean, they're here for a food fest. The commons area is going to be packed with food for twelve straight hours each day for a week starting tomorrow morning at seven. Actually, I believe sunrise is six forty-something. The fest opens with sunrise and shuts down at sunset. Can we get away with giving them something light to last them from here to there?"

"You mean a continental breakfast instead of a buffet?" Tripp considered this before answering. "We might be able to, but we should really ask them about that when they check in. Our website specifically says full buffet breakfast. Either way, the food has to be quality, and we'll need gluten-free muffins or pastries of some kind for a continental spread."

"Let's find some options, then." I glanced through half a dozen recipes in one of the cookbooks he had laid out and in minutes realized gluten-free was complicated. "I don't even know what some of these ingredients are. Do we have any of this stuff?"

"No. I called over to Sundry and talked to Peyton. He said he's got all the different flours—almond, coconut, rice, and potato—and something called xanthan gum, which is listed on a lot of these recipes. He also told me he keeps these things off the shelf and only sells them to people who ask for it."

"Why does he do that?"

"Because people are equating gluten-free with healthy. Gluten is a protein found in some grains. Eliminating it is only a health concern if you have a gluten intolerance like celiac disease. I'm sure that people who have a true intolerance are thrilled with all the options on the shelves now, but it's a serious health thing, not a trend."

The more Tripp learned about food, the more passionate he became.

"It's kind of sexy when you get all worked up that way." I traced a finger across the knuckles of his clenched fist resting on the counter.

He tried to remain serious, then broke into a smile and gave me a quick kiss. "I really need to focus on this."

"All right. I'll behave."

For the next hour, we searched through his cookbooks and websites and came up with ten different recipes he felt comfortable trying. He'd just started putting together a shopping list when we heard the front door open and a group of people walk in. Pine Time had been open for business for a month, and I still had to stop myself from yelling at people for walking into my home without ringing the doorbell. At least I was stopping myself now. The first few guests I had scolded were worried they were staying in a crazy person's home.

In the foyer, I found six people looking around and exclaiming about what a beautiful house it was.

"You must be the Wakefield party," I greeted. "I'm Jayne O'Shea, owner of Pine Time."

A woman with coppery-red hair that draped past her shoulder blades and a huge blinding-white smile spun toward me and held a hand out like she was there to close a business deal. "Ms. O'Shea, what a true pleasure to meet you. I'm Gin Wakefield."

Working for the Madison Police Department before moving here, I'd met a few celebrities. Most of them were from the political world and not instantly recognized by that many people, but to me, anyone who was regularly in the public spotlight qualified as a celebrity. Gin Wakefield's face was not quite as familiar as her name, which was on every product she sold, but a thrill still rushed through me upon realizing who this effervescent woman was.

Mid-forties, five foot seven, ivory skin, medium-blue eyes, round build but not overweight. She wore a small black hip pack with a red first aid cross on it around her waist. Was Gin Wakefield diabetic?

"Ms. Wakefield, the pleasure is mine."

Her smile softened, and she shook her head as she wrapped my hand in both of hers. "I knew your grandparents. I'm so very sorry to hear about what happened to your grandmother. Lucy was a woman who, I must admit, intimidated me as a child. But as I grew older, and especially after I opened my own business, I realized how strong she was. It took me years to understand that she had become a sort of silent mentor to me and that I had modeled myself after her. No-nonsense, always considering what was best for the majority first. Hers is a true loss."

While I was still thrilled to meet the woman, I had to say the initial sparkle faded quickly. She seemed pleasant enough, but her admiration of and eulogy-like words for Gran seemed forced, as did her smile. It's not that I doubted her words, but they felt rehearsed, as though she had prepared to say them to a camera instead of just me. I suppose that happened when someone was in the public eye so much.

"Thank you," I said. "I appreciate your words. I assume these are your employees?"

"They are. This is my A-team." She beamed and proceeded to introduce everyone starting with the two men. "This is Kim Robbins, my Chief Financial Officer."

Mid-forties, five foot nine, two hundred fifty pounds, medium-brown skin, cropped black hair, neatly trimmed goatee.

Professional in jeans and a sports coat, Kim was a big guy. He might do a little too much sampling of the products, though. I suddenly regretted those four half-scones.

He held up his cell phone. "Wi-Fi password?"

"I'll give it to you with your room key," I promised.

"This is Leif Forsberg," Ms. Wakefield continued, "our head pastry chef."

Mid-twenties, lean, five foot seven, sandy-blond hair pulled into a frizzy ponytail, full patchy beard. Leif seemed eager to please, standing just behind Gin as though waiting for her to make a request so he could fulfill it.

Meeka came around the corner, sat directly in front of me, and stared from person to person like a drill sergeant inspecting her troops.

"This is Latoya Craig," Gin continued. "She creates all of our award-winning specialty recipes."

"Specialty recipes?" I asked the woman with choppy short black hair, black plastic glasses, and a variety of tattoos running the length of her right arm. "Does that include gluten-free items?"

"It sure does," Latoya said with a raspy voice and touch of attitude. "Are you gluten-free? Thinking about it?"

Thinking about it? Tripp's words about gluten not being a trend echoed in my head.

"No," I answered. "I'll eat pretty much whatever you put in front of me. Unfortunately, the guests who just checked in to two of our rooms are gluten-free, and we weren't aware of it. My partner and cook, Tripp Bennett, wasn't prepared for that. He found a few things to try but ..."

"I'd be happy to give him some pointers," Latoya offered.

"I'm sorry to interrupt." One of the group members, a woman in black athletic leggings and a black jacket, stepped forward. "I haven't been feeling well for the last hour. I think it's something I ate when we stopped for lunch."

"Sonja," Gin said, "you're still feeling ill? I'm so sorry, why didn't you tell us? Jayne, Sonja is our cake designer. Would it be possible for her to go right up to her room?"

"Of course." I indicated the sitting room to her right. "There's also a half-bath down the hallway on the left, just in case. Go on in and have a seat, and I'll get your key right away."

"The company is paying for the entire weekend," Gin said. "Kim will go with you and take care of the charges."

I did a quick inventory of the group. There were six of them, and they had only reserved five rooms. "Were two of you going to share a room?"

"I told her time and again," Kim said, staring at his phone as though expecting it would magically connect to the internet, "that Leif and I could share a room, but Ginger wouldn't hear of it."

"This is a sort of celebratory weekend for us," Gin explained. "We've had such a wonderful year, I wanted to reward them all for their hard work. In fact"—she waved over a mousy woman still standing by the doorway—"this is Mandy."

The young woman awkwardly raised a hand as her cheeks flamed red. "Misty."

"Misty is one of our dishwashers," Gin continued without missing a beat, as though forgetting the name of one of her A-team members was no big deal. "A kitchen certainly can't run without clean dishes, so we appreciate Misty's service greatly. We had a sort of lottery for the kitchen staff, and Misty won. She gets to enjoy the weekend with us as well. Anyway, I want everyone to have their own space to relax, so no sharing rooms. After all, that is what Mabon is all about. Time for rest, relaxation, and reflection."

"I take it you're Wiccan." I remembered a second later that I already knew the answer to that question.

"Used to be." She held her head high, and her smile left her eyes. "I was the best kitchen witch they'd ever seen around here."

I waited for the megawatt smile to return or something else to break the sudden tension surrounding her, but it seemed she meant every word as well as the attitude attached to them.

"We still haven't worked out the room situation," I stated. "We have one too many people."

"I will be staying at The Inn," Gin announced. "I'm sure everyone will be very comfortable here, and I will be equally so in the village. I'm anxious to reunite with some of my old friends."

With that, Gin Wakefield handed everything over to Kim Robbins, spun on her heel, and left with a little royal wave to her people.

Chapter 5

ONCE KIM HAD GIVEN ME the corporate credit card number and everyone in the Wakefield party had their keys and room assignments, I went back to the kitchen to see if Tripp had finished putting his shopping list together.

"I have no idea if this requires a special touch or not," he said of his gluten-free pastry recipes, "but I guess the best way to learn is to give it a try."

"One of our guests is a specialty baker." I told him about Latoya. "I asked if she would give you some tips, and she said she'd be happy to."

"That's great." He relaxed a degree. "In the meantime, I have to go over to Sundry and pick up the ingredients. Would you like to come with me?"

"Is it sad that I think that sounds like a date request?"

"Not sure. I was thinking the same thing."

While I ran up to my apartment to get Meeka's leash, Tripp checked in with our guests to make sure they had everything they needed before we left the premises. We met at his rusty old pickup truck in the driveway.

"Do you ever think about getting a new truck?" I asked when the passenger's door gave a horrendous screech as I closed it.

"Sure. I think about getting one with lots of power and more paint than rust. But right now, I like not having monthly car payments more than I want a new truck."

At Sundry, the village's grocery store, which was half old-world market and half wild west general store, the owner, Peyton, met us at the checkout counter. Peyton was like a Zen drill instructor. His bald head gleamed, giving him the appearance of wearing a halo, but his sometimes-gruff manner caught many people off guard. When he smiled, though, deep soft crinkles around his eyes and across his sun-weathered face made him look like a marshmallow of a guy.

"I pulled out everything I had in back." Peyton showed Tripp the contents of two cardboard boxes. "Test out your recipes and let me know what works and what doesn't. My staff takes care of day-to-day items, but if you put together an order of your favorite ingredients by late-October, I'll make sure you have all the specialty items you need to last the winter."

"The winter?" Tripp asked. "Are you going somewhere?"

"I am." He set the items Tripp didn't want on a counter behind him. "Much as I love this village, by the end of Samhain, I get a case of wanderlust that about drives me crazy. It's a big world, and I need to explore as much of it as I can while I'm here."

"That's great," I told him as I examined the bag of xanthan gum.

"Best of all, if I combine my travels with searching for new items for the store, I can write it off as a business expense." He pointed to a basket at the end of the counter. "Last winter I went to Peru and found those beauties."

"Purple potatoes." Tripp picked up a few of the long, thin, cylindrical vegetables. "I've heard of these. Never had one, but I hear they're supposed to be healthier. I didn't realize you carry these here."

"If you took time to look around the food section when you come in," Peyton began in that patently brusque way of his, "instead of only hanging out in the home improvement section, you'd find that we carry a lot of unique items."

Peyton gave me a wink and smiled. The marshmallow man returned.

"I'll do that from now on," Tripp promised. "I've been so focused on getting the B&B up and running, it was easier to order from the online restaurant supply place. I'm clearly missing out. Why don't you give us a couple pounds of those? I'll make some for breakfast tomorrow."

"Remember, you do live in Whispering Pines." Peyton weighed out three pounds of the purple spuds. "Any shop that doesn't have a quirky factor doesn't belong in the village."

"Where are you headed this year?" I asked and handed him Pine Time's credit card.

"Slovenia. I understand they've got some amazing cheese there."

With our boxes of gluten-free ingredients secure in the back seat, covered with a blanket to keep Meeka from nosing around in them, we headed for home. We were almost to the west-side parking lot, when Tripp mentioned stopping for dinner.

"That really would make this a date." I grinned at how something so simple made me suddenly so happy. "Where do you want to eat?"

"I couldn't tell you the last time I ate at Triple G. How do you feel about bar food?"

"I could eat bar food."

We had to park in the public lot since motorized vehicles weren't allowed in the village and then walked hand in hand the half-mile to the pub.

Grapes, Grains, and Grub, the village pub, was about half

full tonight. Most of those diners were inside due to the autumn chill in the air, but Tripp and I knew winter would be blowing through soon enough and wanted to enjoy every minute we could outside. After dropping Meeka off in the dog yard, a fenced in area set up for customers' canines, we asked to eat on the deck.

Maeve, the owner, overheard our request and sat us herself. "I've got the perfect spot for you."

She led us through the large building that used to be a residential cottage. The wall between the original kitchen and dining room had been knocked down to make a bigger kitchen, and every other room had been converted into a dining area. We walked past one with only tables for two which made for a more private or romantic setting. A larger room with tables of different shapes and heights scattered about had a festive atmosphere. Still another room held a twenty-foot-long dining table that the hostess filled with random customers. In that room, diners started their meals as strangers and by dessert were friends.

Triple G's outside eating area easily doubled the pub's dining space. The massive deck had multiple layers which we climbed and descended as Maeve led us to the farthest corner. There, we came to a dining platform that was elevated by six steps and tucked into the surrounding pine trees.

"We call this the love nest." She handed us each a menu.

"It's perfect," Tripp said as she flicked on the outdoor heater. "Thanks, Maeve."

"You didn't get the chance to meet Gin Wakefield yet, did you?" I asked Tripp after we'd placed our orders and had received our beers.

"I know that tone. What do you think she did?"

"Nothing. She's just … interesting." I told him about the rivalry between her and Sugar and how Reeva entered the baking competition as well.

"Sounds like more same old, same old Whispering Pines stuff to me." He held my gaze as he sipped from his stein. "Are your instincts tingling?"

He knew me so well. Among the many tools I had at my disposal as sheriff—my deputy, my K-9, my Glock, handcuffs, etc.—possibly the biggest was my intuition. If I listened to that, many times I didn't need any of the other tools.

"They are. I don't know what or why, but she set something off. Maybe it's that I'm not used to dealing with celebrities." I waved a hand in the air as though erasing a whiteboard. "Enough shoptalk."

The next two or so hours flew by as we ate juicy burgers, drank great beer, and talked about where we would go if we structured our lives the way Peyton did. If we closed Pine Time for the month of February like we'd been talking about, there was nothing stopping us from heading down to Peru and searching for our own purple potatoes.

~~~

The next morning, I went over to the house for breakfast early. Normally, we had a quiet breakfast together before I left for work and he opened the buffet at seven thirty. There was a council meeting at five thirty this morning, however.

I entered the great room through the back-patio doors a little before five and stopped cold when I found Leif and Kim already awake and sitting on one of the couches, both poring over cookbooks. Guess even when on vacation they couldn't get away from food. "You two are up early."

"We're bakers," Leif said. "Well, Kim isn't. Normal start time for us is four a.m. Sleeping in until four thirty was a luxury."

"Latoya was up at her regular time." Kim flipped a page in the book he was holding. "She's been helping your partner make muffins or rolls or something."

I gave them a wide-eyed stare. "Are you saying that Tripp got up at four o'clock?"

Kim nodded, and Leif grunted, "Yep."

The kitchen was, once again, a disaster. This time, instead of cookbooks, the ingredients for gluten-free creations were scattered everywhere. Tripp and Latoya stood on the other side of the island, Tripp listening intently to every word she said.

"Xanthan gum is a thickening agent," Latoya said. "It also acts as a stabilizer, which keeps ingredients from separating."

"Couldn't I just use cornstarch?" Tripp asked.

"For some things, yes. Cornstarch needs to be heated for it to thicken so is good for things like sauces. With xanthan gum, you just add it and it does its job. Both are gluten-free."

Tripp scribbled that in his notebook as I paused next to him on my way to get a mug of coffee.

Distracted, he placed a quick kiss on the corner of my mouth and mumbled, "Morning," as he handed me a small plate filled with various muffins and pastries. "Try these and let me know what you think."

Just that fast, his attention was back on his instructor. Looked like I wasn't getting breakfast with my boyfriend this morning.

With my plate of gluten-free goodies and mug of coffee, I rejoined the others in the great room.

"Are those Tripp's cookbooks or yours?" I asked of the unfamiliar books scattered across the coffee table. I popped a bite of a cranberry muffin in my mouth. If I didn't know it was a specialty item, I never would've guessed. It was really good.

"Gin bought them when we stopped in Milwaukee on the way here," Leif explained.

"She's always looking for the next new thing for the stores." Kim glanced at Leif and rolled his eyes. Leif responded with a knowing grin and turned back to the book in his lap. "Sometimes it's a food item. Other times it's a new kitchen gadget to re-create, improve upon, and add to our lineup. Regardless, her mind is always in business mode."

"Unless she's baking," Leif added, eyes still on the book. "When she gets in the baking zone, nothing else matters."

While there was nothing wrong with any of their statements, there was an underlying dissatisfied tone attached to them. A baker being in the zone should be considered a good thing. Leif almost made her sound more like a tyrant than a focused employer.

"It must be interesting working with food at that level." I popped a bite of a cinnamon pastry into my mouth. It was okay but not as good as the muffin. "Tell me about the bakery business."

For the next ten minutes, I listened while Leif explained a normal day for him as the head pastry chef. He was obviously passionate about food, but to hold a top position with Ginger Wakefield at only twenty-five, he had to be talented too.

"Why are you looking through cookbooks, Kim?" I asked. "I thought you were the CFO?"

"This is an assignment handed down by the boss." His expression was initially annoyed, and then he added with a resigned sigh, "And I'm a team player."

I was about to ask what the assignment was, but as I glanced across the room, I saw Misty, the back-kitchen employee, sitting by herself in the corner by the window. She was so quiet and clearly so good at disappearing into the woodwork, I hadn't even noticed her there. I excused myself and went over to her.

"Everything okay?" I asked.

"Oh, sure." She gave me a big smile, exposing a mouth full of horribly crooked teeth. I hoped Wakefield's offered their employees good dental insurance. "I'm just taking in the lake view. It's so pretty here. And so peaceful compared to Chicago."

"I've been to Chicago a number of times. Madison is big city enough for me." I sensed a reason other than the view for her to be in the corner. "Must be a little strange being the only non-chef in the group."

Her smile turned grateful, and in a low voice, she acknowledged, "You have no idea. When I first found out that I had won this trip, I was super excited. To come up here and stay in your beautiful bed-and-breakfast sounded like a lot of fun. Now, I kind of wish I would've asked if I could bring a friend." She glanced at her fellow employees. "Other than working in the same kitchen, I have nothing in common with them."

"You're not planning to move up the ranks?"

Meeka came over to us and sniffed at my plate of pastries. I held my hand palm out to her, the signal to stop, and she dropped to the floor with a huff.

"No, this is just a job," Misty replied. "It pays for my textbooks."

"You're a student? What are you studying?"

"Human resources." She glanced at Leif and Kim again. "It was an interesting car ride up here. Kim, Leif, Latoya, Sonja, and I rode up in the company van. Ms. Wakefield drove her own car." She went mute for a moment and frowned. Remembering the ride? "Anyway, I got to hear the grumblings of the upper-level employees."

"By the look on your face, I'm guessing being part of the upper crust isn't always so great." I realized what I just said. "Food-related pun not intended."

Misty laughed and then agreed with me. "We're never happy with what we've got, are we?"

"Speaking of your fellow co-workers, is Sonja still sick?"

"I'm not sure. I was going to let her sleep for a while and

then check on her."

"We've got a decent clinic in the village. They can't handle major problems, but a stomach bug should be easy enough for them to tackle. Let us know if you think she needs help. Either Tripp or I can tell you how to get there."

Misty nodded in a way that said she had more to say on the topic, so I waited.

"It's a little strange," she finally said, "this food poisoning of Sonja's. She and Latoya had the same thing when we stopped for lunch. Latoya isn't sick, and I don't remember Sonja eating anything else during the ride." Misty shrugged, dismissing the thought. "What do I know about food poisoning? I'm just a dishwasher."

A dishwasher who noticed a lot. Once again, my instincts started to tingle. I would've loved to sit and talk with her more, but I had to get over to the council meeting. I stopped in the kitchen hoping for a proper goodbye from Tripp, but he was still captivated by whatever Latoya was telling him.

I managed to get their attention long enough to say, "No to the cinnamon pastry, yes to the cranberry muffin, and a big yes to the cheese Danish."

For that, I received a, "Thanks," and a quick kiss on the cheek.

This day was starting out strangely. And around here, that couldn't be a good thing.

Chapter 6

CONTINUING WITH THIS MORNING'S THEME of nothing going as it usually did, Emery wasn't at the front desk when I got to The Inn. I couldn't remember a single time I'd come here and hadn't seen him at his post. On top of that, the boardroom was empty. Was I really the first one to arrive? I glanced at my watch. I was only ten minutes early; at minimum, Flavia should be here by now. It was standard procedure for her to be the first one anywhere. That way she could complain about everyone else being late. Guess five thirty was too early even for her. Unless I got the day wrong.

I'd been pacing around the boardroom for maybe a minute, debating how long to wait for the others, when Lupe appeared in the doorway.

"I'm here," she announced, breathing hard like she'd run from her rental cottage a mile away. "I stayed up late into the night and have a proposal ready for the council."

Sure hoped I got the day right, then.

"I can hardly wait to hear it." I stopped her before she could start giving me her spiel. "Don't tell me anything. I really should hear it with everyone else. Have a seat out in the lobby, and I'll come and get you when we're ready."

"But can I just—"

I shook my head, and Lupe frowned as she turned and went to wait out front. A second later, Sugar appeared.

"You have no boxes," I noticed. "Where are the scones? We always have scones."

I should have paid attention to the look on her face before I asked. I knew she'd been in a mood yesterday regarding Gin Wakefield. Today, she was flat-out snarly.

"You want something to eat?" she challenged like a parent who had reached her limit with her demanding kids. "Mabon Fest opens in ninety minutes. Then you'll have all the food you can eat for twelve straight hours."

Okay, don't talk about food.

"I met Gin Wakefield yesterday," I began cautiously and immediately wondered why I thought that was a better topic.

"And you're still alive to talk about it? I'm surprised she didn't chew you up and spit you out. Do yourself a favor and have Morgan help you with a spell to repel that woman. The further away she is from this village the better."

I gave her a minute before asking, "I know there's some bad blood between you two, but isn't it the Wiccan way to forgive and forget or turn the other cheek or whatever code you all live by?"

Sugar's eyes narrowed. "I know Violet gave you her version of my history with Wakefield when you were in the Bean Grinder yesterday. Did she mention how that woman stole the valedictorian spot at culinary school from me by two points?" Sugar held up two fingers and stuck them in my face. "Two points!"

I understood why Sugar was upset, but unless Gin did some "special favors" for the right instructor, she probably earned the spot fair and square. Thankfully, I kept that thought sealed tightly behind my lips.

"She told me," I confirmed.

"And then she calls her business Wakefield's Treats and Sweets. Does that sound familiar to you at all?"

I hesitated, unsure if I was really supposed to answer.

"Treats and Sweets?" Sugar repeated with emphasis. "Treat Me Sweetly? She couldn't even come up with her own name. I can't believe she's able to run her own company. I mean, what exactly did she have to do to earn that last contract? Did you hear about that one? The bakeware?"

Fortunately, Violet walked in at that moment with a smile on her face and a container of coffee in each hand. Maeve followed steps behind her. Grateful for the excuse to escape Sugar's wrath, I went to the cupboard in the corner, grabbed a tray of coffee cups, and set them on the table.

"Is this coffee or did you bring some of that fat chocolate chai?" I asked.

"Sorry, this is just coffee." Violet placed the containers on the table. "The chai is best made to order. Stop in later. We'll get you one."

I poured myself a cup of coffee and, bypassing a still glowering Sugar, went over to Maeve on the other side of the table. "Thanks so much for that secluded little spot you gave Tripp and me last night. I don't know if you purposely kept everyone else at the far end of the deck, but we appreciated the solitude."

"I've been keeping an eye on you two." Maeve added three sweetener packs to her coffee and stirred. "I see you around the village all the time. I see Tripp now and then. I never see the two of you together. You two need to get out more. And sitting on the deck together is not the same thing as a date."

I was touched by the matchmaking, despite the slightly grumpy delivery. Like Peyton, Maeve had a reputation for being prickly at times, but the villagers knew they could always count on her.

"Dinner was good?" She tasted her coffee and added one more packet.

"Juiciest burgers and crispiest fries I've had in a long time. And my business partner is a pretty good cook, so that's saying something."

Mr. Powell, owner of The Busted Knuckle village repair service, walked in then. Living up to his reputation of being the world's klutziest man, he missed the edge of his chair as he sat and ended up on the floor.

"I'm okay." He sprang back up, and as he reached across the table to pour himself a cup of coffee, Violet slid one over to him, preventing another mishap.

At least something was normal today.

A short time later, Cybil and Effie, the village's elder fortune tellers, entered the boardroom. The moment they saw me, they both shot matching evil eyes at me and started muttering silently.

"Have they spoken to you yet?" Jola asked as she snuck in around the two older ladies.

"I think Effie was going to last week, but then she must've remembered that Lily Grace moved in with you."

The two women had never told Lily Grace and Jola that they were sisters. Since I had unearthed their secret while investigating a death from forty years ago, they blamed me for Lily Grace leaving the Fortune Tellers' Triangle.

"How's that going?" I asked. "The roommate situation, I mean."

"Better every day. We did have one fight, but since then, it's all good. We're slowly getting to know each other."

Morgan floated in then, looking as radiant and happy as she had when I'd seen her on her shop porch yesterday.

"Blessed be, everyone. Isn't it a beautiful morning?"

"Careful," I cautioned. "You might outdo Violet in the Happiest Villager First Thing in the Morning category."

She simply smiled and settled into her seat at the table.

Balancing out Morgan's over-the-top happiness, Creed, the circus ringmaster, walked in with an uncommon hating life and everyone associated with it attitude.

"Is there even anything on the agenda today?" he asked.

"Only one thing that I know about," I told him. "Lupe Gomez has something she wants to talk to us about."

"That's it? We all dragged ourselves out of bed before the birds are awake for one agenda item? It couldn't have waited until next month?"

Flavia finally arrived, and a few seconds later Laurel walked in with a huge tray of muffins.

"Thank the Goddess. I'm starving." Morgan grabbed two of the extra-large muffins from the tray before Laurel had even set it down.

"Did Wesley make these?" Violet asked of The Inn's chef. "What kind are they?"

"They're pumpkin with a cream cheese filling and an icing sugar drizzle on top," Laurel explained. "And no, Wesley didn't make them. I did."

Sugar's eyes went wide. "You?"

"Yes me," Laurel snapped back. "You don't have to be a kitchen witch to be able to bake, you know."

While Sugar and Laurel had a crabby debate about baking abilities, and the other members helped themselves to a muffin or two, Reeva shuffled into the room, crossed to her chair, and lowered slowly into her seat, grimacing as she did.

"Are you okay?" I asked, ready to go arrest someone when I saw she also had a black eye. "What happened?"

Reeva turned as though a metal rod ran from her tailbone to the top of her head. "Ask my sister what happened."

Flavia sat straight and primly. "I have no idea what you're talking about."

"You cast a clumsy hex on me, didn't you?"

Oh geez. Woo-woo. The sisters had started battling with each other three weeks ago. Their bickering was making everyone crazy.

Reeva pointed at her blackened eye. "Not only did I run into a door and end up with this, I fell down the stairs and bruised my tailbone, and then nearly cut off my pinkie toe when I dropped a knife while making dinner last night." She held up a heavily bandaged foot as proof, wincing the entire time. "I have never in my life dropped a knife."

Creed laid his head down on the table. "It took forever to clean up after the late performance last night. All I want to do is go back to my trailer and sleep. Can we bring in Ms. Gomez and get this over with?"

Good idea. I jumped up, stepped out into the lobby, and motioned for Lupe to come in. She practically launched herself off the couch and jogged over to me.

I gave her an encouraging smile. "Go ahead. The floor is yours."

"Thank you all so much for this opportunity." Lupe looked pointedly at Flavia as she spoke. Hoping for a positive vote from the mother of the man she'd been dating for the last three months? "I'd like to talk to you this morning about me becoming a resident of Whispering Pines."

Flavia let out a little squeak. Regardless of what Lupe was about to say or do, Flavia would vote against her. She'd done surprisingly well at behaving herself since Lupe and Reed started dating, but everyone knew Flavia was holding her tongue for her son's sake until Lupe's assignment was complete.

The other council members shifted in their seats or cleared their throats or refilled their coffee mugs.

"I've done my research," Lupe continued, "and know that to become a resident, I need to have a job within the village. I already have a job that allows me to work from home so don't need to take one that someone else might need. As you know, I work for an online travel magazine. I also do freelance work, writing articles that I sell to other publications. Since I've been in the village, I've also begun writing a novel." She glanced at me with a mischievous look. "It's about a whip-smart but sometimes sassy detective who stages her own crimes and then solves them in order to be seen as the hero."

I didn't hear the rest of what she said. I was too flabbergasted by her pitch for this proposed novel. Was she serious? I had talked to Lupe one night a few weeks ago, confiding to her how upset I was about some accusations Sugar had made about me. Sugar said she and "some of the other villagers" believed the unusual number of murders in the village started when I arrived here. They didn't accuse me of committing the murders or staging the crimes, but they seemed to feel I was somehow mystically involved with them. They felt that by uncovering some nasty secrets from Whispering Pines' past, I had released some sort of dark demon on the village. To soften the blow of the horrible accusation, Sugar said they also believed I was brought here to chase away these demons and heal the village. Or something like that.

"Jayne?"

I blinked and discovered Morgan staring at me.

"Are you all right? Lupe finished her presentation. Since you put her on the agenda, you should open the floor to questions."

I glared at Lupe, furious that she would even think to turn my distress into something commercial. "Sorry. I checked out for a moment there. You want to stay in the village. Would you tell me again how you propose to do that?"

Lupe cleared her throat. "I told the members that since I already had a job, my proposal is that along with my freelance and novel writing work, I'd like to open my own business. I want to establish a village newspaper."

"Does anyone have any questions about this?" I asked, my voice tight with anger.

The members glanced around the table at each other, no one saying anything. Finally, Flavia spoke up.

"I don't have a question, but I do have a statement. You have been in the village since the start of the summer season, Ms. Gomez. You've seen it at its busiest. You also now understand what the summer season is all about. Basically, once you've seen one, you've seen them all. Other than a new batch of tourists, nothing new will happen here next summer. What could you possibly write about?"

"I interviewed a lot of villagers this summer," Lupe explained. "I haven't written all of their stories yet, but I intend to. On top of that, there are still many more people I can talk to and write about. Everyone has a story to tell, it's just figuring out what it is. I haven't spoken with you, for example."

Flavia stiffened and sniffed again. "My point is, nothing happens here from November through May. There will be nothing for you to write about."

Murmurs of agreement sounded around the table.

"My plan is to do a weekly paper," Lupe continued, "full of special interest pieces about different villagers. I'll spotlight a different villager each week."

No one responded.

"I'll also go to each home and talk to everyone. The paper will be a sort of bridge between the villagers through the winter months. Everyone seems to believe it's important to stay in touch with each other."

"And we do stay in touch," Cybil said.

"We do," Laurel agreed. "We all get together at either The Inn or Triple G every Sunday. We eat together and catch up on the past week. If anyone needs assistance with something, we talk about it and form a plan."

"I've got to agree with them," Mr. Powell said, leaning back precariously in his chair. "As much as I appreciate your enthusiasm, there really is no reason for a Whispering Pines newspaper. We already know each other. What we don't know, we ask."

Heads bobbed up and down in agreement as Lupe's hopes sank.

They were describing Whispering Pines as my grandmother intended it to be. The people here were far more connected than most communities.

"You can't possibly know everything about each other," Lupe insisted. "I can do in-depth pieces on villagers, so you can get to know each other as well as you know your own family members. That's what Whispering Pines is after all, right? A family?"

She started to offer a list of the people she wanted to do pieces on, and Effie cut her off.

"If there's something we don't know about each other," Effie said, "it's because the person doesn't want it known. There's a fine line between caring and invading privacy."

"Does anyone have anything else to add to this?" I asked.

No one offered anything.

"Okay, then," I continued, "we should probably open this to a vote." I held a hand out to Flavia across the table since she insisted on running the meetings and, therefore, calling for votes.

"Seems obvious how this will go," Flavia said with barely concealed satisfaction. "Those against Ms. Gomez's proposal of opening a village newspaper and becoming a permanent resident?"

Eleven of the thirteen board members raised their hands, signifying a negative vote. Only Reeva and I had not voted.

"Those in favor of Ms. Gomez's proposal?"

Literally physically paining her to do so, Reeva raised her hand. Lupe forced a smile of thanks and then turned to me. Slowly, her jaw dropped as she realized I wasn't going to raise my hand.

"Sheriff O'Shea?" Flavia asked. "You have not voted."

"Since it won't make a difference to the outcome," I said, "I would like to abstain from this vote."

"Very well," Flavia said. "The vote is eleven against, one in favor, and one abstention. Thank you very much for presenting your proposal to the board, Ms. Gomez, but the council denies your proposal to start a village newspaper. Since you are not employed by the village of Whispering Pines, we are also denying your request to become a permanent resident of the village until you can secure employment with one of the village businesses."

Chapter 7

KNOWING LUPE WOULD LIKELY HAVE words for me, and that those words would probably be angry ones I wouldn't want anyone else to hear, Meeka and I left the boardroom immediately and hurried to the station. There, I was pleased to find my deputy.

"Hey, Sheriff."

"When did you get here?" I took Meeka's harness off her, and she darted right for her favorite jail cell, jumped up onto the cot bolted to the wall, and curled into a ball. I'd finally gotten her a cushion and placed it in a quiet corner of my office, but when her cell was empty, she still preferred to nap in there. "I didn't expect you until later this afternoon. You'll be here all week, right?"

"Since most of my instructors are cops, they're okay with me being gone in order to back you up. Turns out, word of Whispering Pines' reputation of being a hotbed for murder has spread through the law enforcement communities. So, yeah, here for this week, but I need to be back next week for sure."

"Excellent. I'm happy you're here, but I hope there's nothing for you to do, and you can go back early."

Just then, Lupe burst through the front door looking ready for a fight.

"How could you do that to me?" Her accent was thick, her pace rapid-fire, her fiery Latin blood about to boil over. "You know how important it is to me to stay in this village. I expected you would help me." Then she saw Reed at his desk and threw herself into his arms.

After a minute of their canoodling, I asked, "Should we go into my office and talk about this?"

"I have no secrets from Martin." Her pace had slowed a little, but the accent was still heavy. "We can talk about anything in front of him."

"One of you should catch me up first." He stood and shoved his hands in his pockets. His version of putting up walls and remaining neutral. "What happened?"

"I told you I was going to ask the council about opening a village newspaper," Lupe explained. "Remember?"

"I remember. I take it things didn't go well?"

"Why don't you ask your boss?" Lupe glared at me and muttered something in Spanish.

Why did things muttered in anger in a different language always sound like a curse of some kind?

"First of all," I began, "you know my vote wouldn't have made a difference."

"You have a great deal of influence in this village," Lupe insisted. "If you had voted for me, you may have changed some minds."

Reed gave me almost the same look of betrayal Lupe was. "You voted against her?"

"I abstained."

"Which is just as hurtful as if you would have said no." Lupe frowned and clearly intending to make me feel guilty added, "I thought you were my friend."

I wanted to say that a friend would not use another

friend's distress for commercial gain. Meaning this novel she was so excited about. Now wasn't the time for that, though.

"Lupe, listen to me." Nothing I could say at this point would make a difference. Hopefully, speaking the truth would matter for something. "In all honesty, I agreed with them. You heard what they said; if you did open a newspaper, you wouldn't have anything to write about. There won't be enough going on in the winter to produce a quarterly release let alone a weekly or even monthly edition."

"You all won't even give me a chance."

"Not for a newspaper. Not in Whispering Pines." She couldn't guilt me into agreeing to something that wouldn't work. "Look, I love a good news story as much as anyone, but I'm sorry, it's just not a business that would bring value to this community. Is there something else you can do? It's not like you have one shot at a proposal. You can keep coming to us with all the plans you want. You're a smart woman. I'm sure you can figure out another way to stay here."

She didn't react, but I could tell her brain was spinning with ideas. I'm sure it was just because she was angry at me, but the look on her face made me uneasy. What exactly was she thinking?

By the time I'd finished responding to a couple emails and was ready to head back for the opening of Mabon Fest, both Reed and Lupe were gone. Great, now my deputy would be angry at me as well. I called for Meeka who stretched and yawned before trotting over to the front door.

I bent to attach her harness and asked, "You're not mad at me too, are you?"

She leaned against me and wagged her tail in response. That dog was so good for my self-esteem.

In the commons area, a crowd had gathered near the Pentacle Garden. A buzz of excitement hung in the air as they waited for the fest to officially open. On the beach by the lake between The Inn and the marina, a drum circle had gathered. Jugglers had come down from the circus and were entertaining people with their skills. Clowns circulated through the crowd doing tricks while others taught folks how to paint their faces with clown makeup. There was a tent for poetry readings and literary discussions. I wanted to check out the craft tent if I had time; they'd be holding classes on how to make cornucopias. The small kind, not the fifteen-foot beauties in the garden. Also, the fortune tellers had brought over one of their small wagons and, as always, there was a line for readings. Seated next to the wagon, Effie and Cybil were still giving me evil-eye stares. Honestly, they needed to let this go.

In the midst of the excitement, Jola called out, "Anyone entering the food competitions, please come with me."

Curious, I followed the cluster of twenty-five to thirty contestants to a spot behind Shoppe Mystique. There, Jola covered some rules.

"For some of you," she began once everyone had gathered and quieted down, "this contest is familiar. For others, this is your first year competing. Either way, there are some new rules that you need to know about."

Gin Wakefield appeared from behind me and joined the cluster. It took about two seconds for Sugar to spot her and for the mutual glaring to commence.

"I'm sure you're all aware of the problems with food allergies," Jola continued. "For the safety of our tourists, you all now need to post your ingredient lists. There are no restrictions on what you submit, you can make anything you want, we just need you to be transparent with the contents to prevent any possible problems. Any questions on that?"

Everyone looked around at each other, but no one had a question.

"All right," Jola said. "If you need clarification on anything, such as potentially problematic ingredients or other health concerns, please see me. Now Laurel has further instructions for you."

Laurel, crabbier than I'd ever seen her, stepped in front of the group then and growled for folks to settle down. "You should all have a green wristband. That band is proof that you are registered and eligible to compete." All hands went into the air except for Gin's. "Ms. Wakefield, pleasure to have you here." People gasped and spun to get a glimpse of the popular chef. "I'll get your wristband for you as soon as we're done here."

"The deadline for entry was two weeks ago," Sugar called out. "If Wakefield missed it, she can't compete."

"Sugar." Gin turned to her with that camera smile firmly in place. "How delightful to see you, it's been years. Sweet of you to be concerned about me, but my assistant got my registration in well before the deadline. I just never got my wristband."

"Are there any questions," Laurel asked the others while the two argued, "regarding any of the rules."

"I have one," Sugar called out. "Isn't there a rule about this being an amateur competition?"

"This is a *friendly* competition," Laurel said. "Anyone is welcome to enter. And scoring is blind, meaning all entries are anonymous. The judges won't know who submitted what. Everyone has an equal chance."

"Sugar, I'm curious about something," Gin's voice dripped with saccharine. "Since you feel the contest is for amateurs and you are competing, are you saying that you're an amateur and not a professional?"

Sugar spun on Gin and hissed in return, "Can't be happy with what you've got, can you?"

"Oh, I'm very happy," Gin replied, smiling big. "I've got a blessed life. When someone is fortunate enough to find success doing what they love, how can they be anything but thrilled?"

Sugar's hands were so tightly clenched her knuckles had turned white. She took a step closer to Gin. "Why couldn't you just stay away? You and your mother left years ago. You don't belong here anymore."

The look on Gin's face was pure hatred. It was so intense, I actually took a step away from her.

"Once a villager, always a villager." Despite the look on her face, Gin was as cool and calm as Sugar was flustered. "Not sure why you're so upset. You heard Laurel, it's a blind competition. Maybe this time you'll get the two extra points."

"Today's category for the cooking division is cheese," Laurel called out, eyes locked on the two women. "This means cheese must be the key flavor of your dish. For the bakers, it's a free for all, meaning you can submit anything you want. Younger contestants, you'll follow the same categories as the adults each day, but you'll obviously be competing against your peers.

"Your entry must be on your table by four o'clock each day," she continued, emphasizing each word. "This gives you just over seven hours today. At the end of today's judging, we'll announce tomorrow's category, and you'll then have almost twenty-four hours before your next creation is due. There is no cushion on that deadline. If time is called at four o'clock and your table is empty, you don't compete." Scowling slightly, she let her gaze pass over the cluster of cooks, freezing on Sugar and Gin at the end. "Remember, this is a *friendly* competition."

Sugar stood tall, chin lifted, and turned to Gin. "You know what? It's good that you entered. This way when you lose, everyone will know what a hack you are and that success can obviously be bought."

When Gin took a step closer to Sugar, I finally separated them.

"All right, enough. I know you two have a history, but

let's not let it ruin things for everyone else. Neutral corners, ladies. Play nice." They continued glaring at each other, neither backing down, so I threw out a sort of Hail Mary woo-woo pass. "Remember your karma."

Wiccans believed that whatever you did came back at you threefold. Do a good deed? You'd get three good things in return. Do something bad? You ended up with Flavia's sour life.

Sugar had walked away, grumbling to herself.

"Thanks, Sheriff," Gin said, her tone implying that I'd come to her rescue.

"For what? I wasn't choosing sides. No one gets preferential treatment." I looked down at Meeka, who panted up at me and wagged her tail. "Except my dog."

Gin studied me for a moment. "You consider everyone in the village to be equal? How nice that would have been twenty years ago."

What did that mean? Was she referring to her mom not being allowed to set up a shop here? The council at that time would have been comprised of nothing but Original villagers. Gin's mother had proposed a business that would have directly competed with an Original family's business. I could see why Gin thought they had played favorites, but I also understood the importance of a new business offering something different while still adding value to the community.

"In the eyes of the law, Ms. Wakefield, everyone is equal. Until a law is broken, of course."

She paused before walking away, her entourage of chefs trailing after her.

Chapter 8

SHORTLY BEFORE THREE THIRTY, I wandered across the commons and found Tripp waiting for me between Ye Olde Bean Grinder and Grapes, Grains, and Grub. He was sitting on top of a picnic table with his elbows resting on his knees. The collar of his old beat-up brown leather jacket was flipped up against the chill in the air, and his olive-green slouchy beanie held his wavy blond hair in check. He wasn't doing anything, just sitting there, and was still the sexiest man I'd ever seen.

"Where are they staging the competition?" he asked after pulling me in for a hug.

I pointed over my shoulder toward the lake. "They set up a bunch of tables on the lawn behind The Inn. Judging starts in half an hour."

People started gathering there more than an hour ago. The competition entries would be available for free sampling after the winners were announced, handed out on a first come, first served basis. Unlike the tables around the Pentacle Garden that seemed to have an endless supply of food, once the contest creations were gone, they were gone.

Tripp stared at the crowd and worried we'd never get close enough to see the entries.

"Stick with me," I told him and tapped my sheriff's star. "I have a badge. I always get through."

"Isn't that abuse of authority?" He cocked a judgmental eyebrow at me. When my only response was a blink and blank stare, he shrugged and said, "In that case, let's go check out the drum circle."

We followed the sound of the drums to the marina beach and joined the group of fifty or so people there. Tripp stood with his eyes closed and swayed to the beat. There was something sort of wild and free about him that way.

"This is how you were when you were wandering the country all those years, isn't it? A free spirit with no worries. Well, other than finding your mom."

"Might have been. Couldn't say for sure." He was still swaying, eyes still closed. "I admit, having no real responsibilities and living with only what fit in my trailer was nice." He peeked one eye at me. "It got lonely, though. I like having a home base and someone to share life with."

I was a little envious of the experience he'd had. "I wish I could've known you then."

He smiled and continued to sway. "We weren't ready for each other yet."

I was about to say more when he put a finger over my lips and an arm around my waist. I moved to the music with him but kept one eye open. I was on duty, after all.

A voice over a loudspeaker announced that the judging for the food competition was about to start. Prepared that there could be trouble after the winners were announced, Sheriff Jayne pushed drumbeat-loving Regular Jayne out of the way. I hated being so paranoid all the time, but public safety was my job. Instead of parting the crowd with my badge and uniform, we cut through The Inn and out the restaurant door at the back of the building.

There, a variety of different foods were on display from

simple homestyle dishes to more complex creations. The contestants stood by their tables and proudly explained their recipes to us. Tripp made note of those dishes he wanted to come back and sample after the judging. He was on the hunt for more items for Pine Time's menu. If we stayed open through the winter, he'd have to make three meals a day because the restaurants in the village would only be open a day or two a week.

We stopped at Reeva's table, which was piled with different breads.

"I call this my Tour of Italy." She identified each item. "Traditional Italian bread, herbed breadsticks, garlic knots, parmesan and prosciutto pull-apart bread, and rosemary and black olive focaccia."

"How much kitchen witch magic did you mix into these?" I teased.

She responded with a wink.

"Save a bit of each for me?" Tripp asked Reeva, as he had every contestant. His charming grin ensured he'd get all the samples he wanted. I'd have to roll him home.

"You look much happier than earlier," I told Sugar when we got to her table. "You must feel confident about what you made."

Sugar stood by a three-foot-tall, triple-tiered tower loaded with cookies, bars, and scones.

"These are all our customers' favorites." She adjusted the placement of a couple brownies and then pointed at a still-empty table. "Best of all, Wakefield hasn't come out yet. Maybe she finally realized that mass-produced food is never as good as what's made by hand with care."

"This is the one-minute notice," a village volunteer called over a bullhorn. "Contestants, you have one minute to get your entries to your table."

"Sugar," I began, "you know that there's room for all

types of—"

A gasp rose from the crowd near The Inn's door before I could complete my thought.

The rosy, confident glow on Sugar's face drained as she saw what was coming our way. "You have got to be kidding me."

"What is that?" Tripp asked.

I turned to see Latoya and Leif carrying a ten-foot-tall cone-shaped tower of what looked like doughnut holes. Gin followed closely, hands raised to catch the tower if it started to topple.

"It's a croquembouche," Reeva said in a near whisper. I wasn't sure if the tone was due to her being as awestruck as the rest of us or to keep Sugar from overhearing her.

"It's a what?" I matched her volume.

"I've heard of those," Tripp said," but I've never seen one. It's a French dessert. The little balls are choux pastries."

"Shoe pastries?" I repeated and made a face.

He laughed at me. "Same pronunciation, very different ingredients. They're little cream puffs. Each is filled with a custard of some kind."

"What's holding them together?" I was sure that at any second one of the puffs at the bottom would slip free and cause the whole stack to collapse.

"Caramel," Reeva explained. "Each puff is dipped in melted caramel which sticks it to the others."

There were thin strands that look like gold threads wrapped all around the cream puffs. "What are the threads made of?"

"Spun caramel." Tripp stared in awe. "I want to try that sometime."

"That's what you've said of almost every entry," I teased.

We stepped out of the way as Latoya and Leif got closer. As they did, we could see tiny decorations nestled into the hollows where the round puffs didn't touch.

Tripp squinted at the small shapes. "Moons, stars, pentacles, tiny ears of corn, pumpkins …"

"Decorated for the season," Reeva noted with an appreciative nod. "Very nice touch."

"Time!" the volunteer bellowed just as Gin finished inspecting that the croquembouche was placed exactly as she wanted it on their four-foot-square table.

Another volunteer, a villager who always wore a tuxedo with tails and a top hat—just in case the circus needed a spur-of-the-moment ringmaster, he claimed—stepped through The Inn's door.

"The judges are about to come out," he announced importantly as he plucked the nametags off each table. "All contestants must step away from their tables."

"That's so they don't know which of us made what," Reeva explained.

"Why bother putting nametags on the tables?" I asked.

"They mix us around every day, so we don't take the same spots. It's an extra level of anonymity." She stepped off to the side with the others.

Tuxedo man asked Tripp and me to stand with the other spectators behind a rope surrounding the contestant area. A minute later, the judges emerged from the building. Wesley, The Inn's head cook, and Triple G owner Maeve would judge the hot foods. That group went first as most of those were best at hot, fresh out of the oven temperatures. They started with the children, since they were getting squirmy, and then the adults. Laurel and Sylvie, one of the servers at The Inn's restaurant, were the judges for the baked goods entries. They also started with the kids.

"Sugar is looking upset again," I said softly to Honey on my right. "Is it just because of Gin?"

"Partly," Honey answered. "Gin made a croquembouche

for their final project at culinary school. That one was five feet tall. This one looks to be ten."

"Gin's trying to psych her out," I murmured, and Honey agreed. "Never knew the world of desserts was so cutthroat."

"You have no idea." Honey frowned. "Sadly, too many cooks let taste suffer in favor of presentation."

I leaned over to Tripp and repeated what Honey said about the croquembouche.

"Understandable that she'd win with one of those." Tripp's gaze was firmly on the judging. "It's an impressive dessert."

The tension grew stronger with each table Laurel and Sylvie approached. We were nervous; I could only imagine how the contestants must have felt.

"The judges score every entry on four different aspects," Honey told us. "Ten points each for taste, quality of the bake, presentation, originality, and one point for judge's choice. Reeva's entry is a gamble. If one of her breads is of lesser quality, it could lower her entire score. The judges add their individual scores together, and the contestant with the highest score wins the day. Medals will be handed out at the close of the last day of competition. The scores are cumulative, so everything counts."

When the judges left the area, stepping inside The Inn to calculate scores, Sugar unloaded on Gin.

"What the hell is that?" Sugar pointed at the tower.

Gin gave her a slow, almost slithery smile. "My showstopper. Your first entry in a competition establishes the judges' impression of your ability, so that entry must be what you're best at making. I'm best at jaw-dropping creations." She flung a hand at Sugar's table. "You're best with cookies and scones." She smirked. "Far from a showstopper."

"But melt-in-your-mouth delicious," Honey called out, defending her sister's honor. "Equal points for presentation and taste."

Sugar glared at Honey and hissed, "You're supposed to build me up, not make us equal."

"I—" Honey began then clamped her mouth shut.

"Let's let them hash it out," I suggested and put a hand on Honey's shoulder.

Sugar and Gin reminded me of fighting peacocks, both with tails fanned out and ready to pounce on each other to prove supremacy. I didn't know Gin, only what I had found out since meeting her yesterday and talking with Violet. Competitive and peacock-y could well be Gin's normal personality. Sugar, however, had different temperaments. At times, she could be as sweet as her name. Other times, like now, she could be as sour as Warheads candies.

"Sugar's pretty worked up," I noted.

"She really wants to beat Gin," Honey replied. "If she comes in tenth and Gin comes in eleventh, she'll still consider it a victory."

We all waited in agonizing anticipation for the judges to reemerge from The Inn. When they finally did, we held our breaths as we waited for the announcements. The winner in today's kids' division cooking category was a thirteen-year-old boy with a politician's haircut. He had made a cheese and chicken enchilada stack with black beans and red sauce. On the baking side for the kids, the winner was an intense fifteen-year-old girl in a chef's coat who presented individual pumpkin pecan cheesecakes. As the two posed for pictures, taken by Lupe who had ignored me all afternoon, the judges stepped up to announce the adult winners.

The winning entry in the adult cooking division was awarded to Peyton from Sundry. He had prepared a four-cheese souffle that was golden-brown and had risen tall above the edge of its dish.

"We'd like to remind everyone," Laurel stated before

moving on to the adult baking winner, "that this was a blind challenge. While the contestants were bringing out their entries, all the judges were in The Inn's conference room, which has no windows."

"I've got kind of an itchy feeling," I whispered to Tripp.

"The winner for the first day in the adult baking division is the croquembouche."

Chapter 9

TO HER CREDIT, GIN WAKEFIELD said nothing. She just smiled her camera smile, held her hands with palms together, and bowed in thanks to the judges before waving to the cheering crowd.

"You have got to be kidding me," Sugar demanded of Laurel. "She enters this *friendly* competition with a staff of professional chefs behind her—"

"There's nothing in the rules," Laurel interrupted, "that says only one person has to make the creation. A team of people is fine. Are you telling me that Honey didn't help you?"

Sugar turned a bright tomato-red, huffed a little, and finally clamped her mouth shut in an angry pucker.

"That had to be hard for her," I told Honey.

"Losing to Gin Wakefield," she asked, "or not tearing into Laurel?"

"Yes," I responded after a moment's pause. I'd been thinking losing to Gin, but the second option fit too.

"I have a feeling I'll be helping with tomorrow's entry," Honey mused.

"How do you feel about that?" I asked.

A smile spread across her face and she whispered, "Excited."

Good for her. Sugar would still get the recognition for their entry, like Gin did for her team, but at least Honey would get to play.

A few feet away from us, Sugar closed her eyes, inhaled deeply, and like the professional she was, thanked the judges. Then, just loudly enough that Tripp, Honey, and I could hear her, Sugar leaned over to Gin and hissed, "You'd better bring your A game tomorrow, Wakefield, because it's on."

"Tomorrow's category," Laurel shouted and then picked up the bullhorn. "Tomorrow's category for the cooking contest is barbecue."

Beside me, Tripp groaned. "If I would have known I could use that smoker again, I would've entered."

He had used a smoker for the grand opening party we had for Pine Time and had asked repeatedly since then if we could buy it for the bed-and-breakfast.

"Those smoked ribs of yours would've won, hands down." I petted the back of his head as he pouted. "Next year."

"You can make anything you want," Laurel continued, "but the sauces and spice rubs must be your own creation. Bakers, tomorrow your category is cakes. Any kind of cake is permissible as long as everything is handmade." She paused, waited for questions, and then gave a tight smile. "Congratulations, winners. Good luck tomorrow, everyone."

"Something's wrong with her," I told Tripp.

"With Laurel? Why do you say that?"

I shrugged. "Not sure, exactly. She's always positive and even-tempered. She seems edgy and kind of crabby right now. And really lowkey for a contest coordinator. Usually, coordinators bounce around like over-caffeinated head cheerleaders."

"Maybe it's just the stress of getting all this set up." Tripp jerked a thumb over his shoulder. "I'm going to talk to some of the contestants about their entries. Do you want to wander with me? There will be samples."

"Tempting as that is, I should do a patrol of the commons and make sure everything is under control." So far, the crowd had been so well-behaved I could've let Reed stay at school in Green Bay. There was nothing going on I couldn't handle by myself. "Meet you at the negativity well at seven o'clock?"

"Do you have some frustrations you want to get rid of?"

The negativity well was a gleaming white marble water well at the very center of the Pentacle Garden. Instead of dropping in wishes, the "wisher" whispered their frustrations into their hands, threw them to the bottom of the well, and their problems floated off to wherever negativity went.

"I have zero frustrations in my life." Other than the bickering between Sugar and Gin. And the bickering between Flavia and Reeva. And the evil eye glares Cybil and Effie kept shooting at me. Maybe I could toss them in the well. The frustrations, not the people. I reached up and gave him a quick kiss. "The well is just an easy landmark."

Meeka fought me when I gave a tug on the leash for us to go patrol. She wanted to stay with Tripp because Tripp meant food. Whether cooking in the kitchen or sitting down to eat, Tripp tended to drop crumbs.

"She can stay with me," Tripp offered.

"She's been scrounging up dropped things for the last two hours. A few people even flipped her little pieces of whatever they were eating. She's going to get sick if she keeps eating all this people food."

"Are you saying I'm not a good babysitter?"

"I would never say that … out loud." I gave him a grin and tugged on the leash. Once again, my K-9 pulled back. In a stern voice, I ordered, "Meeka, working."

She dropped her furry head forward and blew a huffy breath out of her nose that was the canine equivalent of a teenager rolling her eyes. Still, she followed the command and moped alongside me. It only took her about ten steps to figure out that other people dropped food too. There were plenty of scraps throughout the commons area and she scrounged up every little bit she came to.

I crossed paths with my deputy in front of Grapes, Grains, and Grub. "Any issues? Was it worth skipping school for a week?"

"If it stays like this, no," Reed said. "Mabon tends to attract a quieter crowd than the regular summer season."

He was right. There were a handful of children, but most of the tourists were adults. I estimated a thirties to seventies age range.

"It's always worth it to come, though." A faint pink color rose on his cheeks. "You never know what could happen."

"Worth it because you get to see Lupe?" I teased. "Is she still mad at me? Are you mad at me?"

"She'll get over it. And I was never mad. I don't understand why you didn't vote, though. Sounds like it wouldn't have made a difference if you did, and then Lupe wouldn't be so upset. At least, not at you."

It had been a no-win situation for me. I couldn't vote for her, I didn't think her idea was a good one. If I would've voted against her, though, she'd be twice as angry as she was now.

"I told her it wouldn't work." Reed looked side to side, making sure Lupe hadn't snuck up behind us. "After Samhain, there won't be anything new to cover."

"That's what your mother told her." Glad we were on the same page. "I'd like for you to stick around through the weekend. If things stay quiet, you can head back to Green Bay on Sunday night or Monday morning."

He agreed and continued his patrol, making his way to

The Inn when I told him that's where I'd last seen Lupe. We were just coming to Shoppe Mystique when Meeka pulled hard on the leash as though she'd scented something. She dragged me to a patch of grass at the back of the shop, ate a few of the blades, and promptly threw up.

"I warned you about the food scraps." I knelt down and rubbed her ears. "Poor girl. Let's go see if Morgan has anything to settle a doggie tummy."

Shoppe Mystique was decked out in all things autumn. Dried flowers in shades of deep purple, warm yellow, burnt orange, and crimson red hung from the rafters. Right inside the shop's front door, we were greeted by a smaller version of the fifteen-foot-long cornucopias in the Pentacle Garden. This one also overflowed with harvest items and dominated the display. It even smelled like autumn with pumpkin spice incense burning on the front counter.

"Blessed be," Morgan greeted as we walked in.

"Hey." Four months in the village and I still didn't know how to respond to Wiccan greetings. "Do you have anything to soothe an upset doggie tummy?" I cast a sad glance at my Westie. "Someone has been eating too much fest food."

We watched as Morgan gathered together small bottles of essential oils. After mixing them together, she called Meeka to her side and rubbed a few drops onto her belly. Then she handed the little bottle of the mixture to me.

"Fennel, coriander, ginger, peppermint, tarragon, anise, and caraway. That should help. Of course, eating the proper food will help more." Morgan arched a dramatic black eyebrow at her, and Meeka turned away as though ashamed. "Rub on a few more drops before bed tonight."

"I knew you'd have something for her. How's the fest been going?"

"As well as ever. It's just such a peaceful time of year."

"Not sure peaceful is the word I'd choose." I swept a hand

randomly at the crowd outside. "There's just so much going on. The smells from the food tables and the constant hum of people talking. Then there's the beat from the drum circle mixing with the karaoke music over at Triple G. All that isn't overwhelming you?"

"I see and hear all of it, but we have to appreciate our visitors while they're here. Come April, we'll be itching for excitement again."

I stared at her, confused. "What about all your talk about 'Whispering Pines as it's meant to be'? I thought you were anxious for winter."

"I am," she assured in her calm Morgan way. "Isn't it wonderful that we always have something new to look forward to?"

I couldn't argue with that so instead told her about the food competitions and who the winners were. "I'm a little worried about this thing between Sugar and Gin Wakefield."

"Why is that?" She finished tidying a rack of grapevine wreaths near the counter and then crossed the aisle to re-alphabetize the apothecary bottles of dried herbs.

"You must know about the fighting between them. Wait, you weren't here when Gin lived in the village. Were you?"

"I was here, but I was very young. I heard murmurings of a kitchen witch named Ginger every now and then. Some of the older villagers kept track of her after she left, and when her business in Chicago started doing well, they'd start in with the 'remember when Gin' stories." Morgan chuckled at the memories, but only a little. "Inevitably, the fond stories turn to those of the sweet shops feud. That's what they called it."

"Was it ever resolved?"

"The feud? Unfortunately, no. The way Mama explained it to me, Gin and her mother packed up their belongings and left the village in the middle of the night without saying goodbye to anyone. They were so hurt." Morgan tilted her head in question. "What are you thinking?"

"First, I was thinking that there are an awful lot of rumors surrounding Gin. Everyone says something slightly different about her. Also, I was remembering something you said a few weeks ago, about buried things festering and causing problems when uncovered."

She straightened the items on her Lotions and Potions cosmetics table. "The same thing can hold true with unresolved anger."

"That's what I'm worried about."

Morgan faced me and played with one of the many necklaces at her throat as she pondered this. "Normally, I'd say you worry too much. In this case, however, it might be wise for you to keep an eye on Sugar and Gin."

Chapter 10

WELL BEFORE THE FOOD VENDOR tables shut down on the first day of Mabon Fest, I was ready to call it a day. This crowd was so calm and quiet, there was no reason for either Reed or me to be there. Not in an official capacity, at least. If anything did happen, someone could contact me via walkie-talkie. I went in search of Tripp and found him still hanging out in the competition area behind The Inn talking to the contestants.

"I'm ready to head home," I told him. "How about you?"

He hesitated, not quite ready to walk away from these people he had clearly bonded with. He promised to come back tomorrow and all the way home he talked about Peyton and Gino, a man who had entered a fire roasted five-cheese pizza that had come in second in the adult division.

"Gino has an actual pizza oven." Tripp's eyes glazed with envy. "I'm going over to his house to see it next week."

"So you want a smoker and a pizza oven?"

"Okay."

"No, I wasn't—" I shook my head and swatted his arm with the back of my hand.

As we emerged through the woods that flanked our

driveway, we discovered all the lights were on in the great room.

"What do you suppose is going on in there?" Tripp asked.

"We'll find out soon. I'm going to change clothes first. I'll be right there."

Instead of running around the yard, barking at invisible intruders like she usually did, Meeka patrolled the perimeter at more of a slow trot tonight, her tummy still not feeling well. That would hopefully teach her not to eat everything that smelled good.

After changing into leggings and an oversized flannel shirt, I went to the house and found Gin Wakefield and her employees spread out in the great room.

"What are they doing?" I asked Tripp who was in the kitchen prepping for tomorrow's breakfast.

"Brainstorming their next entry. They said it's more private here. Too many people wandering around The Inn."

He beat whatever was in the mixing bowl in front of him with a little more aggression than was usual for my boyfriend.

"Something bothering you?"

"How many times did Laurel say this was a friendly competition?" He tipped his head toward our guests. "I overheard their conversation when I walked in. Sounds like Ms. Wakefield is determined to win every event."

"I've heard that she can be extremely competitive. I'll go listen in, see what I can learn."

"So nosey," Tripp chastised with a smirk as I walked away.

"No, not red velvet," Gin was telling her people. "Not only is it cliché, it doesn't fit with an autumn theme."

"She's right." Leif held up a piece of paper. "Our scoresheet shows we got full marks for presentation with a handwritten note praising us for including fall colors and decorations."

"We need to think bigger," Gin demanded. "Think out of the box. We need something no one else will do."

"Dark chocolate with salted caramel filling?" Misty offered.

Gin cocked her head and gave the dishwasher a smile that was somewhere between appreciative and condescending. "Better. The caramel color is seasonal, at least. How can we make it different, though?"

"What about making a healthier version?" Misty continued, encouraged by the smile from her employer. "I was talking with the local beekeeper about his honey today–"

Just that fast, Gin went from smiling at her kitchen helper to practically screaming. "Are you trying to kill me? Why are you even contributing to this discussion? You're not a baker. You wash dishes."

The mousy young woman cringed and shrank back in her chair.

"Settle down, Ginger," Kim said in a firm voice while Latoya comforted Misty with a pat on her shoulder. "We asked Misty to be here to give a different perspective. Sometimes the public can give you the next great thing, and she's had some good ideas. She couldn't possibly know about your allergy."

"Anyone who knows me knows I'm allergic to honey and bee stings." Gin slumped back in her chair and put a hand to her forehead.

Kim sighed. "She wasn't implying that you should eat it, Ginger."

"That's actually a great idea," Latoya agreed and immediately followed up with, "Not the you should eat it part. I mean that I've got some great recipes for cakes using alternative sweeteners. That woman with all the different breads today—"

"Reeva Long," Gin informed. "She's one of the villagers."

"Reeva," Leif traced a finger down his paper. "She came in second. I chatted with her afterwards. She said she got a note of praise for having more than one item on her table."

"That's where I was heading with my idea," Latoya said. "I've got probably half a dozen recipes for honey cakes. We could—"

"No honey," Gin repeated, leaving no room for further discussion. "You know full well I don't put out anything with my name attached to it unless I've sampled it myself or used it in my kitchen. I can't very well sample anything with honey in it, can I?"

The employees went mute and stared at each other across the room. They all looked exhausted.

Gin stood and blew out a heavy sigh. "I'm going outside for a breath of air. I want an answer by the time I get back. We have until four o'clock tomorrow afternoon. The sooner we get this done, the sooner you all will be able to enjoy some of the fest and the village." She paused when she saw me standing behind her and asked, "Is there any alcohol on the premises? I'd kill for a glass of wine right now."

She stormed out of the room, and after the patio door had closed, it took about two seconds for the grumbling to start.

"I thought we were supposed to be relaxing this weekend," Leif said.

"Right?" Latoya ran her hands through her hair, making the already-spiky locks stand straight up. "This was supposed to be an R&R reward for a successful year."

"And isn't this supposed to be a friendly competition?" Leif asked and looked at me.

"That was my understanding," I said when it became obvious he wanted an actual response from me. "I'm sorry things are getting so intense."

Maybe the council needed to discuss allowing amateurs only in this thing. Although, that wouldn't necessarily make things less competitive.

Latoya and Leif turned to Kim as though expecting him to fix this. He threw his hands in the air. "You all know what she's like. It's because of this woman. Sugar."

"Maybe we should accidentally let her sample a honey cake," Latoya suggested.

Everyone in the room, myself included, was horrified by this.

"Not to kill her," Latoya insisted. "Sheesh. Just enough to cause a reaction and send her to bed for a day or two."

Leif frowned at her. "Toy, that's really disturbing."

Kim's gaze darted from them to me and back. "You do realize there's a sheriff standing behind you?"

Latoya laid her head on the back of the sofa and turned to me. "Just blowing off steam. Nothing illegal about saying it."

"No," I agreed, my eyes fixed on hers. "There's nothing wrong with saying things." I left the great room, trying to convince myself she was just frustrated with her boss, and returned to Tripp in the kitchen. He was measuring flour of some kind from his basket of specialty ingredients. "It's getting a little intense over there."

"Something we need to be concerned about?" he asked when I told him what Latoya had said.

"I hope not. Say, do we still have wine left from our last wine and cheese gathering?"

He thought and then laughed. "I bought three cases, thinking it would last for at least two gatherings. We only have three bottles left. The last group really sucked it down."

"Guess you're getting good at choosing wine."

He gestured with an elbow at the pantry. "Red is on the shelf in there. White is in the cooler."

What we called the pantry used to be my grandmother's office. The space was far too small for an office but perfect for storing food and small appliances. We also put a wine cooler in there. Recently, we had to add a lock to the door after Tripp found a guest in the kitchen preparing a late-night meal for himself and his wife.

Gin hadn't specified white or red, so I took a bottle of each along with two glasses and a corkscrew. I'd heard a lot of stories in the last twenty-four hours from many villagers about Ms. Wakefield's time in Whispering Pines. It would be nice to hear her version.

I opened the back-patio door and found her standing there, staring out at the lake. She spun and relaxed when she saw it was me.

"Sorry for that little display of frustration you witnessed." Her gaze landed on the bottles in my hand. "Please tell me one of those is for me."

"A whole bottle?" I joked.

"If we didn't have a cake to make, I'd say yes. Is one a red?"

I held up one of the bottles, indicating it was indeed a red wine. After setting the bottle of white aside, I opened the red, poured a healthy glass for her, and a little for myself as well.

She took the glass and asked, "Is there a beach to walk along by this section of the lake?"

"There is a bit of a shoreline, but it's very rocky and I wouldn't recommend walking along it at night. We could sit on the dock."

Gin took a sip of her wine, smiled, and motioned for me to follow her. "Is this a Malbec?"

"I have no idea. Tripp is the wine guy in this relationship. I just drink it and tell him if I like it or not. I do like this, by the way."

Gin stared pointedly for a moment and then nodded at the bottle in my hand. "What does the label say?"

I felt myself blush as I checked the bottle. "It says Malbec."

As we walked to the end of the twenty-five-foot dock, I thought of how we'd have to haul it out of the water for the winter soon. When the water froze, the dock would surely be destroyed, but for now, it was still available for guests. More people than I had anticipated came out here to sit. We'd set out Adirondack chairs in the spring.

Over the summer, I'd developed a liking for kayaking. Getting into and out of a kayak without flipping myself into the lake, however, was something I couldn't seem to master, so Tripp lowered the dock to make it easier for me. This meant Gin and I needed to either take off our shoes and dangle our feet in the ever-cooling water or sit with our legs pulled up on the dock.

"Has Whispering Pines changed much since you lived here?" I sat with my legs in crisscross.

"What you're really wondering about, Sheriff, is this animosity between Sugar and me."

"True, but I'm wondering about other things as well. Such as why you didn't return to the village after culinary school. I heard a version from Violet and a little more from Morgan, but it would be nice to hear about it from you. If you want to tell me."

"I'm not sure who Violet is," Gin stated and sipped her wine.

"She runs the coffee shop."

"Ah, yes. She is a curious one, isn't she?"

I snorted as I drank from my glass. "That's an understatement. She never knowingly spreads false information, though."

I sat and listened for a good ten minutes while Gin told me about moving to the village when she was twelve years old. She confirmed what Violet had said about she and Sugar becoming fast friends. They became competitive when they were old enough to enter their creations in the Mabon baking competition.

"They've lowered the minimum age since then," Gin said with a hint of jealousy. "I don't know about Sugar, but I was certainly ready to compete at thirteen. It was torture having to wait until we were sixteen. And then, of course, I won with every creation I entered."

I noted the pregnant pause at the end of that statement. "Every entry?"

"Well, I may have let Sugar win once or twice."

Let her win. By the tone in her voice, I didn't think she was joking.

"I really did love it here." She stared thoughtfully across the lake. "After graduating from culinary school, I was fully prepared to come back to the village. The tourists were starting to come, and everyone could see that it was possible to make a living doing what you loved here."

"Violet told me your mother wanted to open a shop."

"Mother wanted me to. Her idea, but my place. We talked about it a lot. Treat Me Sweetly sold ice cream, scones, and a few types of cookies. They didn't do cakes or breads or more involved desserts such as eclairs." She smiled. "I love eclairs. Anyway, that's what I decided I wanted to do, sell pastries and cakes. I love taking my time and making desserts that people take in with their eyes before tasting."

"The council turned down your proposal."

"They did. Sugar was furious that I had earned the valedictorian spot at school. I assume you heard that part."

"I did."

"Maybe if I'd come in second, things would've turned out differently, but word of mouth is the most powerful promotion, you know, and she had nothing positive to say about me." Gin took another sip of wine. "Sugar's parents were council members, and I expected they would vote against me. I hadn't expected a unanimous vote, however."

She sipped again. "One sweet shop, they said, was more than enough for such a small village."

Treat Me Sweetly was insanely busy during the summer season. I saw people walk away rather than wait in the line that almost always extended out the door and yards down the red brick pathway. The village could easily support a second sweet shop. Sometimes, both then and now, the council wasn't forward thinking enough.

"Morgan told me that you and your mother were so hurt by this that you left in the middle of the night without saying goodbye."

A dark shadow passed over Gin's face. "Morgan is correct. My mom—" Her voice broke, and she needed a second to compose herself. "It was really hard for Mom to leave here."

There was more to this. Gin was getting emotional talking about this topic, though. Time to lighten the mood a little. "It seems things worked out okay for you."

Gin laughed at that. "Yes, I have had a great deal of success. I must admit, though, this has stuck in my craw. Being denied by the people that supposedly loved and accepted me was a very hard pill to swallow."

"Is that why you entered the competition this week? Are you trying to get revenge of some kind?"

She tossed back the last of her wine, took the bottle from where it sat on the dock behind us, and added more to both her glass and mine. "Honestly, I'm not sure."

"How can you not be sure about something like that?"

"Because I've had tremendous success. I've received dozens of prestigious awards and am often told that I am among the best of the best bakers. Beating Sugar at this point would hardly feel like redemption."

"Is that what you believe you are? The best?"

"You think I'm just bragging? Or full of myself?"

I wasn't about to answer that question. Instead, I met her eyes over my glass and took my time letting the jammy and slightly chocolatey wine fill my mouth. I preferred sweeter whites, but this was tasty. It made me want a wedge of cheddar cheese, though.

"I have three very popular stores in the Chicago area," Gin informed. "We're opening another in Milwaukee in a few months just in time for Christmas. My line of retail desserts sells better every year. Earlier this year, a company offered me a multimillion-dollar contract to put my name and face on a line of bakeware." She slurred her words a little, getting tipsy now. "I told them the last thing this country needed was another line of bakeware. They upped the offer and told me that people want the best and associate anything from Gin Wakefield with being the best. So, you tell me. Taking all that into consideration, what else am I supposed to believe about myself?"

It didn't sound like she was bragging, just listing items on an impressive resume. Someone had to be the best. Why couldn't it be her?

I held my glass up to her in a toast. "You are absolutely one of the best."

"Thank you for the wine." She handed me her once again empty glass. "I should get back in there and see if my staff has come up with my winning entry for tomorrow."

"I'm sure it will be fabulous even if you don't win."

She narrowed her eyes at me and then, apparently deciding I was joking, gave me a wink. I wasn't joking.

This week, according to the Wiccans, was supposed to be a time to relax and reflect. It seemed Gin Wakefield was doing quite a bit of reflecting, but I had yet to see either her or her employees relaxing. Why had she come here? If not to bask in her own success around those who had denied her so long ago, what had she hoped to achieve?

As I crossed the yard to go back to the house, Meeka came racing around from the front yard barking. I figured one of those predators in the woods only she could see had freaked her out. But she came straight to me, sat in front of me, and barked again. This wasn't playing. This was her *red alert* bark.

"What's going on, girl?"

She ran ahead a few yards and looked back to make sure I was following.

"All right. Show me what's upsetting you."

She did the run ahead and look back thing twice more until we were at the front corner of the house nearest the trees. Meeka stood perfectly stiff, doing her Pointer impersonation, and stared up at either the second floor or the roof. Now, I was getting concerned. She may be a joker sometimes, but when she did this, something was wrong.

I knelt beside her and tracked her gaze. The only thing out of place was the corner window on the side of the house. Lights were on in that room. The window was open wide and the curtain was hanging outside. Except, every window had a screen. Why was the screen off this one?

We had installed a fire ladder, the kind with a half-circle cage around it to prevent falls, near that window. For a moment, I worried someone had broken in using the escape, but the ladder was still pulled up, ready to be released with the flip of a latch up at the top.

"That's what has you upset? A curtain?"

Meeka pranced her paws and let out a little *ruff*.

"I didn't realize you actually patrolled when you patrolled."

She headbutted my leg.

"Nothing wrong with having a window open. I do wonder why the screen isn't on, though. And I suppose if someone had climbed the ladder, they could have pulled it back up at the top. Good job, Deputy. Let's go check it out."

She wagged her tail proudly and followed me into the house. We stopped in the kitchen first where Tripp was still hard at work.

"It's getting late," I told him. "Are you planning to make breakfast in the morning?"

"Keeping it simple." A yawn sneak-attacked him. "A couple different muffins, some pumpkin bread, and fruit. Coffee and juice of course. I polled everyone this morning, and they all agreed that simple was fine considering they'd be eating a ton during the fest."

"Then I say it's time for you to go to bed." I took the towel out of his hand and hung it to dry over the sink. "Since I'm here, can I walk you up to your room?"

He held his arm out to me, and I slid my hand into the crook of his elbow. At the top of the stairs to the second floor, we turned left, went halfway down the hallway, and took the flight of stairs there that went up to the attic. It was a decent space, well-lit with a view of both the lake and the trees, and plenty of room to accommodate an apartment conversion. Along the outside wall to the right was a raised landing, two-steps high, tucked into an alcove. We'd decided it was the perfect place for his bed. If he had a bed. Right now, there was nothing but an old sofa for him to sleep on.

"This will be our project this winter," I promised. "I don't like thinking of you sleeping on this old couch."

He pulled me close. "You know that there's an easy fix to that problem."

He meant him sleeping in my bed. As tempting as that option was, it wasn't time yet. Not that I felt us sleeping together would harm our relationship, but I was enjoying things so much just the way they were right now, I didn't want to rush and miss out on this courting part. Slow and easy, that was the Whispering Pines way.

I wrapped my arms around his neck and pulled him in for

a long goodnight kiss. "Sleep well. I'll see you for breakfast."

Before he could say a word, I started down the stairs and at the bottom, took a left instead of a right. I needed to stop by that room and see if there was a problem with the window screen. At the door to the room in question, nicknamed "The Treehouse" because the only view was of the pine trees surrounding the property, I heard music or the television. Who had this room? I thought back to checking in the Wakefield party and was pretty sure the sick woman was in here. Sarah? Was that her name? No, Sonja. I hadn't seen her since they checked in. Gin introduced her as their cake designer. Tomorrow was cake day, and she hadn't been downstairs to brainstorm with the group. She must really be sick.

I knocked. "Sonja? It's Jayne O'Shea. I just wanted to see how you're doing."

The television volume lowered, and after a good thirty seconds, I finally heard the slide of the chain on the door and the click of the unlocking deadbolt. The door opened a few inches, and Sonja's face appeared. She was flushed, and her breathing was unsteady.

"Ms. O'Shea, thanks for checking on me. I'm starting to feel better. Not a hundred percent yet, but definitely better." She opened the door a little further. "This was quite a bug I caught. The timing is awful, but isn't that the way things seem to go?"

"Illnesses do seem to have a way of ruining plans. I think it's because our stress levels either rise or fall in anticipation of an event." I pointed into her room. "My dog noticed that your window curtains were hanging outside the window. Is there a problem with the screen?"

She looked over her shoulder and then back to me. "Good watchdog. No, there's no problem. I was feeling a little claustrophobic." She gave an embarrassed smile. "Not used to being in one room all day. I stuck my head out to get some fresh air. Guess I forgot to put the screen back on."

"Do you need help with it?"

"Oh, no. I just forgot."

"All right. Glad you're starting to feel better. I know the folks over at Unity, the village medical center. They'll take good care of you if you do need them."

She nodded and smiled. "Misty mentioned that to me. I appreciate the offer, but I think I'm okay. Hopefully, I won't miss out on all the festivities."

Sonja thanked me again and closed the door. I heard her slide the security chain and relock the deadbolt. Funny thing was, the flush to her face had improved during the few minutes we spoke, and her unsteady breathing had evened out. In fact, she struck me as being a very healthy-looking sick person. The thin layer of sweat on her forehead and tint on her cheeks could have been from a fever. But when she opened the door, it seemed almost purposeful, so I could see her with her hand to her stomach. Rosalyn used to do that when she didn't want to go somewhere. She'd find us in whatever room we were in, drop onto the closest chair, and moan with her arms clenched around her midsection. Proof that she was too sick to go to school or wherever.

Sonja's sweaty sheen and flush could also have come from strenuous exercise. Or climbing up the fire escape? Other than watching TV, talking on the phone, and maybe reading, what else would a healthy person do in their room if they were pretending to be sick? This, of course, raised the question, why was she pretending?

Chapter 11

TRIPP AND I WERE SIMPLY not meant to have morning quiet time together this week.

"I thought you all started baking at four," I told the Wakefield group when I found them in the great room, eating bananas and drinking coffee at six o'clock.

"We were baking over at The Inn's kitchen until one in the morning," Leif said. "Once we had all the cakes baked and crumb coated—"

"And they'd gotten Her Highness' stamp of approval," Latoya added with an eyeroll.

Leif mirrored her expression. "After that much was done, we were cleared to get some sleep."

"What's a crumb coat?" I asked.

"A thin layer of frosting," Latoya explained, "that locks crumbs in place and keeps them from showing up on the surface of the final layer of frosting."

"Gotcha," I said.

"We have to be back by seven to start decorating." Latoya popped the last bite of her banana into her mouth and dropped the peel into a zip-top bag. Then she held out the bag for Leif's and Kim's peels as well. At my questioning look, she explained, "We save them for our compost pile."

It was too early in the morning to question transporting garbage from northern Wisconsin to Chicago, so I shrugged and continued to the kitchen.

"How's Meeka this morning?" Tripp asked.

"I rubbed some more of Morgan's magic juice on her belly before we went to sleep. She seems okay now. She ate some but not all of her kibble this morning. I think she's afraid to get sick again."

Tripp placed a mug of coffee in front of me on the kitchen bar then leaned in close and whispered, "Did you know Gin didn't get her registration in on time?"

"For the competition? I was there when Laurel asked about wristbands. Gin said she hadn't received hers."

"Sounded to me like Laurel pulled a favor for Chef Wakefield. They were grumbling about it this morning. 'It was supposed to be a long vacation weekend.' 'If only that woman didn't let her into the competition at the last minute.'" He took a swig of his coffee. "There's been a lot of grumbling coming from them. They clearly don't know how good the acoustics are in this house."

"Anything else I should be concerned about?"

"I don't know that you need to be concerned. It just sounds like frustrated employees complaining about their boss."

I told him my suspicion about Sonja pretending to be sick.

"Or maybe she was starting to feel better and decided to try some aerobics." Tripp was more of an optimist than I was.

"Keep your ear open for any more grumbling, would you?"

"Are you deputizing me?" He leaned across the counter. "Do I get handcuffs?"

"No, but I'll thank you properly for any information later." I gave him a sultry smile, and he waggled his eyebrows at me.

I drank my coffee and nibbled a muffin while Tripp set out breads, fruit, and beverages for our guests. I wished the group good luck with their entry today and found Meeka by the boathouse, licking the grass again.

"Tummy still upset?"

She whined and nudged the blades with her nose.

"Let's put on some more oil. Then we have to get to work."

Granted, I was more cynical than most, but I think she was playing it up to get a belly rub. Which I would've given her anyway.

I parked the Cherokee in the lot behind the station, placed a ticket on the windshield of the convertible BMW whose owner somehow missed the massive "Employee Parking Only" sign attached to the building, and went inside to check emails. Most were spam. A few were advertising for conferences or workshops. One was from Deputy Evan Atkins of the County Sheriff's Department.

Hey, Jayne. Just wanted to give you a quick update on the Donovan situation.

I had met Donovan Page shortly after coming to the village with the original assignment of getting my grandparents' house ready for sale. When I'd first walked into his shop, Quin's clothing shop, now Ivy's Boutique, he seemed like a fine person. By the time I'd made my purchase and was ready to leave, the man was making me itchy. Turned out that not only was he my half-brother, whom my father had never told us about, Donovan had also been responsible for the accident that caused Gran's death. When Deputy Atkins brought him in for processing, Donovan managed to escape custody and had been on the run for the past two months.

A report came in early this morning that a man matching Page's description was seen in International Falls, Minnesota. The officers in the area are searching for him, and we're sending a squad to help.

The last time a report came in on Donovan, someone had seen him on Mackinac Island, Michigan. By the time the officers got to the reported location, he was nowhere to be seen. Deputy Atkins and I guessed that from there, Donovan made his way north and slipped over the border into Canada.

My guess is that he's crossing into the States every now and then. Maybe to see if we've given up. Maybe just to play games and see if we'll catch him. Don't worry, we haven't given up and won't. I'll get regular updates from the deputies in International Falls and will report back to you with anything important. If you don't hear from me, that doesn't mean that we lost him, it means we don't have anything new for you.

Donovan was working his way back to Whispering Pines, I'd stake my life on it. He was a patient man and would wait until the time was right if there was something he wanted. In this case, what he wanted was either revenge on me for busting him or some twisted claim to my family. Or both. He never thought he'd get caught for Gran's death. I'm sure he expected to live out the rest of his life in Whispering Pines, hiding his secret like everyone else here hid theirs, and then I caught him. I had no idea what he'd do when he came back, but I was positive he would reappear in the village at some point. My instincts were on high alert for that day. I'd be ready for him.

Turning my attention back to my emails, I found one that was a promo for a conference being held in New Orleans this winter. That might be a good thing for Tripp and me to go to—not that he could attend the conference, but he could certainly go to New Orleans with me. I was reading over the details when the front door opened. I peeked around the corner to find Flavia Reed standing in the main room.

"I'm looking for Martin," she informed before I could ask. "The only good thing about this festival is that my son came home." She crossed her arms and tapped her long twiggy fingers on her elbows.

"I thought Wiccans loved autumn."

"Autumn is fine, but this festival is ridiculous."

"Any particular reason you don't care for it?"

I had a pretty good idea. It was common knowledge that Flavia had no skills in the kitchen. She offered me a cup of tea when I was over there one time, so I assumed she could boil water, but Reed was overjoyed when his aunt Reeva gave him some cooking lessons.

Flavia fixed a cold stare on me. "We all have our own talents, but we don't get a festival to show them off. Kitchen witches are such braggarts." She pursed her lips and dismissed the topic with a crisp shake of her head. "Do you know where my son is?"

"Nope. I've been here for half an hour and haven't seen or heard from him. Is there a problem?"

She cleared her throat. "Only in that I never see him anymore. If it's not that Gomez woman, it's you sending him away to college."

I plugged a pod into the nearby coffee machine and hit the start button. Flavia declined my offer of a cup.

"For the record," I said while the machine gurgled, "he decided all on his own that he wanted more education."

"He already has a job. What does he need more training for? What could possibly happen in this village that would require all that?"

I couldn't decide if I was more offended by her disregard for higher education or her attitude that Whispering Pines wasn't worthy of it.

"There's more to college than education," I told her. "It's learning how to deal with different types of people. It's learning responsibility by not only handing in assignments when due but by ensuring you get yourself to class on time."

I turned away from the coffee station with mug in hand to

find Flavia straightening Reed's desk and ignoring me.

"Has Martin ever done his own laundry?" I asked.

"Why would he need to?" She capped all his pens and put them in his top desk drawer. "He has me to take care of his domestic needs."

Obviously. I was a little worried she was going to spit shine his computer monitor next. "What if he ever decides to get married?"

This caught her attention. "Do you know something I don't? Is that why this Lupe woman plans to stay in the village? Has she convinced him to marry her?"

"I haven't heard that. I think you know what I'm trying to say, though. What will happen when he finally moves out of your cottage and has to take care of his own place?"

"Move ... out of my ...? Why would he do that?"

The possibility of him moving out upset her more than him getting married. Had she expected her future daughter-in-law to move into her house? Poor Lupe. Or whoever.

Returning to her reason for coming here, I asked, "Have you checked the commons area for him? That's probably where he is."

Without another word, Flavia scurried off down the Fairy Path. Once I'd finished my coffee, Meeka and I headed that way too.

At the edge of the Fairy Path, between Treat Me Sweetly and the resale shop, was where the fortune tellers had set up their wagon. This was a smaller version of the large, gingerbread-trimmed wagons permanently set up in The Fortune Tellers' Triangle—a clearing almost directly north of my house and across from the campground. The wagons at The Triangle were big enough for not only a table and chairs at one end, but a loveseat and overstuffed lounge chairs at the other. This little one couldn't hold more than a table and a few chairs.

Before I could change direction, I found myself heading

straight for Effie and Cybil. I could feel them staring at me, shooting their evil eyes my direction, and the next thing I knew, I tripped over my own feet. I windmilled my arms, trying to prevent myself from falling, got twisted in Meeka's leash in the process, and then bounced off a small pine tree before coming to a stop. I would've made less of a spectacle of myself if I'd landed on my face. And maybe then I would've gotten a little sympathy from passersby instead of chuckles.

Meeka stared and then turned away as though embarrassed to be seen with me.

"No such thing as an evil eye," I told her. "If anything, it was a karma smack. I picked on Flavia, so the Universe picked on me."

I headed their way, determined to finally have it out with Effie and Cybil. Regardless of what their nasty looks could or could not do, this had been going on for three weeks and had to stop. By the time I got to the wagon, the elder fortune tellers were gone. Probably off having a good laugh at my expense.

I spent the afternoon talking to tourists. Some people came for Mabon Fest every year. Others had heard about the village from friends. One retired couple had been passing through, stopped for lunch, and decided to stay a few days.

Shortly before four o'clock, I was waiting for Tripp near The Inn and noticed a woman dressed entirely in black. As in every square inch of her skin was covered. And not just black clothes, but a floppy black hat, balaclava, gloves, and sunglasses. The only thing not black were her hot-pink shoes. She wandered from table to table and chatted with the cooks at each one.

"Always has to be one in the crowd, doesn't there?"

I turned to see Reed standing next to me. "Always. There's something familiar about her, but I can't narrow down what it is."

"Maybe it's the fact that she's so odd that she fits in

perfectly around here?"

"That's possible," I said with a laugh. "I was thinking, why don't you take tomorrow off and spend time with your girlfriend and then head on back to school whenever you're ready? Oh, you may want to spend time with your mother too before you leave."

"She found me about an hour ago." He narrowed his eyes at me. "Did you tell her I was moving out?"

"No, I did not say you were moving. Or getting married."

The color drained from his face. "Married?"

Just then, the competitors started bringing out their creations for today's competition. The cooks looked at ease with their barbecue dishes, while most of the bakers appeared frazzled. After Gin's croquembouche yesterday, it seemed they had all upped their game. The cakes were amazing. Most were quite tall, averaging two feet in height, but once again, Reeva had a display to admire. From tiny bite-sized petit fours, to mini cakes the perfect size for two people to share, to a multi-tiered beauty large enough to feed a couple hundred people. They all looked perfectly decorated and delicious.

I found Briar standing next to a table with a six-tier display of what appeared to be very thick cookies stamped with pentacles and Triple Moon Goddess symbols.

"Did you make these?" I asked.

"I did." She beamed. "Aren't they cute?"

"Were you in the competition yesterday? I didn't see you."

"I enter every year," she said, "but only for cake day. I'm not interested in a medal. I just know no one will make mooncakes, and Mabon Fest isn't complete without mooncakes."

Her pocket-size marvels were tinted a variety of colors. Some were the standard tan-cookie shade. Others were sage green, scarlet red, golden yellow, or chocolate brown.

"Mooncakes?" I asked. "I've never seen these before. What are they, exactly?"

"They're traditionally a Chinese treat, but I put a Wiccan twist on them." She explained that the outer pastry was a simple dough made of flour, syrup, oil, and water. The inside was where the magic happened. "When you cut them open, you'll find a salted egg yolk. It looks like a little reddish-yellow moon suspended inside different fillings." She tapped the different cakes as she said, "Spiced walnut and red bean paste. Traditional custard. This one, the black sesame paste, is everyone's favorite. The illusion of a little moon suspended in a black sky is very fun."

"Sounds like a lot of work."

"It takes me a full day to make these. The garden forgives my absence for that long, but any more than that and the weeds grow at triple speed."

I studied her, trying to decide if she was being serious. In the Barlow garden, anything was possible. "They sound amazing. I'd love to try one."

"I'll save one for you and one for Tripp," Briar promised.

"What are you saving for me?" I turned to see Tripp standing behind me. He placed a kiss on my temple, and I let Briar explain her mooncakes to him.

All but two of the teams had brought their entries to their tables. With five minutes to go, The Inn's door opened, and Sugar and Honey walked out carrying their cake on a board that was almost the size of their table. Once they'd set it down, Tripp and I went over to see their creation.

"Is that the Pentacle Garden?" Tripp's mouth hung open.

That's exactly what it was, a three-foot-square to-scale model of the Pentacle Garden. The replica of the negativity well at the center even had water in it. Or what appeared to be water. In each of the pointed sections of the pentacle, they had created miniature versions of the huge cornucopias. There were hay bales and tiny pumpkins and even tinier gourds and ears of corn. They'd even included the benches where people sat to view the lake or the shops, depending on which side they were on. Rightfully, Sugar beamed with pride.

"This is truly amazing," I told them.

"The two of you must've been up all night," Tripp said.

"Almost," Sugar confirmed. "I made the cake and covered it with fondant icing. While I did that, Honey formed all the little decorations."

"You didn't just make the cake," Honey said, never one to take credit that wasn't due, "you shaped it all."

"But you made all these little hay bales and teensy flower petals by yourself, Honey?" As I got in close to inspect the detail, I thought of the replica of Pine Time they had brought to our grand opening party. I thought the detail on the house cake was mind-blowing, this one had ten times the detail. And in less than twenty-four hours.

"I've been practicing a long time," Honey acknowledged, "but Sugar was right there by my side. She was able to do quite a bit."

"Well," Tripp said, "I can't imagine what could beat this."

Just when we were all sure that the Wakefield crew wouldn't make the deadline, they did it again. With less than a minute to go, they exited The Inn with their own cake creation. Theirs was a two-foot-tall replica of what looked like one of the village cottages. A closer inspection showed that it was Treat Me Sweetly.

"How am I supposed to react to someone re-creating our business?" Sugar asked, both astonished and suspicious. "I know she's bitter about our shop, but couldn't they have chosen someplace neutral like The Inn? What does this mean?"

"I don't know what it means," Honey said, "but you've got to admit it's great promotion."

The man in the tuxedo stepped out of The Inn and announced that it was time for the contestants to move away from their tables, the orders of which had been mixed up from yesterday to maintain anonymity.

"This seems like a risky move on Gin's part," I told Honey, again standing to my right. "I mean, if they see Treat Me Sweetly, won't they assume that the two of you made it?"

"They could," Honey agreed. "Depending on how Laurel's feeling about us today, that could work for us or against us."

I was with Sugar on this one. What was Wakefield up to?

Laurel, Wesley, Maeve, and Sylvie emerged, and the judging began. It seemed to take forever for them to sample all the different barbecue submissions. Even longer to go through the baking entries. Other contestants had caught on to Reeva's tactic of displaying more than one item, and the judges had to sample everything.

"I hope there's a stash of insulin nearby," Tripp whispered in my ear. "One of them is sure to collapse from sugar overload."

The judges spent a long time inspecting Sugar and Honey's Pentacle Garden cake. If the *oohs* and *aahs* meant anything, they were very impressed. It was almost heartbreaking to watch them cut into it, but flavor was worth a quarter of the points. They spent an equal amount of time on Gin's sweet shop replica. Honestly, I didn't know how they were going to choose. Both were overflowing with detail and produced by bakers with equal skills. To me, both teams should get full points for presentation. It would likely come down to how the cakes tasted.

When the judges had finished viewing and sampling, they went back inside to tally their scores. At that point, the contestants were free to return to their tables. Before standing behind her miniature Pentacle Garden, Sugar stopped by the

Wakefield table to inspect Gin's cake. Her smile faded and then her face turned an angry beet red as she stared at something the rest of us couldn't see.

Worried that her sister was having a heart attack, Honey rushed to her side and grabbed Sugar by the arms. "What's the matter? Are you okay?"

"Look at what she did." Sugar shook her sister off and flung both hands at the sweet shop cake.

It took Honey a moment to figure out what she was so upset about and then she too, a woman I'd never seen angry, glared at Gin Wakefield.

"Judges are returning," tuxedo man announced. "Contestants to your tables."

"It doesn't matter who wins this one," Sugar hissed at Gin loud enough for all of us to hear. "You want a war, you've got one. You'd better watch your back, Wakefield."

Murmurs hummed through the crowd as people wondered aloud, "Did you hear what she said?"

"Was that a threat?"

"Will death by cake be the next murder in Whispering Pines?"

Unamused, I spun to see who had said that, but all I found was a sea of faces. When Honey returned to my side, I asked, "What did she do?"

"Exact replica of our shop." Honey's voice was strained as though she was fighting off angry tears. "Except the sign says, 'Wakefield's Treats and Sweets.'"

Chapter 12

"YOU'VE BARELY SAID TWO WORDS since we left the fest." Tripp turned on the outdoor heater on the deck outside my apartment and sat next to me on the sofa. "What are you so deep in thought about?"
"The baking competition."
"It's a nail-biter, isn't it?"
He meant because Sugar and Honey won today. The sheer amount of details—the flowers, pumpkins, haystacks, and the "water" in the well, whatever that was made from—put them over the top.
"Yeah, the competition is close," I agreed, "but that's not what I mean. It's the comments Sugar made to Gin. The crowd was buzzing with talk of death threats. And you know the village's reputation for murder."
"Yeah, but—"
"And did you see Laurel's face when Sugar saw the Wakefield sign on the sweet shop cake? I swear she was excited, as in thrilled. What was that about?"
"I'm not—"
"And why did Gin even do that? I mean, what was she thinking? What could that sign possibly mean? Was she

issuing a threat of some kind to Sugar and Honey?"

Tripp flipped me from sitting to on my back and kissed me. His hands roamed up and down my side and over the curve of my hips. I threaded the fingers of one of my hands through his curly blond hair while the other glided over the strong expanse of his back. The touch of his hand to my abdomen, the skin-to-skin contact beneath my shirt, sent electric waves through me. When his kisses went lower and lower down my neck, I had to put on the brakes.

"What was that?" I asked, breathless.

"A distraction." He collapsed on top of me, his heart pounding so hard, I could feel it through our clothing. "Did it work?"

"I'm not sure." I pushed him off of me, smoothed my hair, and straightened my shirt. "What were we talking about?"

He grinned as he slouched back into the sofa and blew out a heavy exhale. "*You* were talking about the competition. I was thinking about unhooking your bra." He grabbed my hand and laced our fingers together. "I was also thinking that you're making too much out of this. Sugar and Gin have been rivals for three decades and probably haven't seen each other in two. They're just being women, duking it out in the best way they know how. In the kitchen."

I was about to scold him for being a chauvinist but stopped because first, he was a cook himself and never thought that a woman's place was in the kitchen. Second, he was right. They were both professional bakers and very, very talented in their own ways. Their battlefield was the kitchen.

"You're right," I finally said. "It's just been a war of words and fondant. Nothing more."

Tripp chuckled. "I like that. Words and fondant." He looked sideways at me. "Do you know what fondant is?"

"Yes." I stuck my tongue out at him while making a mental note to check the internet once he left.

We left the fire in the tabletop pit off so we could appreciate the full, blinding-white moon shining off the lake tonight. We had a thick blanket and body heat keeping us warm. I snuggled in against his chest as he draped an arm over my shoulders. In the distance, a wolf, probably one from the circus, gave one long, lonesome howl. Otherwise, it was a perfectly calm and quiet night.

"After this week," I began, "we'll have one last Wiccan holiday—"

"Halloween." Tripp actually wiggled with excitement. "I can hardly wait. That's always been my favorite holiday."

"Really? I always figured you to be more of a Christmas guy."

"Christmas is all right, but it was always kind of a letdown for me. Every year I expected my mom would show up, like a gift delivered by Santa, but she never did."

My heart hurt a little for him.

"Don't feel sorry for me," he said. "I got over it a long time ago."

"Still, maybe we can find something special to make this one a good Christmas for you." That came across as more loaded with inuendo than I had intended.

I always loved Christmas. Not that I got all the gifts I wanted or that my family celebrated in some fabulous way. We didn't. Dad was usually out of the country at some dig site, so it was just the three of us. Mom ordered dinner to be delivered, and sometimes we'd watch a movie together. Otherwise, it was a day like any other day. What made Christmas special to me was the hope and promise of good things to come that it always brought.

"What I was going to say," I tried again, "was that after the Samhain celebration, I'll be home a lot more. I remember Sheriff Brighton telling me that he almost always worked from home in the winter."

"That sounds great." He paused before asking, "Wonder how long until I drive you crazy?"

I shrugged. "I'm willing to test it."

We sat there for another half hour and then Tripp said he was heading to bed. Meeka followed him across the yard and stood outside the patio doors and gave a soft bark, as though saying goodnight, and then made her final patrol of the yard. While she did her thing, I pulled the blanket tight around me and stood at the railing. I took in a long, deep breath of the crisp night air and watched the moonlight reflecting off the small ripples on the surface of the lake. The towering pines stood over me like ever-present protectors. Or maybe spectators. Those trees had witnessed a lot. Sometimes I wished they really could whisper. Then they could tell me about the secrets yet to surface from Whispering Pines' past. Then again, knowing what was coming didn't always make the revelation easier.

~~~

I tried one more time to have breakfast with Tripp this week and was surprised to find the great room empty at five thirty.

"No bakers this morning?" I asked.

"Not yet. What are they supposed to make today? Picnic food?"

"Something like that." I filled a coffee mug for myself and topped off his. "Does this mean we can actually have our routine today?"

This excited me too much. I really needed to learn to be more flexible.

While we ate together, we tossed around ideas for the attic renovation. It was going to be so cool, we could hardly wait to get started. Tripp was just putting breakfast together for our guests when Latoya and Leif came down the stairs a little after six.

"You guys got to sleep in?" I asked.

"We did. Crazy, hey?" Latoya glanced at Leif with a look that made me wonder what they'd been up to last night. "Today's entries are pretty easy. Nothing that required us to stay up half the night prepping."

"We have to make portable food," Leif began, "that doesn't require refrigeration or utensils to eat. Something self-contained that could be taken on a hike or a picnic."

"That's right," I said. "Now I remember." That's where Tripp got picnic food from.

"We ate dinner at the fest," Leif continued, "and then did our planning at The Inn. We made sure we had all our ingredients and measured everything out. Then we got back here at a decent hour. It was, what, a little after ten?"

Latoya agreed with a nod but said nothing.

"Good luck today," I told them and caught Tripp in the hallway, bringing a tray full of food to the dining room. "I'm going to head into work."

"Meet you at four o'clock again?" he asked.

"Make it three. That way we can hang out at the drum circle for a while or listen to some poetry readings before the contest judging starts." I went back to my apartment to put on my uniform shirt and load my cargo pockets with all the necessities.

I had just strapped Meeka into her harness when my walkie-talkie squawked.

"Jayne? Are you there? It's Violet."

A feeling of dread came over me. A summons on my walkie-talkie this early in the morning couldn't be a good thing. I pulled my unit off my belt and depressed the talk button. "This is Jayne. What's going on, Violet?"

"Nothing you'll like. There's a body on the Fairy Path."

After getting specifics from her as to where the body was, I ran back over to the house to let Tripp know.

"Any idea who?" he asked.

The conversation in the dining room was boisterous enough this morning that there was little chance they would hear me. Still, I kept my voice low.

"I didn't let her give me any details. Not even if it's male or female." I rubbed my hands over my face and through my fingers mumbled, "After yesterday, there are two people who come to mind."

Tripp wrapped me in a hug that helped center and calm me. "I'll assume we won't be meeting at three."

"I'll call you if that changes." Now fully in cop mode, I left the house.

~~~

As she promised she would be, Violet was standing sentinel over the body. I hadn't stopped in the station for the investigation kit, but I always had a pair of latex gloves in a pocket of my cargo pants. I snapped on a pair and felt for a pulse on the victim while Violet told me her version of the events of the morning. She knew nothing other than that Ruby had found the body on her way to work at The Twisty Skein and that the victim appeared to be Gin Wakefield.

As Violet jogged off, to first ask Ruby to come talk to me and then take over for Meeka on guard duty a little further up the path, I turned my attention back to my victim. This was the sixth death in Whispering Pines in the four months I'd lived here. Dead bodies showing up in the village didn't surprise me anymore, but the who, how, and why always did. As did the number of ways a person could die. I prayed, to whatever force in the Universe was watching over me, that I never became desensitized to those details.

The last I'd seen Wakefield, she was alternately cursing out her team for not putting enough detail around their Treat

Me Sweetly replica cake, giving Sugar smug looks over tacking her company's name onto Sugar's family business, and deflecting "watch your back" threats from Sugar for the offense. What had happened after that?

Out of nowhere, our time together on the dock the other night, sharing a good Malbec, flashed in my mind. I felt like I'd bonded with her, like I got to know a bit about the woman behind the treats. As I stood there, it struck me how remarkably tough the human body was, able to bounce back from all kinds of use and abuse. That same body could also be unbelievably fragile. One wrong move, and we were dead.

I blew out a breath and stepped back a few feet from the body to take in the scene. Wakefield's left hand was tucked beneath her, her right arm above her head extended at a forty-five-degree angle away from her body. My guess was that she had fallen.

I'm falling. My right arm …
Or maybe she collapsed.
I drop to my knees and hold myself up using my right arm. My left …

Why was her left arm beneath her? Perhaps she'd had a heart attack and was clutching at her chest.

"Hey, Sheriff."

I turned to see Reed coming from the west, from the direction of the village commons. Travel mugs, presumably filled with coffee, in hand. Good man.

"You walked to work?"

"Had to since I walked home last night. It was a nice night with the full moon and all." He handed one of the mugs to me and looked down at the victim. "Is that Ms. Wakefield?"

"I'd say there's a ninety-nine percent chance of that."

"Any immediate thoughts on what happened?" Reed tilted his head to the side, stepped closer, and bent at the waist to get a better look. "What's wrong with her hand?"

"I was just wondering the same thing."

Her right hand was puffy. Not as in she'd had too much salt and was retaining fluids but swollen to the point that her fingers look like bratwurst links. The skin across the back of her hand was expanded tight and smooth like a balloon about to pop.

"Maybe she broke it?" I gestured north. "She was probably on her way to Unity to get it checked out."

Reed made a face and shook his head as he did every time I said the name for the village's recently combined healing center and yoga studio. While far from an old fogey, Reed sometimes had a hard time with change.

"How did she get from broken hand to face down on the Fairy Path?" I wondered out loud. "People didn't die from a broken bone. At least, not this quickly. It is possible for a blood clot to form from a broken bone, break free, and travel to the heart. That could kill her. I've also heard of situations where fat tissue from bone marrow released into the blood stream and caused an obstruction in a blood vessel. That would require a break from a larger bone, though, like the femur."

"You know the weirdest things," Reed said. "Oh, I called Dr. Bundy before I left home like you asked. He's on his way."

"Great. Thanks." There wasn't much we could do until the ME got here. "I really doubt we'll find anything, but we can search the area for anything suspicious while we're waiting for him."

"I'll run and get the crime scene kit." Reed started toward the station then paused and asked, "How are we going to keep this one quiet?"

Good question. "There's no way we'll be able to for long. The best we can do is try and keep it under control once the news gets out."

"I hate to even think this, much less say it, but you know

who looks guilty for this."

He meant Sugar, of course. The question of her guilt played over and over in my mind as I stood over the body and recalled the events of the last forty-eight hours. Was the two women's rivalry so severe that all these years later a simple baking competition could end in murder?

"I do know. We'll deal with that when the time comes."

While Reed hurried over to the station, I decided to try and determine the level of rigor mortis. This would be a very unscientific test and would only satisfy my own curiosity. A very rudimentary way to determine how long a person had been dead was to feel the body. Rigor mortis started within two or three hours of death. The body would slowly stiffen for the first thirty-six hours and then the muscles would gradually start to relax again. If a body was warm and soft, that indicated a recent death, one that had happened within the past two or three hours. A warm and stiffening body meant death had occurred within the past three to eight hours. A cold and stiff body meant eight to thirty-six hours. And a cold but no longer stiff body meant the person had been dead for more than thirty-six hours.

I spotted Meeka trotting my way, coming from the east.

"Violet standing guard now?" I asked her.

She gave a little bark that sounded like *yep* and then stopped in the middle of the path upwind from the body, her attention locked on our victim.

"At ease, Deputy."

She sat but still faced Wakefield. Blue the cat, so named because of her almost neon-blue eyes, wandered out of the woods then and sat next to Meeka. I met Blue a few weeks earlier. She was the village's cat which meant she belonged to no one and made herself at home wherever she was accepted. Normally wrestling or chasing each other, the two all-white pals sat respectfully now.

I turned back to Wakefield. I'd last seen her around five o'clock last night. Leif and Latoya told me that they were with her until about ten. It was now almost seven and Ruby had reportedly found Wakefield around six fifteen. That rough timeframe meant Gin had been dead no more than nine hours. Since rigor started at the head and worked its way down the body to the feet, I would do my highly unscientific squeeze test on the lower half of her body. After first feeling my own calf to get a baseline of what living flesh felt like, I pressed my gloved finger against her leg.

"What's the determination?" Reed asked and set the crime scene kit down a few feet away.

"I can't determine warmth through all these layers, but rigor is starting to set in. She's been dead for at least three hours. Did you see her at all last night?"

Reed stared off into the trees, recalling the events of last night. "Lupe and I hung out in the commons area until all the food tables shut down at seven. After that, we went over to Triple G for a couple beers, and then I walked her to her cottage. We took the south route around the Pentacle Garden going past The Inn. That would have been around ten o'clock. I didn't see Ms. Wakefield but did see some of her employees coming out of The Inn at that time."

I couldn't help but smile at this detailed recounting. If I would've asked him this type of question four months ago, he would've said something like, "I don't know. There were people everywhere." His observation skills had improved drastically.

"You walked Lupe to her guest cottage from Triple G? That's more than a mile. And then all the way to your house from there? Why not drive?"

He shrugged. "I had some things to think about."

I gave him a suspicious look and then asked, "Do you remember which employees you saw coming out of The Inn?"

"The two men and the woman with the tattoos."

"They would be Kim Robbins, Leif Forsberg, and Latoya Craig. That's it? Just the three of them? Misty Wagner wasn't with them?"

"Who's Misty Wagner?"

"The dishwasher. Early twenties, quiet, stringy light-brown hair."

"Didn't notice anyone like that."

Poor girl. Hopefully she hung out at Triple G drinking beer and playing pool and didn't just sit alone in her room all night. I loved the idea of her having a secret party-girl persona.

"Leif and Latoya came out of The Inn first." Reed continued and paused to stare into the trees again. "Kim was saying something to someone in the lobby, I didn't see who."

"What did he say? Could you hear?"

"Something like have a good night and he'd see whoever it was in the morning."

"Probably Gin, but I suppose it could have been Laurel. They seem friendly with her. Maybe Wesley, but he opens the restaurant early so would probably be home by that time of night."

"Most likely it was Ms. Wakefield. What does that give us for a timeframe?"

"Using what you saw and my rigor test, we've got a time of death window of between ten last night and four this morning. Dr. Bundy will pin it down more for us."

With nothing else to do but wait for Dr. B, we started a search of the area. Since Wakefield was face down, it was possible she'd been shot. We could be looking for a bullet casing. Of course, "shot" also had a different meaning. Maybe we'd find a hypodermic needle. Possibly she'd been strangled, and we were looking for a length of rope. Really, neither of us expected to find anything. This was something to keep us busy until Dr. Bundy got here and we could roll the body over and get a better idea of what we were dealing with.

We had been searching the forest floor for about five minutes, when a woman came our way at a fast clip.

Chapter 13

"WHO IS SHE? IT'S GIN Wakefield, isn't it? Oh, my Goddess. I can't believe she's dead. What happened?"

Ruby McLaughlin had two speeds: mellow and meditative to do her crafts or high-strung. Right now, high-strung was fueled by the agitation of having found Wakefield's body.

"Ruby," I said in a stern yet soothing voice, "I need you to calm down and talk to me."

She placed her hands palms together at her breastbone and took in a long breath through her slender nose, then pursed her lips and blew it out. Ruby was striking. Her white hair hung in choppy chin-length layers on the right side and was shaved to about a quarter inch on the left. Her ivory skin was as flawless as porcelain and created the perfect backdrop for her signature ruby-red lipstick. She appeared to be in her early-twenties, but rumor had it she was in her late-thirties. Whatever variety of Wiccan witch she was, she'd clearly found a spell to keep her young looking.

"Okay," she said in a breathy, mellow voice, "I think I'm better now. Sorry about that."

"No need to apologize. Finding a dead body can be very

upsetting. Tell me what happened this morning."

"Sorry to interrupt," Reed said. "I'm going to start taking pictures."

"Great." I pulled Ruby a little farther down the path, out of his way, and repeated the question.

"The day started out normal," Ruby began. "I left my house to head to work right around six. I just love Mabon Fest. I've been doing my paperwork in the morning this week rather than after we close, so I can be with everyone later."

"At what point did you find Ms. Wakefield's body?"

She gasped at the confirmation. "I knew it was Gin." She stood with a hand over her mouth and then, assuring herself more than me, said, "I'm fine. I live on the west side of the village sort of near the parking lot. You know, the area where Violet, Honey and Sugar, Flavia, and most of the other Wiccans live."

"I'm familiar with the area. So you were on your way to The Twisty Skein this morning …"

"Right. Since I've been staying up a little later at night and waking a little earlier than normal in the morning the last couple of days, I decided to stop at Ye Olde Bean Grinder for one of Violet's coconut chai latte's today. Have you had one? They're delicious."

"I had one made with regular milk and chocolate. That was good too."

Ruby's mouth pinched in disapproval at my choice of non-vegan milk. "After I got my drink, I secured it in the basket on my bike and continued on to work. That's when I came across poor Ms. Wakefield."

"Do you know what time that would've been?"

She tapped her fingers against her chin, thinking. "It takes me not quite ten minutes to get to the Bean Grinder from home which means I got there no later than ten after six. I stayed and chatted with Violet for a few minutes, so what would that make it?" She did a quick calculation. "I probably headed for Twisty about six twenty and found Ms. Wakefield about six twenty-five."

Her voice broke, and I gave her a few seconds to regain control.

"After you found the body—"

Ruby flinched at my procedural way of referring to the victim.

"Sorry. After you found Ms. Wakefield, what did you do?"

"Well, I got off my bike, of course. I was riding along the wooden plankway and didn't want to ride on the forest floor. You never know what you might crush when you go off the path."

My cynical little mind immediately thought, *right, you don't want to crush a fairy*, then I silently smacked myself. Respecting nature could only be a good thing. Especially around here.

"What I'm asking is," I tried again, "at what point did you go back and ask Violet to contact me?"

"Ah, I understand. Obviously, I didn't continue to Twisty. Blue the cat was watching over Ms. Wakefield almost like a security guard when I found her. That's not really an important detail, but I thought it was sweet, her protecting her that way. Anyway, I know they have a talkie at the Bean Grinder, so I turned around, rode back over, and told Violet what I had discovered. That's when she called you on the talkie. I was standing right there when she did."

That lined up with Violet contacting me at six thirty. "Okay, this is good. It gives me a solid timeline."

"Are all these details important?" Ruby asked, curious.

"We never know which detail will be important and which won't be until we get further into an investigation. This is why I ask as many questions as I can right away. Everything is still fresh in your mind now, as well, so you'll be able to give more details than you would tomorrow or even later today."

"That makes sense. Is there anything else you need from me? Any other details I can provide?"

"I do have one more question."

Ruby fidgeted a little at my serious tone.

"This could be important so think carefully before answering. As you were riding around this morning, did you see anyone else? It was quite early, so another person probably would have stood out to you."

Ruby closed her eyes again and took in a long breath. Her long slender fingers waved about in the air; she seemed to be drawing a map of her route through the village while she thought. She started at her left shoulder and drew a line that curved down and back up in a half circle, indicating she must have gone south around the Pentacle Garden rather than north which would have been a straighter route for her from the Bean Grinder.

Her eyes shot open. "There were a few people setting up their food tables. A few, as in maybe four. People, not four tables. They had the path blocked outside Shoppe Mystique, so I went down and around the garden instead of straight across. Laurel was outside The Inn."

Laurel? The times when she had seemed uncharacteristically crabby over the past couple days flashed in my mind. That didn't mean anything, though. Certainly nothing that would make me connect her to a death.

"Laurel was outside The Inn," I repeated. "What was she doing?"

"Just standing there," Ruby said. "Have you ever seen her do that? Usually, it's to soak up the sun. Since I don't normally come to work this early, I don't know if that's something she does in the morning as well. I wouldn't be surprised, though."

I wouldn't either. That was Laurel. She only needed a few minutes alone to reset and be able to deal with her demanding guests. Being outside was the way she did it. Unfortunately, since Ruby mentioned her, now I was going to have to talk to her about Gin.

"Okay, good," I encouraged Ruby. "You saw Laurel and the four people near the Pentacle Garden. Anyone else?"

She paused for a second and then shook her head. "Just Violet and Basil in the Bean Grinder."

"Was anyone else in the coffee shop at that time?"

"Not a soul." She released a wistful sigh. "If I didn't have work to get to, I would have loved to sit in there for a while. You know what I mean?"

I smiled. I knew exactly what she meant. It was a tight race between Ye Olde Bean Grinder and Shoppe Mystique for coziest cottage in the village, but the coffee shop won by a nose. That was because while Morgan's shop was fun with all its different items, the Bean Grinder smelled like coffee and with its short ceiling, I felt like I was getting wrapped in a hug every time I walked in.

"Oh, wait." Ruby held her hands out in a stop motion. "Lily Grace was there. She was sitting in a corner quiet as a snowflake doing her homework."

For half a second, I wondered if Lily Grace was someone I should speak with and almost burst out laughing. I shoved the absurd thought to the back of my brain. If any possibility, no matter how remote, came to mind I'd pursue it. For now, it was a definite no.

I jotted down some quick notes about Ruby's statement. "I'm sorry your morning was so traumatic. I'll stop by your shop if I have any more questions, but for now you can go on back to work. It would be great if you could keep quiet about this for as long as possible. I'm sure you can imagine the chaos that will descend on the village once word of this gets out."

I shuddered as I envisioned news crews from Milwaukee, Madison, and possibly Minneapolis and Chicago invading Whispering Pines. Once that happened, it would surely be the end of Mabon Fest. I'd been here long enough to know how much the Wiccans loved their celebrations. What would happen if this one, one of their favorites, was cut short?

As Reed took pictures, I scanned the woods again for any evidence while waiting for Dr. Bundy. He appeared about fifteen minutes later.

"We held a lottery," the pudgy, gray-bearded man said in lieu of greeting. "How long before the next death in Whispering Pines?"

"You bet on us?" I asked and frowned. "Or would that be you bet against us?"

His balding head tilted to the side as he considered this. "I'm not sure. Joan won, by the way. Her bet was that it would be tomorrow."

Joan was his receptionist. "She plays a lot of bingo, doesn't she?"

"Goes down to the Potawatomi Casino in Milwaukee every Saturday. How'd you know?"

I shrugged. "Just a hunch."

"What have we got this time?" Dr. Bundy tugged on a pair of latex gloves and peered around me at the body on the wood plank path.

"I won't know until you turn her over, but I believe this is Ginger Wakefield—"

"The baker lady?"

"Is that look of shock because she's a celebrity or because you're a fan of her baked goods?"

He patted his bulging belly. "Definite fan. What a shame. Well, all deaths are."

Donovan's silver ponytailed head flashed in front of my face. "Maybe not all."

Dr. B squinted at me but ignored my statement and asked Reed, "Are you finished taking pictures, Deputy?"

"I am from this angle." Reed stepped aside. "I'll need to take more once she's facing upward."

"Very good." The ME motioned for the paramedics who'd arrived with him to turn the body over. He blinked, startled, when they did. "Wasn't expecting to see that."

Gin Wakefield's face was swollen to the point that her eyes were nearly closed. Her lips had puffed to three times their normal size.

"Allergic reaction?" I recalled the discussion in the great room the other night. "She's allergic to honey and bee stings."

Dr. Bundy was on his knees, his hand to Gin's thigh.

Startled by the action, I asked, "What are you doing?"

"Looking for a pulse, which I'm sure you already did. Everywhere else on her is too swollen, so I'm checking her femoral artery. Nothing, by the way." To the paramedics, he said, "Hand me two bags, would you?" He pointed out a spot on the back of her hand as he secured a plastic bag around it to preserve any evidence on her skin or under her fingernails. "See this mark?"

I knelt next to him and saw a tiny raised mark surrounded by tiny red dots.

"Bug bite?" How had he noticed that so quickly?

"Possibly. But since we already know she's got this allergy, and she clearly suffered a severe reaction, my guess is it's a bee sting." He grunted as he got back to his feet. "I'll test her for bee venom. Go ahead and finish taking your pictures, Deputy."

"If she was that allergic and was stung by a bee—"

"Bees," he corrected. "Multiple places on her body are swollen. A bee only stings once. Hornets, wasps, and yellow jackets are the little buggers that will keep attacking. I'll know for sure when I examine her, but I'm guessing I'll find numerous little stingers with venom sacs attached. The mark on her hand is easy to see, but I can almost guarantee there will be more. I'll find them."

"All right, if she was stung by bees," I indicated the path she had presumably been taking, "it's a safe assumption she was on her way to the health center to get help."

"If she was that allergic," the doctor corrected me again, "she would've had an epinephrine pen on her at all times. I'll check during the exam to see if she injected herself. Maybe she got a faulty pen. That doesn't happen often, but it does happen. Or maybe she needed two injections and only had one pen with her. I'm just guessing now."

While Reed continued with his pictures, I noted that Wakefield was dressed in green plaid pajama pants, tan suede slippers with no socks, and an oversized white T-shirt with "I Love Maldives" and a palm tree on the front. That was it. It got chilly last night and she didn't even have a sweater. So, whatever happened to her, it seemed safe to assume it didn't happen here on the path. She wouldn't be out and about dressed that way.

When Reed had finished, Dr. Bundy instructed the paramedics to place Wakefield in a body bag and then bring her to the ambulance. Dr. Bundy, Reed, and I stood in respectful silence as they did this. Once they'd left with her, I asked, "Any way you can keep this quiet for a while?"

"I'm not the one you have to worry about," Dr. Bundy replied. "Her people will know soon, I assume."

"They will." I shook my head and groaned. "News stations and reporters are the last things we need around here."

Dr. Bundy gave me a consoling pat on the shoulder and told me he'd be in touch as soon as he had preliminary results. "I can do her autopsy right away. We've got a little lull in the action now that we're past Labor Day. Things will pick up again once winter sets in. Slippery roads, reckless snowmobilers, ice fishing folks who refuse to wait for the ice on the lakes to get thick enough." He sighed, waved goodbye, and went on his way.

"Let me guess," Reed asked, "you'd like me to stick around instead of going back to Green Bay."

"That's a big yes. I have a feeling that things are about to get crazy around here."

Chapter 14

AFTER DR. BUNDY AND THE paramedics left, Reed and I spent another half hour scanning the woods for anything that might indicate someone had been involved with Wakefield's death. We found nothing remotely suspicious. Looked like bees were both the weapon and the killer. Although, until the autopsy results came back confirming that, I wanted us to start an investigation as though this was a murder. It wasn't an unreasonable assumption. Since I arrived in the village, almost every death here had been murder or manslaughter.

Once done with our search, we stood in the middle of the Fairy Path not only trying to decide how to proceed but also taking advantage of a few more minutes of peace. Once we stepped off the path, we'd get swarmed. And when word of Gin Wakefield's death got out, chaos would descend on the village.

"Let's do it this way," I suggested, "I'm going to start talking to people and find out if anyone knows anything about what happened to Gin. I've got a special assignment for you."

Reed pushed his shoulders back and stood taller. "Special assignment?"

"Don't get too excited, it's not *that* special." He knew

about Wakefield's allergies, and I told him that Dr. Bundy felt she had been stung by bees. "I'd like you to find information on allergies to bee stings and honey. Good to be informed since it's a safe bet that's where this is headed."

"I can do that." He took a half-step toward the station, ready to go. Reed liked doing research. "Anything else?"

"Just man the fort. I'm sure something else will come up soon. Restock the crime scene kit before anything, would you?" We turned and headed off in separate directions. "Oh, let Violet know she can go back to Ye Olde Bean Grinder."

He gave a salute. "Aye, aye."

When Meeka and I got to the end of the path, we found a crowd. A dozen or more tourists wanted to know why they couldn't stroll through the woods with their morning coffee. For the first time in weeks, Effie and Cybil, standing next to the little fortune tellers' wagon, gave me questioning looks instead of evil eye ones. I responded with a quick shake of my head, indicating I couldn't say anything right now. The one person I was afraid I'd run into was there as well.

"What's going on, Sheriff?" There was acid in Lupe's too-loud voice.

"You're mad at *me*?" I whispered to her. "You treat me like I'm the reason your proposal was denied, and now you think I'm going to share information with you?"

She stood with her arms crossed. "Yes, I'm mad at you. I thought you were on my side."

The crowd, which was slowly closing in on us, wanted to hear my response to her "what's going on" question.

"Everything's fine now, folks," I called out. "You're free to use the Fairy Path now. Thanks for your patience." I jerked my head to the side, indicating Lupe should come with me as I made my way to The Inn. "What did you expect me to do? Plead your case to the council?"

"I expected you'd do *something*." Lupe blinked back tears.

"You know how badly I want to stay in the village."

"Wanting to stay isn't good enough around here." My irritation with Lupe was starting to rise. There was nothing wrong with asking, but she seemed to think that was all she had to do to get what she wanted. "Look, Tripp wanted to stay here as badly as you do. The council denied him too."

"And now he's living with you."

I narrowed my eyes at her. "So, what, you think I should let you move into my B&B?"

Very subtly, she shrugged.

"Lupe, Tripp is my boyfriend. Not only that, he's my business partner." I had a memory flash of my grandmother letting families move in with her. When every room in the house was full and people were still coming, they started building the cottages. "I'm sorry, but I'm not the answer to your problem. If you want to permanently rent a room at Pine Time, that could be arranged."

As Lupe fought off tears, I looked away. Meeka and Blue were playing tag. First Meeka nipped at Blue's tail and then Blue swatted in return. Meeka yelped; Blue must've snagged her butt with a claw.

"You abstained," Lupe blurted.

I stretched my neck side-to-side, trying to release the tension forming there. "Your idea wasn't a bad one. If you had presented it to any other community, it probably would've been accepted. You know Whispering Pines is different from most places, though. There just isn't a need for a newspaper here."

She shook her head. "There's more to it than that. Why did you abstain?"

I took great pride in my instincts and being able to read people. Lupe's instincts were just as good, and she was using them against me.

"The plot of your story." I waited for her to fill in the blanks. When she didn't, I spelled it out. "Your main character sets up her own crimes? I told you in confidence that Sugar had said that to me. You know how offended I was, and still am, by that. Now you're turning it into a novel?"

Lupe's jaw dropped. "You think I'm writing about you? Honestly, Jayne, you have to see that it's a good storyline. I never once thought Sugar was right; I know you're not setting up the deaths around here. But like Dexter, that TV show about the serial killer who only kills bad people, the writer in me knows this is too good to pass up." She put her left hand in the air and her right over her heart. "I swear this isn't about you. My main character in no way resembles you. She's Latina, so if anyone, she resembles me."

The two of us were equally stressed out but for very different reasons. I'd been set up by some of the villagers to be the savior of Whispering Pines and had no idea how to fulfill that edict. Lupe was fighting for her professional life and seemed to be losing the battle.

"Truce?" I asked.

Her entire body relaxed. "Truce. Now, tell me what was going on in the woods this morning."

That was Lupe, straight to the story. "Let me start by saying that, other than myself, there are only a handful of people who know who the victim is. I need to keep this quiet for as long as possible, so if it gets out, it won't be hard for me to figure out who leaked."

"*Ay, dios mio,*" she muttered. "Will you please stop with that." It was a command, not a request, her accent growing stronger with each word. "We have this discussion every time you give me information. I want the scoop. For the last time, I won't abuse that privilege."

I took in a breath and blew it out. "Gin Wakefield is dead."

"No! Gin Wakefield? What happened?"

"We don't know much yet. Dr. Bundy is putting a rush on

the autopsy. I've got Reed back at the station doing some research. I'm on my way to The Inn to talk to people there."

As always, Lupe perked up at the mention of Reed. "What is Martin researching?"

There were plenty of things I was willing to share with her, but in the case of a murder, only the killer would know the means of death. That was the one piece of information I never revealed. If that detail got out, the whole case could be compromised.

Realizing I wasn't going to answer that, she let it go. "Fine. What can I do? How can I help?"

"Like I said, all I have is a body and a possible means of death. I have no idea if there's something nefarious going on or if this was simply bad fortune on Wakefield's part. For now, you can help me by keeping things normal. Keep talking to people at the fest today like you have been. Ask your subtle questions and see if there's anyone who doesn't love the woman."

"I can do that."

"I'm sure you can guess what's going to happen around here once word of this gets out."

"*Ay, sí.* There will be television and newspaper people from everywhere. Gin Wakefield is a national celebrity."

"Exactly. I don't know how Whispering Pines is going to handle that kind of attention."

"It won't be for just a day or two," Lupe warned. "People will keep coming for months to see the place where one of the nation's favorite bakers died."

Egad. I hadn't thought of the long tail effects of this. "I promise, if there's something you can help me with, I will come to you. The best thing you can do for me right now is to keep working on your article."

Lupe clicked her heels together, stood at attention like a soldier, and then headed for the center of the Pentacle Garden.

Inside The Inn, there were a few people sitting near the fireplace in the lobby. A few more were standing at the registration desk waiting to speak with Emery, who'd recently been promoted to head desk clerk. Assistant Manager had to be next; he knew almost as much about this place as Laurel. He was currently giving a couple in their mid-fifties directions to a few good hiking trails in the area.

"I'm sorry to interrupt, this will just take a second," I told the couple and leaned down to whisper to Emery. "Has housekeeping started their rounds yet?"

"Shouldn't have yet." His voice cracked, as it often did. "They should start in the next twenty minutes or so. What's up, Sheriff?"

"I need them to stay out of Gin Wakefield's room. I'm going to put some 'Do Not Enter' tape across the door. No one but myself or Deputy Reed goes in there."

Emery's eyes bugged out. "Is there a problem with Ms. Wakefield?"

"Nothing that I can talk about right now and nothing that should be mentioned to others. Do you understand?"

He clamped his lips together and nodded.

"Do you know where Laurel is?"

"Last I saw her, she was in the dining room getting ready for today's competition."

"Which room is Ms. Wakefield's?"

"Ten," he replied without hesitation. Emery really knew his guests.

"I'm going to run up there quick. If you see Laurel, let her know I'm looking for her and will be right down."

He gave me a passkey for Wakefield's room and verified that only she had a key for it. Then he picked up the phone to tell housekeeping to stay out of the room.

On the third floor, I inspected the door to room number ten before opening it. It was closed but not locked. There were no signs of foul play such as forced entry. I was itching to investigate inside, but I had no equipment with me. Not even gloves since I'd used my only pair at the site. Instead, I used a tissue from a box on a table in the hall to press on the very end of the lever knob, preserving any possible prints.

I opened the door and was instantly assaulted by the smell of overripe bananas. It was almost overpowering. Along with that, the room had been torn apart. The bedding was in a tangle, and Wakefield's possessions lay scattered across the floor like someone had been searching for something.

Meeka stuck her nose just over the threshold and sniffed. She didn't alert on anything, so no drugs. More importantly, no bodies.

"Stay here."

She took a few steps back into the hallway and sat as I announced, "This is Sheriff O'Shea. Is anyone in this room?"

I waited a few seconds, called out again, and when I still didn't get a response, I entered, taking care to not step on anything. I took three steps and peeked around the corner into the bathroom. It was clear, no one was in there, and not trashed like the main room. Either Reed or I would need to get over here with the investigation kit ASAP.

I closed the door again, insured that it was locked, and secured an X of yellow "Do Not Enter" police tape to the frame. I considered the looky-loo factor, meaning that when other guests saw the tape they'd start asking questions about what had happened. I almost took it down, but the bigger risk was that housekeeping would enter and clean the room. I'd deal with guests' questions as they came up.

When I got to the bottom of the narrow, creaking, popping staircase and passed in front of the registration desk, Emery gaped at me as though I might be a bomb about to go off. I gave him a pointed look, and he returned to the guests standing in front of him.

Considering there was a food fest going on outside, The Inn's restaurant was closed, dining room empty. First time I'd seen that. There was almost always someone occupying a table. I wandered through the swinging doors that led into the kitchen, searching for Laurel, and instead found Wesley, The Inn's head chef, and one of his employees hunched over a notebook.

"Sheriff O'Shea," Wesley startled at my sudden appearance.

Five foot ten, short dark-brown hair, fifty pounds overweight.

Gran always said, "Never trust a skinny cook." She must have loved Wesley. He had the rounded, wholesome, happy appearance of a man who liked to eat and didn't apologize for it. His homestyle cooking was very good. I'd be fifty pounds overweight too if I could cook like that. I paused, realizing Tripp could. Good thing I had to do so much walking in this village.

"Sorry to startle you," I said. "I thought the restaurant was closed."

"We're not serving," Wesley explained, "but we are working. We use Mabon Fest as a time to reevaluate our menu. I'm one of the judges for the cooking division of the competition. Occasionally, there's an entry that fits our old-world theme and stands out enough for us to take a closer look. We won't have many patrons from now until Memorial Day, so we test new dishes with them to see what's good enough to get added to next season's menu. Sorry, that's more than you wanted to know. Was there something you needed?"

"No need to apologize. Tripp and I are running a mini-Inn now. Always good to know how the pros do it. I was looking for Laurel. Have you seen her?"

"Oh, she's around here somewhere. She was getting ready for today's competition. Hard to pin that woman down. She never stops moving. You might want to check outside."

I thanked him and took two steps away before turning back. "Actually, if you have a minute, you might be able to help me with something else."

Wesley's expression changed to one that I was well familiar with. As soon as a law enforcement officer started asking questions, people assumed either something bad had happened or they were in trouble.

"The Wakefield party has been taking over your kitchen the last few days," I began. "How did that come about?"

"Laurel insisted," Wesley said simply and with obvious frustration. "What could I do? It's my kitchen in that I run it, but Laurel owns the building."

"You don't seem happy about the invasion."

He chuckled, but not in a happy way. "Invasion is the right word. Letting another chef in here this way is akin to blasphemy. Honestly, if it was anyone other than Gin Wakefield, I would have put up a big fight. But to let someone of her status and celebrity bake in my kitchen is almost like putting a blessing on the place."

"Did you hang out here while they were baking?"

"I did the first night. Fernando, my sous-chef, did too." He indicated the man standing nearby. "To watch them creating that croquembouche was a true honor. Even though they all usually work in separate areas of their bakery, they came together that night like a single unit. Gin stood back and supervised every movement while the other two did the work." He paused and amended that. "There were five of them altogether. Chef Wakefield, the two bakers, their dishwasher, and the other guy. I don't know who he was."

"He's the CFO," I explained. "What, in your opinion, were the attitudes of the others?"

Wesley paused like he didn't quite understand the question. "They followed orders like any good kitchen staff does."

Fernando laughed and then covered it up with a cough.

"Something you'd like to contribute, Nando?" Wesley asked.

"No, nothing, Chef."

"Fernando," I began, "I'm actually conducting a formal investigation. If there's something you think I should know, please feel free to say it."

"Sheriff," Wesley asked, "what's going on?"

"I can't say much at this point." I chose my words carefully, not wanting to reveal Wakefield's death. "A crime has been committed—"

"Involving the Wakefield party?" Fernando asked. The "yes" had barely left my mouth, and he had more to say. "Any chef worth working for is demanding of their staff. Chef Wakefield was extremely demanding. It was nothing unusual, but whenever she would leave the kitchen, the others would grumble about her." He shrugged. "Just normal banter."

"You all grumble about me when I leave the kitchen?" Wesley asked him.

"Of course we do. By the end of the summer season, you're a bear to work with, Chef."

"Do you recall anything in particular that Ms. Wakefield's people might have said?" I asked.

"You mean anything suspicious?" Fernando's expectant expression was one I'd seen many times. It said he was eager to help solve a crime.

I did my best to remain neutral and not lead him. "What's labeled suspicious in one workplace could be normal in another. I don't know what would be considered an odd discussion between kitchen employees. Was there anything you felt was unusual? Anything at all?"

Wesley and I watched as Fernando seemed to scan his memory for anything worth telling me about.

"I was doing some work of my own at the time," Fernando qualified, "and may not have heard exactly. One of them, one of the guys, I didn't see which, said something about Ms. Wakefield being 'in it for herself.' He didn't give details, but it seemed to me he was talking about something specific. I assume the other two knew exactly what he meant because they agreed with him. Then the first guy said something to the effect of everything will be taken care of soon."

Wesley crossed his arms and rested them on his belly. "That sounds like conspiracy of some kind."

"That's what I was thinking." I looked squarely at Fernando. "Are discussions about conspiracy standard kitchen banter?"

He hung his head. "No. This was the first night they were here, and I admit, I was a little starstruck by them. Guess I like to believe that when you make it that big"—he turned to his boss—"nothing against you or The Inn, but when you get to work with someone like Chef Wakefield, I'd like to believe that you're happy with your job so didn't think of it as being something illegal." He shrugged. "I guess that's sort of naïve of me."

"Does this help you with your investigation, Sheriff?" Wesley asked.

"Honestly, I'm not sure yet. We're still putting together the details of exactly what happened. I never know what will matter and what won't, so it could end up being important. Thank you for this information."

"You know where to find us if we can help more," Wesley offered, and Fernando agreed.

"I need the two of you to keep this to yourselves. Like I said, we're just starting to pull things together, and we don't want rumors spreading."

Meeka and I left the kitchen, crossed through the dining room, and went out the back door to the competition staging area. As Wesley predicted, Laurel was there, lying on one of the lounge chairs, not moving.

Chapter 15

I ADMIT, FOR A SECOND I thought Laurel was dead. Not an unreasonable assumption around here. Then I saw her chest move and realized she was just soaking up some sun.

"Laurel?" I asked softly.

She put a hand over her eyes like a sunshield and peeked one eye open at me. Half a second later, she sat straight up. "What's the matter? What happened to Gin?"

I must give off an aura of some kind when I showed up to question people. I saw Laurel often, almost daily, and she'd never had that reaction to seeing me before. How did she know that this time something was wrong?

"What makes you think something happened to Gin?" I asked.

Laurel stood from the lounge chair and came over to me. "Her crew was here this morning, but she never showed up."

"When were they here?" I took out the little notebook and pen from my cargo pants pocket to take notes.

"Let me think." Laurel rested her hands on her hips and stared at the ground as she ran through the events of her morning. "Since I'm a judge, it wouldn't be right for me to have any knowledge of what contestants are working on, so I asked Emery to grab me some coffee from the kitchen. He mentioned no one was there yet. That was at seven thirty."

"You're sure of that time?"

"Yep. I had an eight thirty phone call and wanted to go over my notes first. Right before the call, Latoya poked her head in and asked if I'd seen her. That means they got here sometime between seven thirty and eight thirty."

Tripp planned to serve breakfast at seven, a little earlier than normal to accommodate their baking schedule, so this matched up with that. "That's later than the other days. Did they plan a late start?"

"Today's entries are less intricate than yesterday's, so they didn't need to get here as early. That's what Gin told them before they left last night. I was in the lobby when the three were leaving and overheard the statement. I know that Gin runs her kitchen like a military operation. If she says they're going to start at eight, they'd all better be here by seven fifty."

"On time is late," I quipped.

"Exactly."

"What did you tell Latoya?"

"That I hadn't seen Gin and suggested they see if she was in her room. Did you check there?"

"I did. No sign of her."

Laurel stiffened at my response. "Jayne, what happened to Gin?"

As soon as I let her know that Gin Wakefield was dead, getting answers from her would become much more difficult. I sidestepped the question. "Were you aware of any troubles going on with the Wakefield team? Business troubles, I mean."

Laurel gave me a look that clearly said she knew I was holding back. "No, I haven't heard of any troubles. Then again, I wouldn't be privy to that information. What kind of troubles are you talking about?"

I repeated what Fernando had told me about Kim, Latoya,

and Leif complaining about Gin whenever she left the kitchen.

Laurel laughed heartily at this. "I know the last thing you are is naïve. Employees have complained about their bosses since the first employee/boss relationship. I did, you must have. Martin may follow every word you say like it's scripture right now but give it time. He'll grumble about you soon enough too."

That felt unnecessarily nasty. "You seem awfully grumpy lately, Laurel. I thought this was supposed to be the Wiccans' favorite time of year."

"Why don't you ask me what you came to ask me?" She twisted side to side, her spine cracking as she did.

"Ruby from The Twisty Skein reported seeing you outside this morning around six twenty."

Laurel just stared. Guess I needed to rephrase that in the form of a question.

"Were you standing outside The Inn this morning around six twenty?"

"I was. I often take advantage of moments to myself. You know that. A few minutes of sunshine and fresh air throughout the day helps me destress and stay focused."

"You seem more stressed than usual. What's going on?"

"You've seen how crazy it is around here right now. Not as bad as at the height of the summer season, obviously, but I'm not organizing and judging a cooking competition in the summer on top of managing The Inn and a couple guest cottages. I've been getting up early and spending a little time outside before my workday gets going. Is there a problem with that?"

"Of course there isn't."

I took a half-step back and studied her. Laurel was constantly busy but handled everything with ease. Work stuff never bothered her. She thrived on it. Whatever was going on, she wasn't herself. I waited in silence for a minute or so for her to start talking, but she remained equally, stubbornly mute. There was only one way to get her to tell me what was really going on, and there was no easy way to deliver this kind of news. It would probably come across like a slap to the face, but unless I was telling a family member or close friend, I always went with the rip off the bandage approach.

"Laurel, Gin Wakefield's body was found on the Fairy Path this morning shortly before six thirty."

I took a step closer when Laurel paled and swayed a little. I'd had people faint on me too many times to not be prepared to catch them when I delivered bad news. If the person already seemed shaky, I had them sit before I broke the news. I guided Laurel back down onto the lounge chair and took a seat next to her.

"What happened?" Laurel asked when the shock wore off a bit.

"We're not entirely sure yet. The medical examiner is going to do the autopsy today."

As though coming out of a daze, she asked, "Wait a minute, do you think I had something to do with this?"

"No, but you have been acting odd lately, so I think you might know more than you're revealing. Is it true that you arranged some last-minute favors for Gin?" When she didn't respond right away, I added, "Tripp overheard her staff talking about how she didn't get her paperwork in on time, but you let her enter anyway. Why would you do that?"

Laurel took a long moment before answering. "Another Whispering Pines secret. Well, the village has nothing to do with this one. Everyone knew how close Sugar and Gin were when they were kids. In fact, a lot of people felt bad for Honey when Gin came along because Sugar started spending all her time with Gin."

Her words were crisp and clipped and tinted with attitude.

"You were jealous?"

"I was," she admitted without hesitation. "But not because they were friends. I had my own good friends, the kids in the Pack. Besides, Sugar and Gin were five years younger than me. No, I was jealous of them because, as teenagers, they could cook and bake like no one's business."

"You wanted kitchen witch skills."

"I did. Hospitality has been a part of my world since my mom opened The Inn. I can set up a room that will make you feel more at ease than in your own home. I can ensure that you want for nothing while you're here. A visit to The Inn will leave you feeling refreshed, cared for, and ready to come back the moment you leave. That's my 'witchy' talent, as some might call it. The only thing missing from my repertoire is being able to prepare meals for my guests."

"But you made those muffins the other day and they were really good."

She inclined her head in thanks and immediately shrugged it off. "There are a handful of things I can make that turn out all right, but nothing like what Sugar, Gin, and Reeva can do. I was so envious of them I couldn't sleep some nights." She shook her head sharply, trying to dismiss whatever memory was tormenting her. "I've gotten past it for the most part. I truly love my life and am very happy running The Inn. It's satisfying to know that my guests leave here feeling better than when they arrived. But once a year ..."

"Mabon Fest brings it all back," I completed the thought for her.

"It does. All the food and praise for the cooks is front and center, and the old envy comes back. The villagers who have known me for years are used to it. They don't know why, but they expect I'll get crabby at the end of September. It's standing out to you because you've only known me for four months. I can put on a happy face for my guests, so they have no clue anything's bothering me. I admit, this year is harder. With Gin being here and all." She released a little groan of sorrow. "I still can't believe she's dead."

"If her being here made this harder for you, why did you do all the favors for her?"

She threw her hands in the air. "She asked. My job is hospitality. I'm trained to accommodate whenever possible." There was more to it than that. I waited, silent again, and this time she eventually admitted, "I felt bad about what they did to her after culinary school."

"You mean denying her a shop of her own?"

"Right. It was uncalled for either way, but with her mom being sick and all, it was even worse."

"Her mom was sick? I didn't know that." I thought of my conversation with Gin on the dock. This explained why she got so emotional when the topic of her mother came up.

"Yeah, I'm not sure with what exactly. Something neurological, I think. Whatever it was, it was chronic. Tons of medical bills."

"When is the last time you saw Gin?"

"Last night." She put her hands over her face and then blew out a hard breath. "Her team used either the boardroom or the dining room to come up with their plan last night. They wrapped up around ten o'clock, and after the others left, Gin and I sat in the lobby and talked for another hour." The tears she'd been trying to hold back finally fell. "It was a lovely conversation. I told her how I envied her career that took her all around the world. She said she envied mine for being able to stay right here in the village." She sniffed. "She really did love it here. We were going to have dinner together tonight."

"She went up to her room around eleven, then?" I noted this on my timeline.

"Right."

Her statement fit with my rigor mortis estimation. It also

fit with what Reed had told me about seeing her employees leaving around ten o'clock.

"Do you know when she died?" Laurel asked and then quickly amended the question. "Do you know approximately when she died?"

"Sometime between eleven and four is all I can safely estimate at this point. What you just told me fits with that. I have one more question. When you were outside this morning, did you see anyone else walking around the Pentacle Garden? In particular, was anyone near the Fairy Path?"

She stared out at the lake as she thought. "A handful of people were setting up their food tables. I saw Ruby ride past on her bike." She frowned and then met my eyes. "There was one person over by the Fairy Path. You're not going to like this answer."

"It's not my job to like or dislike answers. My job is to gather the facts and figure out the truth. Who was it?"

"I saw Sugar."

Chapter 16

LAUREL WAS RIGHT, I DIDN'T like that answer. In fact, it was the last one I wanted to hear.

"You saw Sugar near the Fairy Path this morning?" I verified.

"Shortly after I saw Ruby," Laurel said.

"Have you ever seen her out there that early before? I understand bakers are up before the sun."

"Sometimes. She and Honey are usually to the shop by five, and they open at nine."

"But this time was different?" Laurel wasn't being very free with the information now. I had to practically pry it out of her.

"If I see her early, she's usually just walking around the cottage. You know, checking the landscaping and getting a little air. Sometimes she'll make a loop around the garden. This time, she was walking away from the shop with a purpose, if you know what I mean. Not a leisurely stroll, more like she was off to get something."

"Do you know where she was going?"

"No, just that she was headed east. Maybe it was just a walk, but if I had to guess I'd say she was going to Sundry."

A mental map of the village popped up in my mind. There was a south trailhead for the Fairy Path that exited closer to Sundry. She could have entered the path at that end, come across Gin, and the two got into a fight. A fight that ended in death over a cake?

No, this didn't fit. Laurel saw Sugar around six thirty. Wakefield would have been dead for two or three hours by that point.

"Sundry makes the most sense," Laurel concluded, interrupting and echoing my thoughts. "She probably needed some ingredients for her entry today."

"Sundry isn't open at six thirty in the morning."

"No, but Sugar runs a sweet shop. You can be sure she's got a hotline to Peyton."

That was true. As far as I knew, Sugar and Honey ordered all their ingredients from the restaurant supply place they'd given Tripp the contact information for. Things happened, though, and if they ran out of something, Peyton could certainly help them out until their next shipment came. Like every other shop owner around this village, all Peyton wanted was for his customers to be happy. He'd be available twenty-four hours a day for them.

"You saw her going that direction, did you see her come back?"

Laurel shook her head. "I wasn't out there that long. It wasn't even five minutes after I saw her that I went back inside."

I made a note of the approximate times and details. "We need to keep quiet about this. News of one of the villagers being involved in this will be a big shock."

Laurel frowned at me. "Don't tell me you really think Sugar did this."

"I can't ignore the things she said yesterday afternoon. Everyone heard her tell Gin to watch her back."

"And you consider that a serious threat?" Laurel gave a skeptical laugh.

I'd heard many kinds of threats that turned serious during my time as a cop. Some were as simple as someone pointing a finger gun at the eventual victim. Others were verbal threats, like what Sugar said to Gin. Still others contained explicit descriptions of what one person was going to do to another. Humans could be awful to each other.

"You never know what's genuine and what isn't. What I know for sure is that I'm not doing my job if I don't at least check it out."

~~~

The bell above the door at Treat Me Sweetly rang out happily as I entered. Honey was by herself, dusting the huge brown wood shelves that held dozens of apothecary jars filled with old-fashioned candies. She turned and gave Meeka and me a bright smile when she saw us standing there.

"Well, hey there, Sheriff. And Deputy. Our freezers up front here are empty today due to the fest, but I can put together something in back for you if you want."

"Thanks, Honey, but that's not what we're here for. Is Sugar around?"

She positioned a jar of jaw breakers on the shelf. "No, she had to run an errand."

"Now? Shouldn't you two be putting together your entry for the competition today?"

"That's why she had to leave. Someone bought every banana over at Sundry."

Instantly, I thought of the intense aroma that came out of Gin's hotel room when I opened that door. This simple thing tying the two women together made my instincts flare from a little flame to a raging inferno. Had Gin somehow known that

Sugar would need them and bought them out of spite? On the flipside, Sugar left town when she should be baking for the competition that meant so much to her right after her nemesis was found dead. Was she really running an errand?

"When do you expect her back?"

Honey dusted a jar of lemon drops and returned it to the shelf. Then she started on a jar of root beer barrels. "It depends. She could be back any minute. If she can't find what she needs, she'll drive over to Ashland—"

"Ashland? That's quite a drive. Are bananas really that important?"

"It's a theme," Honey said with a small tired sigh. "She's planning eight different banana dishes. Six if we don't have enough time. You know Sugar; her mind is like a bear trap. She gets something set in there and it's got to happen." Honey turned her attention to a jar of Pixy Stix next. "What do you need Sugar for, Jayne?"

The tone in her voice made it clear she knew I was here for official reasons. Once again, I had to be projecting some special aura. This was exactly why Whispering Pines didn't need a newspaper. We all could tell just by looking at each other when something was wrong. And I'd only been here four months. The people who had lived here most of their lives, if not all their lives, mustn't even need to speak to each other to have a conversation.

"I talked with Gin Wakefield the other night, and she told me about growing up here. Tell me what you know about Sugar's history with Gin."

"Oh, they were like any other teenage girls." Honey finished with a jar of Necco wafers and then turned to me. "Sometimes they couldn't live without each other for more than five minutes, other times they couldn't stand seeing each other's face."

"But it got even worse than that, didn't it? Gin claimed

that your mom and dad were responsible for her not being able to open a shop here."

Honey sat at the closest café table and pointed for me to take the chair across from her. She let out a sigh that seemed to come from the furthest depth of her soul. "I don't know for sure what happened between Sugar and Gin when they were away at the culinary school. Sugar got accepted first and was so excited. I think she was disappointed that Gin chose the same school. I understand that. She wanted something just for herself. That's hard to have in a village this size. Everyone means well, but they all know what's going on in your life before you've barely had time to celebrate it. That's exaggerating a little bit, but you know what I mean."

"The good and the bad of living in a small town. Things were pretty bad when they graduated from the culinary school, weren't they?"

"Sugar worked so hard and had maintained the top spot in their class for the entire last year. Then right at the end, Gin swooped in and took it from her. Sugar was never able to let that go."

"Is that why your parents denied her a shop of her own?"

Honey got very quiet, and when she finally responded, there were tears in her eyes. "It had nothing to do with punishing Gin. What no one in the village knew was that Daddy was dying of cancer." She paused and through a pained expression added, "Guess it is possible to keep secrets around here."

"Keeping secrets isn't the problem. Preventing those things from happening in the first place is."

"That's true. Anyway, Sugar and I had found out about Daddy after her first year at the school. Mama told us there was no way she could handle the shop on her own, and Sugar immediately said she would take over running it when she graduated. Sugar loves Whispering Pines, always has. It wasn't a hardship of any kind for her to take over that shop and stay here forever."

"You lost me. What does that have to do with your parents saying no to Gin's shop?"

"They were trying to protect us. Mama and Daddy decided they would leave the village once Sugar was comfortable with everything in the shop. They went to live with Mama's sister in Oregon. That way Daddy would be away from the well-meaning villagers here as he got sicker, and Mama would have someone to be with after he died. They asked us to go with them, and when we said no, they wanted to be sure we could take care of ourselves. That meant no competition in the village that could potentially shut us down or hurt our sales enough that we couldn't support ourselves. Both were real possibilities if Gin opened a shop."

"So they made sure that didn't happen."

Honey tilted her ear to the back room. Making sure Sugar wasn't back there? "Everyone knew that Gin was more creative than Sugar, but no one can outbake Sugar when it comes to homestyle things. Not even Gin Wakefield can bake cookies, bars, and simple breads the way Sugar does. Gin could outshine her in the more technical areas—pastries, cakes, pies, more involved desserts, that kind of thing. I guarantee a shop of hers would've taken business from us."

"You think that's what happened with their final project? Gin simply outshined her?"

"I do. I wouldn't be surprised if Gin held herself back all that time just so she could wow and amaze the instructors with her final." She considered that and backed off a bit. "That might be a little extreme."

"That's why it was so important to Sugar to beat her in this competition? Home turf wars between two rivals?"

"You got it. Sugar doesn't care about Gin's popularity or financial success. All she cares about is this village." Honey folded her dust rag and placed it in a neat square on the café table. "Why exactly are we spending so much time talking about Sugar and Gin? I assume it's not just chitchat until my sister gets back."

I tried to tear this bandage a little more slowly. "There's no easy way to say this, Honey. Gin was found dead this morning."

Honey accepted this news with a silent bow of her head and then burst into tears. She cried for almost two minutes before the tears dried up and her expression turned stony. "You think my sister is responsible."

"There was a lot of animosity and a threat or two tossed around over the last couple days. Yesterday, when Gin produced a replica of your shop, your sister was furious. Everyone saw that."

"She didn't do it." No other explanation offered. The certainty in Honey's voice almost convinced me to let it go right then and there.

"Do you have proof of that?"

"She didn't do it."

"I want to believe that," I told her with all sincerity. "And I really hope I'll be able to prove that she's innocent. Right now, however, she is a suspect, and I need to bring her in and question her."

"She didn't do it." She crossed her arms and turned away from me.

Now she was starting to aggravate me. "Honey, not only did she make threats in front of the entire village, she left town. You told me she should be back soon. I really hope she is because if she doesn't show up in the next hour, I'm going to have to call the County Sheriff's Office and put out a BOLO on her."

"Speak English, please." I'd never heard such anger in Honey's voice.

"A BOLO is a police order that stands for 'be on the lookout.' If I issue one and an officer finds Sugar, they will arrest her. If you can get in touch with her, I suggest you do so and tell her to get back to the village as fast as she can."

Chapter 17

I STEPPED OUTSIDE OF TREAT Me Sweetly and pulled my walkie-talkie off my belt. I was about to call Reed and tell him about Sugar, and then remembered there were ten other active units around the village. I couldn't let anyone else hear about this.

"Looks like we're hoofing it back to the station," I told Meeka. But when I started walking, she dug in her paws. "What's the matter?" And then I realized, no biscuits. "Sorry, girl. No way am I going back in to ask Honey for some."

Meeka was determined to get her treat, though, and dropped to the ground. Spoiled little furball.

Since nearly every shop in the village handed out treats for furry visitors, I thought one of the tables might have pet treats. It didn't take long and I spotted a banner with paw prints all over it.

"Okay, let's go see if we can find some."

Meeka jumped up, tail wagging, and followed me to the table. The woman there, a local Wiccan who took in every stray animal that crossed her door, had little parchment bags filled with different flavored treats for dogs and cats.

"You've got something marketable here," I complimented

when Meeka devoured one biscuit and begged for another. "Meeka rarely begs. She thinks it's beneath her."

I tossed Meeka another biscuit, and the woman slipped another little bag to me. "It certainly can't be a bad thing for the community's K-9 to like them."

"Do you need a spokesdog?" I teased.

"Possibly," the woman said. "I am working on setting up a website to sell them."

I wished her luck and returned to the station where I found Reed glassy-eyed at his computer.

"Still looking up bee stings and honey allergies?" I asked as I filled Meeka's bowl from the water cooler in the corner.

"Why is research so addictive?" Reed replied. "I had answers more than an hour ago, but reading about the different ways people have died from these things is fascinating." He paused. "That's probably insensitive, isn't it?"

"No, it's scientific. What did you find out?"

"Did you know that a honey bee will die after it stings because its stinger has a tiny barb on it that gets stuck in its victim? When it tries to pull out the stinger, all its guts go with it. Even then, the venom sack keeps pumping venom through the stinger." He held a hand up with his fingers all pinched together at the tips and opened and closed them. This was presumably meant to represent a venom sack pumping venom.

"Dr. Bundy mentioned something about probably finding stingers and sacs on the victim, but his description wasn't quite so graphic. What did you find?"

"Tons. For someone who isn't allergic, it would take approximately five hundred stings to die from venom toxicity. That's for an adult. It would only require between thirty and fifty for a child."

"That's for a nonallergic person," I noted. "Gin Wakefield was highly allergic."

"Right. I read about cases of people dying from a single sting. The allergy is to the venom, which is kind of obvious, I guess. The actual cause of death would be anaphylaxis which can occur in seconds." Reed scrolled through a page on his computer. "With honey, it's actually pollen in it that causes the problem."

"I wonder if she suffered from hay fever as well."

"Speaking of that, here's something interesting." He sat a little straighter, ready to present his fun fact. "There are studies that show if a person consumes honey that has tiny bits of the pollen that he or she is allergic to, it could actually help with the allergy."

"That is interesting. It acts like a vaccine."

"Maybe Ms. Wakefield accidentally ate some honey."

"It's possible, but she was so swollen, I'd think it was anaphylaxis to bee venom."

"A strong allergy to honey can result in anaphylaxis as well." He pointed at his computer, indicating his research taught him this.

"I agree that it's possible she ate some, but unlikely. Everyone was supposed to post a list of ingredients for their food, and she was obsessive about the stuff. One of her employees mentioned making a honey cake, and she went ballistic."

"What are you thinking?" Reed asked when I let my sentence trail off.

"Latoya Craig made a joke about 'accidentally' feeding Wakefield honey. She insisted she wasn't serious and that she didn't mean to give her enough to kill her."

"But still." Reed scowled and shook his head. "Not funny."

"Not at all. Well, thanks to your research, we have a better understanding of what might have happened to Wakefield. Now we just have to wait for the autopsy results. Good work."

"How did your interviews go?" Reed made a sad face as he reluctantly closed his browser. He really liked doing research.

I filled him in on my discussion with Wesley, Fernando, and Laurel at The Inn. Then I told him about the things Honey had said.

He didn't seem surprised. "You didn't really expect a different reaction from Honey, did you?"

"No. It actually went a lot better than I'd prepared for. Speaking of which, that's the main reason I came back here. I was going to contact you via walkie-talkie, but there are too many villagers who might overhear us. We can't discuss anything regarding Gin Wakefield that way."

"Agreed. What did you want to tell me?"

"Sugar left town to run an errand"

"She left town? That's not at all suspicious."

"Exactly. That's just another check in the suspect column for her. If you see her before I do, bring her in immediately."

He gave a salute of understanding. "As for people finding out, have you spoken with her employees yet?"

"That's the next item on my list. They were at The Inn but left to look for Wakefield. I'm going to give Tripp a call and see if they went back to Pine Time. If they're not there, I guess I'll start searching the village. In the meantime, I need you to go over and investigate Wakefield's room at The Inn."

"Me? By myself?"

Reed had been a deputy prior to me coming to Whispering Pines, but Sheriff Brighton treated him more like an administrative assistant than a law enforcement officer. A real shame. Reed had great instincts, just not a lot of self-confidence until he performed a task on his own a time or two. The sheriff had no idea what he was missing out on. Or maybe he did. Sheriff Brighton was in on various coverups. Maybe he held Reed back so he couldn't figure things out.

"You've investigated crime scenes with me. You know to take tons of pictures. As for the contents of her room, take your time going through it. If anything seems suspicious, bag it and bring it in. You've got this."

"I knew I forgot something." He smacked the heel of his hand to his forehead. "I forgot to restock the kit."

He took a laminated checklist of kit items from his desk drawer and got to work. While he did that, I called Tripp.

"How are things going?" he asked. "Was the victim someone we knew?"

Despite the heaviness of the topic, I smiled at the fact that he now used cop-speak like me. "Are the Wakefield employees there?"

He paused before answering. "No, they left after breakfast. Any reason you're avoiding my question?"

"There's a reason I need to speak with them," I said each word slowly putting emphasis on the word 'them,' hoping he'd figure it out without me needing to say more.

He gasped. "You're kidding. *Her*?"

"Her."

"Wow." He paused then asked, "Why are we talking about this in code?"

"Because I'm being a dork. I'm worried about this getting out and news crews taking over the village."

"That would be a nightmare. Well, they left after breakfast, around eight, and none of them have been back. At least none that I've seen. I assume they're over in the village somewhere."

"They all left? Sonja too? Or is she still up in her room?"

"She popped down for toast and tea, then went right back up to her room. The other three left."

"Hang on." This group was wearing me out. "We're missing someone. I assume, by the three, you mean Kim, Latoya, and Leif. Sonja stayed there. What about Misty?"

"She's so quiet, I forget about her. She was in her room until around ten. I saw her as she was heading out the door. Said something about going for a walk."

"Interesting."

"What's interesting?"

"She didn't go to The Inn with them."

"She doesn't bake."

"I know, but wouldn't she need to be there to help clean up while they make today's entry?"

"You would think so."

"I need to look further into this. Thanks for the info. I need to go find the other three." I was about to hang up and said, "I didn't forget about us meeting over here. I'm just not sure it's going to happen."

"No problem. I'll be there either way so hunt me down if you have time."

His words were relaxed, but there was an edge to them. Or maybe it was just guilt clogging my ears. Even if we didn't get together, I was glad he'd go hang out at the fest. I had Morgan. He needed a friend in the village too. Maybe that guy with the pizza oven.

I stepped out of my office to see Reed getting ready to leave with the investigation kit and camera bag strapped to a dolly.

"That thing is heavy when it's fully stocked," he said of the kit.

"I have to go back over to The Inn," I told him. "I'll walk with you."

When Emery saw the two of us enter, he shot to his feet. "Both of you. What's going on? Is there a problem? Do we need to evacuate The Inn?"

"Calm down, Emery." I glanced over my shoulder at an elderly man in a wingback chair with his feet propped up on the hearth. Not only was he snoring softly, he was the only other person in the room, but I still spoke in a low tone. "Deputy Reed is going to investigate that room upstairs now. You made sure housekeeping stayed away, right?"

"Oh, yes," Emery assured. "They both came down here and asked me if I was sure they needed to stay out. It had been two days since they cleaned, after all."

"Hang on." Reed held up a hand. "Two days? Ms. Wakefield didn't have her room cleaned yesterday?"

"No." Emery shook his head and then stopped abruptly. "Wait … No, that's wrong. They cleaned yesterday morning, but one of her employees told us that Ms. Wakefield didn't want turndown service last night, which was kind of weird. She made such a big deal about it when she checked in."

"Turndown service?" I asked.

Emery shrugged. "It's kind of a silly thing if you ask me. Some people like it when we go up and turn the covers down for them at night. Then all they have to do is slide into bed and lay down. We'll also leave a light on and adjust the room temperature. Ms. Wakefield was very specific about her service. Usually, we just fold the blankets back far enough that the pillows are exposed. She wanted the covers pulled down halfway, the light on the night table turned on, and the temperature in her room adjusted so that it would be sixty-three degrees by ten o'clock. Oh, and she wanted a fresh carafe of water and a water glass left on her dresser."

"That is specific," Reed said.

"You have no idea the requests we get."

"Who told you she didn't want service?" I asked.

Emery shook his head. "All I know is that it was a female employee. Whoever it was talked to housekeeping, not me."

"Ms. Wakefield's employees are all physically distinct. It would be easy to figure out from a few details. Who in housekeeping did the woman speak to?"

"Gardenia. She's gone for the day."

I made a note to ask Gardenia about this if necessary. "So other than the housekeepers, no one else tried to get in there?"

"Those three other chefs were here," Emery said.

"When was that?" Reed asked.

"This morning. They were supposed to meet Ms. Wakefield, but she never showed up."

"That must have been before I talked to you," I noted. "You didn't let them in the room, did you?"

"No." Emery stiffened like I'd asked him to break a law. "I can't give other people room keys unless the person whose name is on the room contract says it's okay. That woman with the tattoos got a little insistent. She claimed Ms. Wakefield said it was all right, but I said I needed to hear that from Ms. Wakefield herself. She kept trying, but don't worry, I didn't let them in."

"Good man." My momentarily elevated heartrate returned to normal. "Deputy Reed is going to check over the room now. He'll let you know when he's done and if housekeeping can go in and clean it. We may need you to keep it off limits a little longer, though."

"Okay, Sheriff. No problem."

"I need you to do something else," I told him.

Emery sat a little straighter, eager to help as always.

"If any of Ms. Wakefield's employees come back here, call me right away. It's important that I speak with them."

"On the walkie-talkie or at the station?" he asked.

My mind spun through the pluses and minuses of each option. Urgency won out, but we needed to keep things as generic as possible. "Use the walkie-talkie and just say 'you asked me to call' and nothing more. Got it?"

"Because we're keeping this on the down-low," Emery said with a dramatic wink. "'You asked me to call.' Got it."

It was impossible to not smile at the dependability of Emery.

Chapter 18

AFTER HELPING REED CARRY THE equipment upstairs, even though he insisted he could do it on his own, Meeka and I made our way through the Mabon Fest crowd searching for Kim, Leif, and Latoya. I didn't have pictures of them, which would have made it easier, but we found one guy right away who had watched the judging and knew who they were.

"The woman with the tattoos and that guy with the beard and big ponytail?" he asked.

"That's them," I confirmed. "There would've been a large man wearing a suit coat with them too."

"I saw them maybe thirty minutes ago." He pointed toward the marina. "They were down by the drum circle."

When I got to the drum circle, the trio was nowhere to be seen. A woman there knew Latoya from her website.

"I saw her," the woman said and gave an excited wiggle. "Toy is so cool. I asked her to sign my shirt." She unzipped her jacket and showed me the back of her T-shirt as proof.

I agreed that the autograph was cool and asked, "Do you know where they went?"

"She said something about going to get something to drink." The woman pointed toward Triple G.

No Wakefield chefs at Triple G, but a man who had clearly sampled too much of the pumpkin ale said he saw them in a sandy place. Assuming that meant the public beach, we went there next. There were a handful of people at the beach, all parents lounging on blankets while their little ones burned off some steam by racing around on the sand. They had also seen the Wakefield crew and thought they were going to the Meditation Circle. The folks at the Meditation Circle sent us to the negativity well.

Of course, by the time we got back to the well, they were nowhere to be seen. Exhausted from running all around the village, I needed to rest for a while. All the garden benches and picnic tables were full, though.

"Blessed be, Jayne."

I didn't even realize we were standing in front of Shoppe Mystique. Morgan was on her deck looking radiant, like the Queen of the Fest gazing out at the crowd. At me, she frowned.

"You appear to be dragging, Sheriff. What's going on?"

There were a handful of people in the village who I knew I could trust implicitly. Tripp, obviously. My deputy. Morgan and Briar also fit this bill.

"I need something to eat," I told her. "We've been walking all over the village looking for ... I'll tell you in a minute."

"Of course. Grab something from one of the vendors, and I'll meet you in the reading room."

As I stood in line at a nearby table to get the largest pulled pork sandwich I had ever seen—honestly, the thing had to have a good six inches of meat stacked on a six-inch bun—I saw the woman in black again. Some people stared at her. Some backed away. She chatted with a few. I couldn't see her mouth moving through the balaclava but assumed the bobbing of her head to be an indication of conversation.

Honestly, it was kind of a fun way to be in disguise.

When it was my turn in line, I realized that the vendor was one of the carnies from the Whispering Pines circus.

"I like to grill for the troupe when not performing." He handed me a fork along with my monster sandwich. "I like things big." He gave me a wink as he added a huge serving of grilled potato planks on the side. "You can't eat my sandwich without a fork. Unless you like things messy."

I was so hungry and tired it took two more food-related inuendoes before I realized he was flirting with me. I took a step back, narrowed my eyes at him, and then felt heat rise around my neck.

For the nighttime adults-only circus performance, sexy was the theme. A group of women in short, low-cut super-sexy Harlequin costumes and men in skintight diamond-patterned leggings, jester hats, and nothing else were the pre-show warm up. They roamed the crowd, flirting shamelessly.

"You're one of the jesters, aren't you? Didn't recognize you with a shirt on."

The man took a step back from his table and gave a low, flourishing bow. "Jester at your service."

I heard "at your service," but he might have said "ready to service."

I waggled a finger at him. "First, I have a boyfriend. Second, don't make me arrest you for …" I was so flustered I couldn't finish the threat.

He chuckled, added a pickle spear to my plate, and dragged his fingers across mine as he slid his hand away slowly. "Come back if you want more, Sheriff."

Willow, Morgan's assistant, eyed my plate as we walked into Shoppe Mystique. "That smells delicious. Why are you so flushed? It's only fifty degrees out there."

I held the plate out to her, ignoring the question. "Help yourself to a potato plank. I'm hungry, but I'll never eat all this."

She took two and bit one in half immediately and pointed toward the back of the shop. "Morgan is waiting for you."

I passed at least a dozen people as I walked through. Morgan, however, was the only one in the reading room, sitting peacefully in her usual spot on the worn velvet loveseat. I set my plate on the small square coffee table in the center of the room and then got a cup of water for Meeka from the complimentary drink station around the corner.

"I made you some Mabon tea," Morgan called out.

When I returned to the room, Meeka was sitting by the table staring at my sandwich.

"Didn't you learn your lesson yesterday?" I scolded. "You can't eat people food."

I pulled the extra sack of dog biscuits from my pocket and set it on the floor at her feet. One sniff and she was content.

"What's Mabon tea?" I took a sip before she could answer. As with all her teas, it was yummy.

"Apple, rose hips, hibiscus, and raspberry." Morgan gave me a few minutes to eat some of my sandwich and then asked, "What's going on? You said you've been all over the village today."

"There's been another death." I tilted my head toward the reading room doorway and whispered. "I'm trying really hard to keep it quiet."

"Don't worry, no one can hear us in here," Morgan assured.

"There's no door." I flicked a hand at the opening that was double the width of a normal doorway.

Morgan responded with the tiniest of smiles. A look that told me she had done something to ensure our conversation would not be overheard. She wanted me to believe that she had worked some sort of witchy woo-woo silence spell. I was more inclined to believe it was simple acoustics.

"Who died?" she asked and nearly fell off the loveseat

when I filled her in. "I certainly understand why you're trying to keep that quiet. What happened?"

"We don't know yet. I'm not going to bother Dr. Bundy for autopsy results this time. I nearly drove the poor man batty with all my calls last month. He promised he would get the report to me as quickly as possible, so I'm going to wait it out this time." I ate another forkful of pulled pork, moaned at how good it was, and then explained it was possible Wakefield had been stung.

"How horrible. Who have you been looking for?"

"Her employees. Honestly, I'm becoming a little suspicious of them. Lots of people, almost too many, have seen them around the village."

"Too many people? Why is that a concern?" Morgan asked.

"Because to stand out to that many people, a person would have to either be really unique in appearance or do something to draw attention to their self. It was almost like the three were making sure they were seen. Like maybe they were trying to establish an alibi."

"Or you're being suspicious."

"It's my job to be suspicious."

Morgan stared, eyebrows arched.

"Fine, maybe I'm wrong. Even if I am, I still need to find them because they need to know what happened to their boss." I stabbed another forkful of meat. That jester really knew his pork. Before filling my mouth again, I said, "Let's talk about something else. What happens after the fest is done?"

"At the conclusion of Mabon, the Whispering Pines summer season is officially over. We will have a gathering for Samhain in approximately four weeks, but that's only two days and won't be anywhere near as large as this."

"Two days?" I snapped my fingers. "No problem."

"Between then and now, Mama and I and the other green witches will put our gardens to rest. That means harvesting anything that's left to be harvested and collecting seeds to be started indoors this winter for planting outside in the spring. Tender plants need to be moved indoors because a hard frost could strike at any time now." She leaned back in the loveseat and sighed. "After all that's done, we get to settle in for the winter. Nesting, I suppose you could call it. Have you and Tripp decided on your plans for Pine Time?"

"Tripp keeps talking about limiting stays to long weekends, being closed Tuesday through Thursday, and shutting down altogether for February. We're going to convert the attic into an apartment for him over the winter too."

Morgan grinned at me. "For him? How long are you going to stretch this out?"

"What are you talking about?" I shoved two potato planks into my mouth. I was getting full, but the food was so good.

"Don't you think it's a little bit silly for the two of you to live in separate buildings on the same property? Why don't you just move in together?"

"I told you, we're taking things slow. A month ago, you were telling me to slow down and live in the moment. Now you're pushing me to speed up this relationship?"

"A month ago, we talked about you living in the moment by not living in the past or jumping into the future. Are you keeping all this distance between the two of you because you want to keep things slow or because you're afraid of reliving past events?"

She meant Jonah. We'd been together for seven years, that was a lot of time. I truly thought I was in love with him and wanted to spend the rest of my life with him. It took seven years for me to figure out he wasn't who I thought he was. Tripp and I had only been dating for two months.

"Quit analyzing me," I said through a mouthful of potato. Morgan chuckled to herself.

"You're in a really good mood lately," I noted. "Did River stop by for another visit and you didn't tell me?"

Three weeks after he had visited our little village, folks were still murmuring about River Carr, a man who looked like a cross between a warlock and the angel of death. It seemed Morgan had snagged a good one, and many of the people in town, women and men alike, were green with envy.

"I told you," Morgan said, "he won't be coming back."

"That's not what he told Tripp," I teased in a singsong. "Tripp says he has every intention of coming back."

Morgan tried and failed to bite back a smile. "Those may have been his parting words to Tripp, but no, he hasn't come back, and I haven't heard from him."

I patted her knee. "Poor witchy."

She laid her head back on the loveseat and closed her eyes. "I assure you, I will be fine if he never returns."

"But you wouldn't mind it if he did, would you?" I set my plate, which still held half a sandwich and a good number of potato planks, on the table in front of us. "I'm going to explode if I eat any more. And I need to go and search for Gin Wakefield's employees again. Can you do some sort of locator spell?"

Morgan sat upright and clasped her hands together. "Of course I can. We'll need four blue candles, a goblet of water, a variety of incense cones, and—"

"Never mind." I held up a hand to stop her. "I've known their location all day, they're just never there when I get there. What I really need is a stay-where-you-are spell. You got one of those?"

"I could come up with something." She meant it too.

"I'll come back if I don't find them by the end of the day. They haven't checked out of Pine Time, so if nothing else, I'll camp out in the hall outside their rooms." I gave Meeka a soft nudge with the toe of my hiking shoe, and she jolted awake. "Time to go, girl."

She yawned and stretched and snuffled around for any last biscuit crumbs she might have missed.

"Blessed be," Morgan said, accompanying us to the shop's front door. "Good luck with your search."

We had taken maybe ten steps along the red brick pathway and ran smack into Sister Agnes.

"I'm not used to seeing you traveling on foot," I told her.

Agnes Plunkett rode around the village on a bicycle while wearing a full nun's habit, preferred hot-pink toenail polish, and had been kicked out of her church years ago. She wouldn't say why she'd been excommunicated but still used the title "Sister" and claimed to run an "un-church" somewhere on Whispering Pines' two thousand acres. To further complicate things, she called out Wiccan greetings as she zipped past on her bicycle but insisted she wasn't Wiccan. Basically, Sister Agnes confused the hell out of me.

"I tied my bike to a tree near the Fairy Path." She pointed in that general direction. "Too many people to ride around the garden today. Speaking of the Fairy Path, I understand there was some trouble over there today."

Play dumb, Regular Jayne whispered to Sheriff Jayne. *Good idea*, Sheriff Jayne replied. "What trouble?"

Agnes frowned. After a second, understanding cleared her expression, and she gave me a knowing wink like we shared a secret. "Gotcha."

Did she know about Gin Wakefield? Had she been riding through the woods this morning? I should ask her these questions but didn't want to open that topic out here in the middle of the crowd. Instead, I asked, "What kind of trouble did you hear about?"

"I didn't hear anything." She gave me another wink and

changed the topic. "When are you coming to un-church?"

The more times I spoke with Sister Agnes, the more I believed she was not merely quirky, but mentally unbalanced.

"You never told me where un-church is, Agnes. I can't visit if I don't know where to go."

She waved vaguely to her right. "It's up north."

"That's not exactly helpful."

She giggled and gave my arm a playful swat. A second later, she turned stone cold serious. It was kind of creepy.

"So much death." Her voice sounded a little like Lily Grace's when she was in a fortune telling trance. "It must weigh on you horribly. You must have so many questions."

"Not really." What was she up to? "I always get my answers."

She paused for a long moment before saying, "Not always. There's one question you've been struggling with for months. One you can't get an answer for. Come to un-church when you're ready."

The first thought that came to me was that she knew where the Wakefield folks were. That wasn't what she was talking about, though. That had been hours, not months.

Before I could ask, Agnes turned, her habit billowing around her, and merged into the Mabon crowd.

I had no idea what that was all about, but the gooseflesh crawling up my arms told me it was something sinister.

Chapter 19

THE COMMOTION IN THE COMMONS area became too much; Meeka and I were both overstimulated. She needed a nap, and I wanted a few minutes of quiet to review what I'd learned this morning. We were heading back to the station, on the Fairy Path, at almost the exact spot where Wakefield's body was found, when my walkie-talkie squawked.

"Sheriff O'Shea?"

I pulled my unit off my belt. "This is Sheriff O'Shea. Who's this?"

I should've been able to guess since the cracking voice at the other end had nothing to do with the connection. "This is Emery. You asked me to call."

The Wakefield crew was at The Inn. So much for downtime. "Be right there. Don't let them leave."

We reversed direction, heading back toward the commons, and had just passed the trailhead when we met up with Reed.

"All done with the room," he informed.

I held up a hand, stopping him from reporting any findings. "Emery just contacted me. The chefs are back at The Inn. I'm going to interview them. My brain is so full right now,

I can only concentrate on one thing at a time. We'll talk about what you found when I get to the station."

"Works for me. I'll download all the pictures and start writing my report."

I entered the lobby and rushed right over to Emery. "Where are they?" To the woman standing at the registration desk who I had startled, I added, "Sorry for the interruption."

"In the kitchen," Emery said. "Anything I can do to help?"

"Not right now." I gave him a firm pat on the shoulder. "Thanks for the call."

With a small proud smile, Emery returned to his guest.

The Wakefield crew had fully taken over the kitchen. Flour, sugar, butter, eggs, and a small mountain of other ingredients lay scattered across one of the four stainless-steel worktables. Leif and Latoya were working at separate tables, on different items according to the ingredients around them. Kim sat at a smaller table off to the side, seriously studying something on his laptop. Misty was up to her elbows in dishes and bubbles in the sink. As usual, the only member missing was Sonja.

They all turned to us as Meeka and I walked in, and immediately Latoya said, "No pets in the kitchen."

"Meeka isn't a pet," I informed her, "she's a sheriff's deputy. I'll keep her over here away from your food, however." Way to put me on defense before I'd even said a word. "Stay here, girl."

Meeka crawled beneath a cabinet close to the door and laid her chin on her paws. Great. It was probably gunky under there and she'd need a bath tonight.

"What can we help you with, Sheriff?" Kim asked while closing his laptop's cover.

"I've got some news for you regarding Gin."

Misty dropped her head forward but otherwise kept her attention on her dishes.

Latoya glanced up from her task. "Is there a problem?"

"Have any of you seen her today?" I asked.

"We haven't." Leif brushed flour off his hands. "We were looking for her this morning. All around the village. Did you find her?"

"I'm very sorry to inform you," I began, tearing the bandage very slowly, "that Ms. Wakefield's body was found early this morning."

"Her body?" Latoya froze in the middle of cutting up vegetables. "Are you telling us Gin is dead?"

"What happened?" Kim demanded, standing from his table.

"She is deceased, yes. We are not sure what happened yet. The medical examiner has her and is doing an autopsy as we speak. If we don't hear from him today, I expect a call right away in the morning."

Kim grabbed the edge of his table and sank back onto his chair.

"I'd like to speak with each of you," I said. "I'm hoping you'll be able to give me information that will help us figure out what happened. The dining room is empty; that would be a private, quiet place for us. Who'd like to go first?"

They glanced at each other, and Leif raised his hand. "I'll go first."

I waited while he washed his hands and then guided him to the back of the old-world style dining room, past wooden tables of different shapes and sizes—some small and round, others large and rectangular, all covered with black tablecloths and decorated with flower arrangements in autumn hues. At a table in the farthest corner, next to the large floor-to-ceiling stone fireplace, I indicated he should take the chair that would put his back to the room. I took the one across from him in the corner, and Meeka sat at attention on the floor next to me.

"This is an informal questioning," I told Leif as I pulled

my voice recorder out of my pocket and placed it on the table between us. "The recording is for my reference later, so I can pay closer attention to what we're saying now."

It would also allow me to focus on his body language as we talked. Sometimes, that spoke louder than words.

His hands folded in his lap and his shoulders rounded forward, he replied with a simple, "Okay."

"For the recording, please state your name and tell me how long you've been working for Wakefield's Treats and Sweets."

"I'm Leif Forsberg and it's been about seven years." Leif smiled fondly and then wiped a hand over his mouth and beard. Just that quickly, he became emotional. "I started working for Chef Wakefield just before I graduated high school doing basically what Misty does now. Kitchen help."

"Did you know anything about baking?"

"I did." His smile returned. "I used to watch YouTube videos and cooking shows on Netflix obsessively. Still do, just not so obsessively. My love of baking started when I was five. I'd hang out in the kitchen and watch my grandmother and aunties prepare meals. They'd talk and laugh, sometimes work in silence, occasionally argue or cry. No matter the mood in the kitchen, we'd all come together at the table in the end. Amazing what you can learn just by watching."

"An apprentice at five years old." His little chuckle said he liked my label. "Sounds like you were destined from the start to do what you're doing."

"I always thought so. I applied for and got the kitchen helper position with Wakefield's. After a year there, I got up the nerve to bring in something I'd made at home for Gin to sample." He blinked, the memory making him emotional again. "Seems silly now, but it was something I used to make for neighborhood gatherings. Everyone loved it. Monkey bread."

I smiled and shook my head, unaware. "What's monkey bread?"

"It's just sweet roll bread formed into little balls." His hands started moving as he spoke, forming invisible dough balls. "You dip the dough in melted butter, then roll it in cinnamon and sugar and toss them into a Bundt pan. Or put the buttered dough into the pan and sprinkle on brown sugar and pecans. It's fun for gatherings. Kids love it because they can pull the little pieces off the big loaf."

"Ms. Wakefield liked the monkey bread?"

He sat tall and proud. "She did. She had me make something simple for her, right then and there in the bakery kitchen, and said I had potential and that she'd love to mentor me but wanted me to go to culinary school first. She said my basic skills were lacking."

"You went to school in Chicago?"

"I did." He pushed his shoulders back proudly. "Got my degree in culinary arts from the same school Gin went to."

"And now you head up the pastry division for the corporation, correct?"

"That's right."

"You moved up the ranks quickly."

He frowned at the observation.

"That wasn't meant to be judgmental," I promised. "I was about your age when I was named detective for the Madison Police Department. Not that I'm that much older than you."

He relaxed again, but his voice quavered. "Gin took me under her wing from the start." He shook his head, seemingly unable to believe his good fortune. "What are the chances? I don't know what the percentage would be, but it's got to be really low. The number of people who get that kind of opportunity, I mean."

"Sometimes the Universe guides us to where we need to be."

He inhaled a shaky breath and blew out an equally ragged one. "I guess it does."

"Mr. Forsberg, it's possible that Gin was murdered." I paused, waiting for a response from him, but didn't get much of one, the guy was already in shock over her death. He shifted in his chair and looked me in the eye, waiting for me to say more. "Do you have any idea who might have wanted her dead?"

He shook his head immediately. "No. I can't imagine who would want to kill that woman. She could be tough, but kind too."

"You're not aware of anyone, whether inside or outside the Wakefield Corporation, who might have a personal or professional issue with her?"

"The only one I can think of," he offered after a moment's thought, "is that woman here. The one that runs the sweet shop."

"Had Gin spoken of Sugar before you all got here?"

"I never heard of her. Gin mentioned her that first night, after we all met with Laurel and Wesley here for a tour of the kitchen. It was really a grumble to herself about someone named Sugar. After that, we gathered to figure out what we were going to make for the first day's entry, and Gin said something about needing to beat Sugar."

Not that it indicated anything to do with Gin's death, but I couldn't help but note his timeline. They toured the kitchen and planned their entry that first night. Not only had Laurel let them in after the deadline, it sounded like she gave them a heads-up on the first day's category.

"Toy and I laughed at the comment," Leif continued. "We figured 'beating Sugar' meant she was starting some ironic new diet. Then she told us that Sugar was a childhood rival." Leif shook his head, a gesture of admiration. "I'd never seen Gin so determined as she was about that croquembouche.

Whatever happened between those two in the past, Gin had something to prove with this competition despite all her business success. She intended to come out on top."

This fit with what I already knew. Unfortunately, Leif just put another checkmark in the guilty column for Sugar. And made me think a little differently about Laurel.

"Anything else you can think of that might help me figure out what happened to Gin?"

He sat back in his chair and stared off into the corner of the ceiling. After a few seconds, with tears forming again, he shook his head. "Nothing. I just don't understand how this happened."

"That's exactly what I'm trying to figure out. Thanks for your time, Mr. Forsberg. That's all the questions I have for you right now. Would you send either Kim or Latoya out next, please?"

Leif shot up out of his chair like a firecracker had just gone off beneath it and practically ran to the kitchen.

Chapter 20

LATOYA CRAIG MARCHED INTO THE dining room like a woman on a mission. She plopped down onto the chair that Leif had recently vacated and adjusted the multi-colored bandana tied around her forehead.

"I realize this is important," she began, "but if we can keep it as short as possible, that would be great."

"Do you have somewhere you need to be?" I hit the record button on my voice recorder.

"No. We have an entry to get done by four o'clock."

This surprised me. "Even after what I just told you about Gin, you're still planning to enter the contest today?"

Her body slumped, and she seemed to wrestle with emotion. She was gentler, more subdued when she spoke again. "This contest was really important to Gin. I think the least we can do for her memory is put our all into this and win it for her." She waved vaguely in the direction of the kitchen. "We're almost done. I just need to put on the finishing touches."

Noble sentiment, but the emotion over her employer's death felt forced and, as she had since I first met her, Latoya struck me as cold. It could be a mask, a self-preservation defense. Often a person's exterior didn't match the interior.

"Let's get to it, then. Tell me about your relationship with Ms. Wakefield."

Latoya was a very animated person. Her tattooed hands waved about as she spoke. Her face twisted into a grimace one minute and turned up in a smile the next. Out of the corner of my eye, I saw that Meeka took notice of her as well. Curious about this woman in motion, she sat at attention, her head cocking left and right then left again.

"This competition is sort of like coming full circle for me," Latoya began. "I met Gin at a Memorial Day employment competition she was holding a number of years ago."

"Employment competition? Meaning the winner got the job?"

"Exactly. Creative, hey? There were multiple rounds that went on all weekend. The public narrowed down the number of contestants by half after every round. Let me tell you, it was high stress. When it was down to two of us, Gin chose the winner. She wanted to expand into specialty items. Gluten-free, nut free, dairy free. You know, all the buzzwords floating around the grocery stores these days. Funny thing was, we didn't even know who we were competing for. It was a blind competition."

"Interesting way to conduct a job interview."

"She's found a number of employees via taste test. Personality also rises to the surface under that kind of pressure." Latoya grew quiet for a few seconds, her lips clamped between her teeth and her gaze far away. "She always said, 'the proof is in the pudding.' She didn't much care that you had a piece of paper that said you could bake. It didn't take talent to earn a degree, she said, just time in school. You heard her the other night, if a product didn't pass her taste buds, it didn't get in the lineup."

"When you found out that your new employer would be

Wakefield's Treats and Sweets, did you accept right away?"

"No, I didn't. I entered the competition last minute. I'd gotten an offer from one of the largest casinos in Las Vegas earlier that week. My creations would be served to tens of thousands of people a day." She gave a little chuckle at the memory. "They offered a nice incentive package too. Anyway, I was young and free, no obligations or responsibilities. I wanted to follow my heart, but logic kept stepping in. So that competition was intended to be a mind-clearing thing that only ended up complicating my decision."

"What made you choose Wakefield's?"

"At that time, Gin was right on the fringe of becoming big. Trust me, it was a hard choice. Everyone was talking about this up and comer, but all she had at that time was a single bakery that was doing well and a growing catering business. She put me up in a room on the top floor of a hotel on Michigan Avenue downtown Chicago. She and Kim wined and dined me that night and made all sorts of guarantees."

"You accepted the position based on promises?"

"Educated promises," Latoya amended. "Kim shared their most recent profit and loss statement with me. The numbers weren't huge, but the profit margin was fantastic, which told me they knew what they were doing. They went into detail about how they were planning to open two more locations in Chicago over the next two years with their sights set on another in Milwaukee and possibly Madison. Even back then, Kim was talking about a line of commercial products. Gin had her eyes set on the food, but Kim's baby was the commercial line."

"Is this the huge deal she got recently?"

"It was. He spent years talking with different manufacturers and sponsors. That was part of my incentive package promise for coming on board. I'd be guaranteed a percentage of any commercial deals. Not just the retail food line, I'd get a share of the profits in the kitchenware as well."

I gave a nod of appreciation. "Sounds like a good deal."

She smiled, but almost sadly. "One I couldn't turn down."

"Did you ever regret the decision? Ever wish you went to Vegas instead?"

"I'd be lying if I said I didn't think about it now and then." She inhaled sharply, and her mood perked up just that quickly. "Things have turned out well for me, though. Gin help me establish my name, and now I'm heading in a direction I never thought of before. I've got a specialty foods website and a YouTube channel that has almost half a million followers. I'm also working with a publisher on a cookbook."

"Sounds like you're ready to go off on your own."

This time her smile was happy. "You're very perceptive, Sheriff. That's exactly what I'm planning."

"How did Gin feel about that?"

"About me leaving? I've helped her make a lot of money, so of course she wasn't happy that I wanted to go. She came around, though. I mean, she gets to keep all the recipes I created for Wakefield's. I'm free to change them up a bit and make them my own, but as her employee, she owns the rights to everything I created."

"That has to be very frustrating. I can't imagine putting my heart and soul into something only to get no claim to it."

She shrugged. "That's pretty standard in this industry. Yes, it was frustrating, but I can come up with more recipes. I'm not worried about that."

"What now?" I asked. "I realize you just found out what happened to your boss, but I mean now that she's gone, will the rights remain with the Wakefield corporation, or will they revert to you?"

She tilted her head to the side, the diamond stud in her left nostril catching the dining room lights when she did. "That's a really good question. I'll have to ask our legal department." She grew quiet again for a second and then threw her hands in the air. "Either way, I'll be fine on my own. Creating recipes is what I do. The public is very loyal. If they see Toy's Treats as simply a reproduction of Wakefield's in a different box, they won't likely follow me."

"Is that what you're going to call your company? Toy's Treats?"

"It is. My YouTube followers know me as Toy. I even have a logo drawn up."

"You were ready to move on."

"You know how it goes. You play around with things when you're thinking and dreaming about the future and something real starts forming. There are plenty of websites out there for logo design. I was goofing around one night and, bam, there it was. I put it up on YouTube, and everyone loved it."

"If the autopsy results come back that Gin was murdered," I said, purposeful with the abrupt change in topic and tone, "do you have any idea who might have done this to her?"

The sudden left turn didn't faze her. Instead, Latoya stared me in the eye, leaned forward, and asked her own question. "Any idea on how she died? I mean, if I knew how it happened, I might have a better idea of who might have done it."

I held her gaze. "Sounds like you have someone in mind."

She sat back with arms crossed. "Gin Wakefield was a very wealthy woman. She trampled many smaller bakers in the Chicago area, even put some out of business. This line of kitchenware will surely make a dent in the lines other chefs have on the market. As I'm sure you're aware, Sheriff, when it comes to money, people will do some crazy things."

Her response fascinated me. She started out almost aggressive, leaning in toward me the way she did. If her tone of voice had been different, she would come across as angry or jealous of her boss. Instead, Latoya seemed genuinely interested in figuring out what might have happened.

"I don't have the answer for means yet," I told her. "We're still waiting on the medical examiner's report. In the meantime, is there anyone you feel might be worth my time to look at?"

She pulled a cell phone out of her apron pocket and checked the time. "We're seriously on a time crunch here. Can I make a list and get back to you?"

"Sure. If you don't see me wandering around the fest grounds, bring it over to the station after the judging today. And don't worry, if you forget, I'll track you down."

She gave me a tight smile. "I'm sure you will. I assume you need to talk with Kim now. I'll send him out to you."

"Actually, I need to stretch my legs. I'll wander with you."

I turned off the voice recorder and followed Latoya into the kitchen, Meeka running ahead of us and diving beneath the cabinet so she wouldn't get yelled at again. Latoya returned to her table, tied her apron behind her back, and got right back to work on her part of today's entry.

Kim was still at the table to the side, on his phone now. I stood nearby hearing only enough to decide that he was talking to lawyers.

He turned to me with a scowl. "Something I can help you with, Sheriff?"

"Yes. I need to speak with you about Gin's death."

"I'm on a call with our attorneys at the moment. Can you give me a minute of privacy?"

"Sure thing. I'll just wait over here for you."

Overhearing my comment, Leif looked up and gave a nod when he saw me coming his way.

"What is your entry for today?" I asked.

"The category is portable food," Leif reminded me. "We're going with a picnic theme. I made puff pastry, which we'll turn into different kinds of filled pockets. Toy is doing the 'main course' portion of the meal, filling the pastry with a savory meat and vegetable mixture."

"Sounds great. I assume you'll be doing dessert pockets of some kind?"

"Right," he confirmed. "I'm using the same pastry, that will tie the two together, but I'll obviously use sweet fillings. One will be chocolate and marshmallow cream with chopped graham crackers that will mimic a s'more, and the other will have cinnamon and apple. I was thinking of a third using dark chocolate and raspberry, but that's not very seasonal. Of course, the s'more isn't either."

I stood back and watched them work. The longer I stood there the more unnerved they seem to get. Tripp didn't like it when I watched him work either. Finally, Kim finished his phone call and said he could give me five minutes.

"This is a possible murder investigation, Mr. Robbins." If he was trying to intimidate me, it wouldn't work. "Our discussion may take longer than five minutes."

As we took our seats at the table, and I placed the voice recorder between us, Kim asked. "What makes you believe Ginger was murdered, Sheriff O'Shea? Do you have evidence of some kind already?"

"I like to err on the side of being efficient," I explained. "I never accuse anyone until I have proof, but I find it a better use of possibly crucial time to assume a worst-case scenario from the start. That way if the autopsy results indicate something problematic, I can act on it right away."

"And you believe I may have had something to do with Ginger's death?"

"Right to the point. I see you are a fan of efficiency as well."

"My job is Chief Financial Officer. Running a corporation as large as Wakefield's requires staying on top of things. And there are a lot of things to stay on top of. If I wasn't organized and efficient, it would become chaos."

"You've been friends with Gin for a long time, haven't you?"

"I have. We met many years ago working at the same resort in the Maldives."

"The Maldives?" My mind spun for a second and then I remembered the T-shirt Wakefield had been wearing when we found her. "Where is that?"

"In the Indian Ocean, about nine hundred miles from the southern tip of India."

"Why would you leave an island paradise like that for the windy chill of Chicago?"

"Because Ginger had a dream." Kim smiled, apparently at a memory, his stern expression easing for the first time since I'd met him. "She claimed that she had learned a great deal creating high-quality dishes for clients who expected the best, but she wanted more. Island life is laid-back but sometimes too quiet for someone who has dreams as big as hers."

"Did she expect her dreams to turn into what they did?"

"I believe she did. She talked of opening a bakery that would expand into another and another, and there wasn't any call for that on the island. As happy as she was, she couldn't let go of the idea of that chain of bakeries. Our clientele adored her food. She had a way of creating desserts that made you feel like you were being sinful but were portioned so you knew you weren't. If that makes sense."

"The three-bite rule?" I asked. "My grandmother used to say that three bites were all you needed to be truly satisfied."

"Anything more is a waste," Kim completed the thought.

I burst out with a laugh at that. "Did you know my grandmother, Mr. Robbins?"

His smile tightened again. "I'm sure she was a lovely woman."

I paused involuntarily as an image of the feisty little woman with light-blue fingernails filled my mind. A blink or two brought me back. "You and Ms. Wakefield met working on the island, did you leave at the same time?"

"We did. Ginger had a vibrancy about her that was positively infectious. I loved living on that island out in the middle of the ocean, away from the stresses of society."

I was familiar with the look on his face. I'd seen it on many of our tourists. "You were looking for a place to belong?"

He narrowed his eyes, surprised by my observation. "I was. And I found it. Then Ginger came along, and I believed that if I stuck with her, I would always have a place where I belonged."

"Did you love her?"

"As a friend, as a sister, and as a take-charge businesswoman, I absolutely loved her. If you're asking was I in love with her, I'm gay, Sheriff."

I didn't care about his sexual orientation. What I did care about was the fact that he had deep feelings for my victim. Deep feelings could lead to crimes of passion, one of the main reasons for murder. "How did you decide on Chicago?"

"Ginger talked a lot about growing up in Whispering Pines. She missed it a great deal and wanted to get back to the area." He chuckled. "I used to ask her the same thing you just asked me. 'You want to go back to the frigid north when you could be on a tropical island?' She insisted that she did. She chose Chicago because she said Milwaukee and Madison weren't big enough for her vision."

"Let's fast forward a few years. You leave the resort, move to Chicago, and open a bakery. Was it just the two of you?"

"For a very short time. Following my advice, she opened the first store in an upscale area of Chicago since she was already familiar with that kind of clientele. It took a great deal of money to get that place up and running, but it didn't take long to see a profit. Ginger was tireless. She was up at four every morning and wouldn't stop until eight or ten at night. She made all the food, washed all her own dishes, waited on customers, and cleaned every corner of the store. I took care of the business side and helped her with what I could, but eventually she needed more help than I could give and hired her first employee. When Ginger started getting offers to cater parties, we needed even more staff."

"I think I'm familiar with the timeline after that," I said. "And then came this most recent deal."

Kim stiffened and clenched his jaw. "The line of kitchenware."

Definitely not a positive reaction. Surprising, considering what Latoya had said about this being his pet project. "You weren't happy about this deal?"

"It turned out to be much more work than we anticipated and far less return."

"Less return? Ms. Wakefield told me they upped the price on an already multi-million-dollar deal when she didn't bite right away."

He coughed and cleared his throat. "The percentages could have been better."

Sounded to me like Mr. Robbins was greedy. Possibly a positive quality in a CFO. "I assume she made some enemies over the years."

"Of course she did. No one gets to be as successful as Ginger without stepping on a few toes along the way."

"Anyone in particular you might be concerned about? Someone you feel I should investigate?"

"There were a few employees who had been let go over

the years. Some people that she made promises to and then didn't follow through."

"Are any of those people here in Whispering Pines? This is where she died, after all."

He paused for a few long seconds, seemingly unsure how to answer. "I certainly don't want to speak for my coworkers. You'd have to ask them that question."

"You're not privy to that information?"

"I deal with the financial aspects of the business. Personnel information is handled through our human resources department."

"Oh, come on. You're telling me there weren't any after-hours gripe sessions over a few beers?"

He stretched his arm out until the sleeve of his shirt pulled up to reveal his watch and glanced at the time. "As I'm sure you can imagine, Ginger's passing will lead to a great many things I will need to take care of. I would appreciate if you would let me know the results of the autopsy as soon as you have them."

"Maybe you should give me contact information for your legal department. I imagine they are the ones I should pass that sort of information along to. Since you're only involved with the financials."

His expression turned hard. "Of course."

"You can give that to me now? Since I'm here and your computer is just over in the kitchen."

He shoved away from the table and strode quickly to the kitchen. He woke up his computer and, with a few clicks of his mouse, had an email address and phone number for me. He wrote them down, turned with paper in hand, and startled to find me standing right behind him.

"Let me know if there's anything else I can get you, Sheriff."

"I will. I'm sure we all want a speedy resolution to this

horrible situation." I headed for the door where Meeka had waited on the other side of the threshold. I stopped to attach her leash to her harness and then turned back to the trio. "Good luck in the competition this afternoon. I'm sure Gin would be touched to know that you all are doing so much to honor her memory."

Chapter 21

ON OUR WAY BACK TO the station, Meeka and I passed the fortune tellers' wagon set up in the commons area. We were probably fifteen yards away when Lily Grace emerged with an elderly couple, both of whom were grinning ear to ear. The next thing I knew, the teenage psychic had me by the arm and was pulling me toward the wagon.

"Sheriff O'Shea," she said in an unnecessarily loud voice, "you're just in time for your reading."

Unsure of what was going on, I glanced around at the cluster of tourists who appeared to be waiting for their own readings. If me butting in front of them bothered them, they didn't let on.

Inside the little wagon, multi-colored silk scarves draped the walls and covered the windows. The flames from candles inside metal holders stamped with Middle Eastern designs cast crazy patterns all around. Pillows lay propped against the wall, in case someone wanted to sit on the floor instead of at the table.

Once she'd closed the wagon's door, Lily Grace picked up one of the pillows, held it to her face, and screamed into it.

"Day going that well, hey?" I asked.

"Thank the Goddess you came along. I needed a break in the worst way. I don't know where Cybil, Effie, or any of the other tellers are, but I've been doing readings for three hours straight. It's been all old people, and they all want to know the same thing. 'Tell me what the future looks like for my son.' 'What do you see in my daughter's future?' 'What do you see for my grandchildren?' 'Tell me, if I die first, will my spouse find happiness again?'" She screamed into the pillow once more. "Is that all I have to look forward to when I'm old? Don't any of them want to know the winning lottery numbers or if they'll get to go on that vacation they've always dreamed about? Is the only thing they care about their kids?"

"You say this like it's a bad thing."

"Whatever."

Meeka had crawled beneath a stack of pillows, and Lily Grace unknowingly threw her pillow on top of the Westie who let out a little *yelp* of surprise and then scowled at the girl.

"Can you really see the winning lottery numbers?"

She blinked at me. "Do you think I'd be sitting in this wagon all day if I could win the lottery?"

Good point. "I assume you dragged me in here so you could get a few minutes of peace?"

"Yes! Please, stay." She covered her eyes with both hands. "You can just sit in the chair and not say a word for fifteen minutes if you want."

I lasted a minute before saying, "I haven't seen you in a while. How's everything going?"

"By everything, I assume you mean living with Jola, and that is pretty cool. I can't believe Effie and Cybil waited so long to tell us we were sisters. I mean, we're getting along perfectly."

"Perfectly? Jola told me there was a fight." Which meant they were getting along like sisters.

"She told you that?" Lily Grace looked betrayed. "Yeah,

after a week or so of living in her cottage together, she woke up one morning and blew her top because I ate her yogurt. We ended up in this huge, stupid fight and said all sorts of mean things. After a couple minutes, we both just stopped yelling, stared at each other, and burst out laughing. Next thing I knew, we were both hugging and apologizing. I guess we were being too nice or something."

"You know, it's okay if it's not going perfectly. I'd be worried if it was. You've known each other a long time, spending summers together as little kids, but you've barely seen her for the last seven or eight years."

"True. The fight was like clearing the air, or whatever, and suddenly it's like we've been sisters all our lives."

"That's great. I'm happy for you two. Has she been able to help you with your other decisions?"

"We haven't talked about college or me leaving the village or anything like that yet." She shrugged. "Right now, I just want to be with my sister, you know?"

Not really. I had to admit, I was a little jealous that Lily Grace and Jola were getting this chance. My sister Rosalyn and I had never been super close and probably never would be.

"Since you're here," Lily Grace said, "do you want a reading?"

"Oh, no. You can just sit and chill. I'm okay with that."

"No, seriously. You're always wondering about something."

I was about to object and immediately thought of Gin Wakefield. Could Lily Grace tell me about that? Or maybe she could see what would happen with Pine Time. Would we still be up and running a year from now, or would my parents pull the plug and sell it out from under us?

"Tell you what," she began, "if you just let me tune into you, rather than asking me about something specific, it'll be like wiping my slate clean."

"All right. Give me a minute to focus on something."

I took a seat in the cushioned chair across from her large upholstered wingback one. While she situated herself by pulling her legs up into crisscross and adjusting her long patchwork skirt around them, I used the meditation technique Morgan and Briar had taught me a few weeks earlier. They had encouraged me to take just five minutes a day to close my eyes, clear my mind, and let it wander wherever it wanted to go. I didn't do it every day, but I had to admit, it was relaxing to just sit and be still for a bit.

I got comfortable in the chair, took in a deep breath as I closed my eyes, and rested my hands in my lap as I exhaled. I did my best to clear my mind of all the frustration of the day and thought of the people closest to me—Tripp, Morgan, and Briar. Then, feeling a little guilty for excluding my family from that group, I let my parents and Rosalyn into the mix. There had to be something about one of them that I needed to know.

"Okay, I think I'm ready."

She placed her hands palms up on the table, and I placed mine over them. Lily Grace claimed this was the only way she could do a reading. She never bothered to learn how to read tarot cards and said she only saw her own reflection in a crystal ball. Like this, with our hands barely touching, was the best way for her to connect with my energy. All I had to do was focus on a topic and let her work her magic.

With her eyes closed, she transformed from a self-focused teenage girl to an empathetic fortune teller with just a few short breaths. She swayed side to side and after a few seconds, she began to hum softly. No matter how much she fought it, I think Lily Grace really liked reading fortunes. And no matter how skeptical I was of the other claims of magical abilities around here, the way Lily Grace connected with future events made even me believe that there was some kind of unseen force around us.

"I see a jack-o'-lantern in the woods," she intoned and then swayed and hummed some more, her facial expression remaining perfectly neutral. "I see a keyhole."

The only problem with Lily Grace's visions was that even though they were ultimately accurate, you never realized that until after the event happened. Was the jack-o'-lantern a literal thing or was it symbolic of something else? Same with the keyhole.

After another minute of swaying, she announced, "I see an infant with dark hair and blue eyes."

I froze, which was good because I might have fallen off my chair otherwise.

After another few seconds, she pulled her hands away from mine, placed them palms together, and slumped back in her chair. "What did I say?" When I didn't answer right away, she peeked open one eye. "What's the matter? You look a little green. What did I say?"

"Do you ask everyone about what you saw?" I flexed and stretched my hands to get the blood flowing in them again and breathed deep to get the rest of me flowing as well.

"No, only you. Seriously, what did I say?"

"You saw a keyhole, a jack-o'-lantern, and," I could barely say it, "a baby with dark hair and blue eyes."

Her mouth dropped open, then she slapped a hand over it. Through splayed fingers, she said, "You have dark hair and blue eyes."

"Shut up."

"Oh, my Goddess!"

I shot out of the chair, startling Meeka. "I'm not pregnant. There's not even a chance that I am." We stared at each other for a minute. "Do you have a psychic key for deciphering what any of that meant?"

She shook her head while chewing on her lower lip. "On the upside, Halloween isn't far away. You should have an answer about the jack-o'-lantern in a few weeks. And some visions are for far in the future. Like at least nine months."

"Shut. Up." I grabbed Meeka's leash. "Helpful as ever, my dear. Now that you've traumatized me, are you ready to deal with paying customers again?"

"My slate is wiped clean." She held her hands to her forehead and then flicked them out to the side as though pushing away any remaining stress. "Thanks for the break." She stepped outside with us and, in her mystical fortune teller way, asked the crowd, "Who's next?"

With one hand to my stomach, Meeka and I continued down the Fairy Path back to the station. Reed was waiting for me there to discuss his investigation of Wakefield's room.

"I'm pretty sure all babies have blue eyes when they're born," I told my K-9. She gave me a sideways glance and then trotted further ahead of me. "I think I read that somewhere. So that doesn't mean it's my baby."

Reed looked up when I entered the station and asked, "How's it going?"

"I'm not pregnant," I said as though this was breaking news.

His face went slack. "Were you trying to be?"

"No!"

"Okay. That's good then." He inhaled and changed topics. "I finished my report and loaded the pictures to the cloud."

I gestured to my office. "Let's go over everything in there."

One of Lupe's many talents was the ability to network computers. In between assignments, she networked the station. Now all documents and pictures were in the cloud, so Reed and I didn't need to check with each other on everything.

"Are you ready?" Reed asked as he entered my office.

"Hang on, I didn't even turn my computer on yet."

A minute later, I clicked on the file labeled "GINGER

WAKEFIELD" and then a folder labeled "Photos." The pictures Reed took confirmed what I had seen from the doorway.

"I only took a quick peek into the room," I told him. "I wanted to be sure there weren't any more bodies. It seemed to me that someone had vandalized the place, but after seeing these pictures I'm not so sure."

He pulled up a chair to sit next to me. "What do you mean?"

I flipped to an image of her clothing strewn all over the floor in front of the dresser, back to one of the nightstands on either side of the bed, and another of the small writing desk in the corner. "See how everything is orderly except for in this first picture? I think she was looking for something."

"Right. I see what you mean. The only things messed up are the bed which wasn't made, the contents of the dresser drawers which are all over the floor, and the contents of her purse." He pointed at the scattering of miscellaneous objects on the floor by the lounge chair in the corner, her bag next to them.

"My understanding is that Wakefield was a very methodical person. She ran her kitchen with precision, expecting dishes to be washed quickly after they had been used. She was professional and pulled together every time I saw her." I clicked slowly through the images again. "A vandal would've gone through everything. What could she have been looking for that would've made her do this to her room?"

"EpiPen? We assumed she was on the way to get medical help."

I spun to face my deputy. "Yes. Good. Did you find one anywhere?"

"The trash can in the bathroom held a variety of common items." Reed crossed my office to the evidence locker, which was basically heavy wire mesh fencing bolted to the walls, floor, and ceiling. He removed a large black plastic bag and set it on a table near the locker. From it, he removed smaller bags, reading each label as he did. "This one is from the can in the main room. The other is from the bathroom."

"Holy banana peels." The bathroom bag had six peels. The one from the main room had at least a dozen.

"They were shoved down to the bottom of the can with a bunch of tissues and trash on top."

"I think I know who bought all the bananas from Sundry." I knew it was too convenient for Wakefield's room to smell like bananas and for Sugar to be looking for some.

"Bought them all?"

"That's supposedly why Sugar left town. She needed bananas for her contest entry today, and Sundry was out." I paused and remembered opening the door. "The smell in the room hit me right away."

"Me too."

"What else have we got? What about that EpiPen?" I checked over the contents from both garbage cans through the clear plastic bags. Neither contained an epinephrine pen. "I wonder if she had one on her."

"You mean on her body on the Fairy Path?"

"Right. Dr. Bundy said if she had an allergy that severe, she would have a pen on her at all times."

"We didn't find one along the path," Reed said. "And there wasn't one beneath her when they rolled her over."

"And you didn't find one in the room. You checked under the bed, in the sheets, in her piles of clothes?"

"I did. The only thing I found in the sheets was the television remote. Nothing under the bed. I also told Emery to leave the room as is for another day."

While Reed removed items from the large plastic bag and laid them out on the table, I flipped through the pictures he'd taken. From the bathroom photos, it became evident that Wakefield had two distinct sides to her personality. The bathroom in her *en suite* was large enough to fit a small narrow table. She had lined up all her bottles, tubes, and cosmetics there. Backing up my earlier description of her being orderly, all the items were organized by time of day use. The nighttime products on the right were the common everyday items I recognized from the shelves at Target. The morning routine on the left, however, were obviously high-end. I didn't recognize all the names, but after spending so much time at my mother's day spa, I knew an expensive beauty product when I saw one. Same with her makeup collection in the middle, all of which were from the department store lines that I couldn't afford on a cop's salary.

Analyzing the contents of someone's home, or hotel room in this case, always fascinated me. A person's preferences for food and other items said a lot about them. For some, of course, purchases were made based on financial constraints. For others, money was no object. In Gin Wakefield's case, it was a mixed bag. The items that the public would see, such as her clothes, were obviously expensive. Items that only she would see were probably the same brands she had used as a teenager or struggling new chef, such as the tube of generic lip balm and off-brand hand moisturizer on the bedside table. Two distinct sides to this woman. How well did those two sides get along inside her?

"Want to come and take a look at this, Sheriff?"

I blinked, scattering the swirling image of the complicated Chef Wakefield in my mind. "Yep. What have we got?"

I checked out the array of plastic bags laid out on the table, all neatly labeled with evidence stickers. One item, a small glass jar, stood out to me. "Bees?"

Reed picked up a bottle which held the carcasses of ten or twelve dead bees. "Honey bees, to be precise. I found most of them in her bed under the sheets and the others on the floor near the bed. It's okay that I put them all in one jar, right?"

I nodded distractedly. "How do you know they're honey bees?"

He pointed out that the carcasses didn't have stingers. "Remember what I told you about honey bees eviscerating themselves when they tried to pull their stinger out of their victim?"

"You found the remains of bees, which had clearly stung someone or something, in the room of a woman who was highly allergic to bee stings?"

"That's what we've got." Reed held the little jar closer to his own face, shook it, and watched the little bodies bounce off the glass.

"What do you suppose the chances are of that many bees being in her room?"

"Pretty low. I checked with Emery, and he confirmed that they have an exterminator come through on a regular schedule. Especially in the wetter months, they can get a bad bug problem there."

"I guess we need to look at this from a different angle." I motioned to the portable whiteboard. "The chances are low in that they regularly spray for bugs. We need to factor in the probability that someone might have known that Wakefield had an allergy to bee stings and wanted her dead."

Reed pulled the board away from the wall, erased the marks already on it, and chose an erasable marker. While he wrote, I paced the room. Before I had turned around again, he had written Wakefield's name at the top of the board along with the date and approximate time of her death. Next came *Method of Death* which we had to leave blank for now. Then he wrote *Suspects* and beneath that *Sugar – childhood rival*.

"Any other villagers who wanted her dead? Or at least knew about her allergy?"

Reed blew out a long, low whistle. "Geez, Sheriff, you're talking about half the village. Mother was telling me about her problem the other night. She said it was so bad, everyone in the village knew about it and had been instructed on what to do if she ever got stung or came into contact with honey." He paused and clarified, "The condiment, not the woman over at the sweet shop."

I laughed at him. "I knew what you meant. Okay, we can't start listing villagers, then. Besides, it's been what, twenty years since she lived here?"

Reed glanced up at the ceiling, doing a quick calculation. "That's about right. So instead, we need to figure out who in the village would've had a beef with her twenty years ago."

"There can't be that many. Sugar, obviously. Possibly Honey."

"Honey? Why would you suspect her?"

"I don't really, but you know how close the two of them are. Honey wouldn't hesitate to come to her sister's defense. She is a remote possibility, but I think we should at least put her on the board."

Wordlessly, Reed added *Honey*. "I suppose you want Aunt Reeva up there too."

I took a moment to think about that before answering. Had I seen anything over the last couple of days that could give me reason to suspect Reeva? "Do you know something I don't know? I hadn't considered her."

His high and tight shoulders relaxed a little. "I was thinking baking rivalry, but I don't honestly think Aunt Reeva would do anything to anyone." A second later, he added, "Except maybe my mother."

I wasn't touching that one. "I don't think we need to add Reeva. Anyone else? Anyone Wakefield grew up with who might have been a little jealous—"

Before I could finish, Reed added Laurel's name to the

board. "I know you talked to her and you said you didn't see anything negative there, but you've got to admit, there was some jealousy."

I agreed with that.

Next, he added the names *Kim Robbins, Latoya Craig, Leif Forsberg,* and *Sonja Hall.*

I mentally reviewed the interviews I'd just done with the crew. "Next to Kim Robbins put 'dissatisfied with commercial deal.'"

"I thought she got a boatload of money for that."

As he added the qualifier, I explained what Kim had told me during the interview.

"Was he upset for the company's sake," Reed asked, "or was he hoping to get a cut?"

"Very good question." I jotted that in my notebook. "Next to Latoya Craig put 'planning to leave.' She made it sound like she was ready to go off on her own."

"How does that make her suspicious?"

"Because Wakefield Corp is keeping every single recipe she created for them."

"Dang. What about Leif Forsberg? Anything to note for him?"

"Nothing specific. He was kind of emotional about her death, but I didn't catch anything that might flag him as a serious suspect." I stared at the board. "I haven't spoken with Sonja yet. Or Misty." I dropped my head back and exhaled in frustration. "She's so damn quiet, standing off to the side washing dishes, I completely forgot to interview her."

"I forgot about her too," Reed said while adding her name to the board.

The two of us were sitting in mute concentration, each silently going through anyone else who could possibly have a reason to be jealous of Wakefield, when the front door opened. Before I could get out of my seat, Sugar appeared in my office doorway.

Chapter 22

"MY SISTER SAYS YOU WERE looking for me." Sugar glanced at the whiteboard and her expression turned ugly. "Why is Honey's name on that board?"

"Let's step over to the interview room." I met her in the doorway and held out a hand for her to go to the room at the back corner of the building. Reed headed for his desk, but I called him back. "You should at least listen in. Interview skills are important for you to learn."

There were two plain metal chairs in the center of the interview room along with a table pushed up against the outside wall. I indicated that Sugar should take the chair that would put her back to the wall. Reed stood in the far corner off Sugar's left shoulder, and I took the empty chair across from her.

"That list on the board," I explained, "is anyone we could think of who might have negative feelings for Gin Wakefield. I assume you've heard that she's dead?"

Sugar leaned forward with her elbows resting on her knees, her hands folded with her fingers interlaced. "I heard. I didn't do it."

"I didn't say that you did. We don't even know yet if she

was murdered or if it was an accident."

"You've got my name on a suspect list and you basically told my sister that you thought I was responsible."

"Can you blame me? You've been stomping around the village and barking at everyone since you found out the Wakefield group was coming. You seem to feel she was taunting you, but I didn't see that."

"That's because you didn't know her like I did." Sugar flung her hands around as she spoke. "I know you've been talking to the villagers about us, so I'll just assume you're familiar with everything I'm about to say. Stop me if you need clarification on anything. That croquembouche was a direct message to me. Of all the desserts in the world, she makes that? It was a definite taunt."

"Because she made one that put her ahead of you at culinary school."

"Exactly. The week before our final projects were due, she and I got together, like we always did, and bounced ideas off each other. She mentioned trying to make one of these things, I told her it was risky because it could collapse, but if it stayed together, it would be huge for her. So, of course, she shows up not with an eighteen- or even twenty-four-inch stack, but this five-foot-tall tower of amazement. The fact that it made it to her presentation table without collapsing earned her bonus points."

"You think she was trying to best you?"

"No," Sugar replied immediately. "I've thought a lot about that over the years. It was a two-year program. During the first year, we were pretty much neck-and-neck. Just before the start of the second year, something was going on with Gin's mom. Gin wouldn't talk about it, but rumor around the village was that she had something like MS or Parkinson's. Gin was devastated, obviously, and it affected her grades. Things picked up for her by mid-year, but I was still ranked first. Making that croquembouche was smart on her part. Something like that really had been her only hope of increasing her grade."

"Go big or go home," I quipped.

Sugar leaned toward me. "And she could've gone home. Risking such a structurally precarious dessert could have resulted in an F on her final and that would've meant she wouldn't graduate." She shook her head as though watching someone heading for a cliff and picking up speed. "We fought over her making that thing. I told her it was too risky."

"But it worked. She took a risk, and it worked."

It had been more than twenty years, and Sugar's anger over this was still obvious in her clipped words and the tense scowl on her face. She sat quietly for a moment, left leg bouncing, then released a heavy sigh.

"Look, Gin was my best friend. I honestly wanted her to succeed. She did well most of our time there but struggled with some things after her mom got sick. And I admit, there was a side of me that was jealous that she got valedictorian by two points." I stared at her long enough that she finally asked, "What?"

"I don't believe you, Sugar. I believe that you were angry, but not because you were worried about your friend's grade. I know you. You like things done a certain way. You like being in charge and being the one who's right. You were winning the grades race right up until the end, and then Gin flew in under the radar and bested you. You were furious because she didn't do what you said, and that ended up costing you top honors."

She didn't respond, just pinched her lips together.

"Speaking of parents," I continued, "Honey says your father was dying and that your parents wanted to be sure that the two of you could support yourselves by running Treat Me Sweetly. That's why the council denied Gin's request to open another sweet shop."

Sugar fidgeted at that. "Yeah. Things went completely out of control after that. Mrs. Wakefield really wanted to stay here, but she was sick enough that she wasn't going to be able to work anymore. They needed Gin to earn an income that would support them both, and baking was what Gin knew to do." Sugar's expression turned from understanding to stony. "But that's what I knew too, and I already had a shop to take over."

"You and Gin couldn't have met in the middle somehow?"

Sugar crossed her arms and looked away. "Water under the bridge. Everything turned out fine for everyone concerned."

"Okay, let's skip forward a few decades. You became angry the moment you heard that Gin was coming to town."

"Yeah, I did. I mean, it's been ten years since her last visit. Why did she come back? It's not like she had family or close friends here anymore."

"Did you ask her?"

"No. And now we'll never know, will we? But if I had to guess, I'd say she came to gloat. The last time she was here, ten years ago, I think she'd just opened her third shop. This time, it had to be because she landed that whopping big deal at the start of the year. Mabon Fest was the excuse she used to come rub more in our faces."

Sugar's voice broke. It seemed that despite her anger, there was still a soft spot deep in her heart for her former best friend. Or perhaps it was an overwhelming jealousy.

"Okay," I pushed, "you hear that she's coming to the village, and then you find out she entered the baking contest."

"You mean that she got Laurel to let her enter two weeks after the deadline." At my surprised expression, she said, "Yes, I knew about that. All the contestants did. Laurel is such a suck up." In a whiny, condescending voice that was apparently supposed to be Laurel, she said, "*Poor Gin. Awful what those people did to her all those years ago. Least I can do is let her compete.*"

She remained quiet for a minute or two, probably thinking I'd move on, but I rode out the silence and waited for her to continue. Finally, she slid to the edge of her chair and said, "I'm not paranoid or irrational. You must see how her entries were calculated, direct attacks on me. She could've done anything in the world, and she presents the dessert that lost me the valedictorian position? And then my shop with her name on it? What was that supposed to mean? That she was going to try and take Treat Me Sweetly away from me?"

"That made you angry."

"Damn right, it did."

"Angry enough to kill her?"

Sugar's face went blank and she slumped back in her chair. "I didn't do it."

"I agree, the contest entries seemed like passive aggressive moves. You threatened her in front of that entire crowd, though. Then Gin shows up dead the next morning, and I find out you had left the village."

Quietly, almost as though exhausted, she mumbled, "I just needed more bananas."

I glanced across the room at Reed. He heard it too. She needed *more* bananas, as in, she'd used up all those she'd had? My assumption was that Gin bought the stock to further aggravate Sugar. But maybe Sugar bought them all and put the peels in the garbage cans in Wakefield's hotel room? But why? And how did she even get into the room?

No matter what I said after that, Sugar responded with, "I didn't do it."

After ten minutes of that, I had no choice. "I'm not charging you with murder yet, because we don't know that

Gin Wakefield was murdered. I am holding you—"

"What?" She leapt to her feet, and Reed pushed away from the wall and took two steps toward her.

"The only thing you've said in your own defense is 'I didn't do it.' You look guilty as hell, Sugar."

"But—"

"I'm not done with this investigation," I interrupted her. "We have other names on our board, and we're still waiting on the autopsy results. At this point, I can't trust that you won't leave the village again, so I'm holding you on suspicion of the murder of Gin Wakefield."

I read Sugar her rights and let her call Honey. Then Reed put her in the cell of her choice.

"I didn't do this," she said calmly.

"Then I should be able to prove that," I promised from outside the cell. "I don't want to believe that you're guilty, but right now everything is pointing to you."

As the words were coming out of my mouth, Regular Jayne asked me, *But what about the bees? If Gin died from bee stings, how did Sugar get the bees? And how did she get them into Gin's room? And what's the deal with those banana peels?*

I'd get the answers to all those questions, so mentally shoved her aside, walked away from the cell, and promptly realized I'd forgotten to talk to two of the crew members, not one. Sonja as well as Misty.

"What time is it?" I asked.

Reed checked his watch. "Almost six thirty."

"Today's judging is long done. I'm betting the two I need to interview are over at Pine Time."

"I'll stay with Sugar," Reed volunteered.

"All night?" Someone had to be here with her at all times. For safety reasons, we couldn't leave her alone.

"Sure. It's not like I haven't done it before. Usually, it's drunks sleeping off too much partying. There's a cot on the top shelf in the evidence locker. Okay if I bunk down in your office tonight? Gives me the creepies to be out here in the main room all in the open. Woke up a couple times to the inmates sitting there staring at me." He shuddered.

I couldn't stop from laughing at that visual. "That's fine. Do you need to get anything first? Dinner?"

"Lupe is going to meet me here later. I'll ask her to grab something for us and Sugar, and eat here. And no, she won't stay the night."

"I don't care if you have company. Just, you know, stay aware of our detainee."

He blushed and mumbled something about being a professional.

I grinned and whistled for Meeka. She trotted over to the back door, and as I followed, I glanced over at Sugar. She was sitting on the edge of the cot with her head in her hands, muttering softly to herself. As frustrating as Sugar had been to me over the past four months—happy I was around one day, wishing I'd never come here the next—the sight of her sitting in that cell absolutely broke my heart.

Chapter 23

I PULLED INTO MY SPOT in front of the garage at home and found Tripp bent under the hood of his truck.

"This is a different sight." I usually found him lounging on one of the patios at the end of the day. "Something wrong with the truck?"

He glanced over at me and stood, narrowly missing hitting his head on the hood latch. "Nothing wrong, just putzing. You know, grease and engine fumes. Man stuff." He grunted and pounded his fist to his chest. "You had a long day. Is it over?"

"It can be soon." I let Meeka out of her cage in the back of the SUV, and she raced off to rid the yard of invisible invaders. "Is Misty here?"

Tripp wiped grime from his hands on an old towel draped over the truck's quarter panel and then slammed the hood shut. "She might be. Their van pulled in about forty-five minutes ago, a door slammed like someone got out, and then the van left again. I was in the garage and saw the van but didn't pay attention to who stayed and who left."

I tilted my head toward the house. "I'm going to go see if she's here and have a little chat with her if she is."

"Have you eaten?"

"I had the world's biggest pulled pork sandwich for lunch so just a little something would be okay."

He dragged his hand across his mouth pretending to wipe away drool. "I'll need to get one of those tomorrow. How does bread, cheese, and wine on the deck sound?"

"Good, but how about a beer instead?"

"I can do that." He held out his hand. "Give me the keys to your apartment. I'll feed Meeka and get the rest set up."

Absently, I reached into the cargo pocket that contained my keys, and as my fingertips touched them, Lily Grace's reading flashed in my mind. She saw a keyhole. Was this what that was predicting? Me giving Tripp my keys? I smiled at the accurate but simple vision and held them out to Tripp. He grabbed my hand along with the keys and pulled me into his arms.

"I've been looking forward to Jayne time for hours."

I reached up and kissed him full on the mouth. "That is seriously the best thing I've heard all day. I'll hurry."

I went to Misty's room, the bedroom next to the kitchen. The one away from all her co-workers that Kim asked I give to her when I mentioned its location. I had to knock twice before she opened the door. When she did, she slumped with relief.

"I was sure it was Latoya or Leif coming to get me to do more work of some kind. What can I do for you, Sheriff?"

"Actually, I need to speak with you about Gin. May I come in?"

"It's a mess in here." She stood back and opened the door wide so I could see that her stuff was, in fact, everywhere. "Sorry. I'm a slob, I admit it. My roommate literally put a strip of duct tape down the center of our dorm room floor. My side trashy, hers obsessively neat to the point of sterility."

"Did our housekeeper offer to clean for you?" We'd been happy with both Arden and Holly, and I couldn't imagine either of them not tending to a room.

"Oh, sure. They ask every day, but I say no. I don't usually have housekeeping come in when I stay somewhere. Kind of freaks me out, you know? People being around my stuff when I'm not there." She shivered. "Is there someplace else we can talk?"

I guided her to the sitting room across the hallway from the dining room.

"I don't think there's anyone else in the house right now," I told her. "Unless you know of anyone. Sonja, maybe?"

"No, the others went back to the village. I saw Sonja about ten minutes ago. She was going for a walk. Said she needed to clear her head."

As in, she wanted fresh air after being cooped up for three days? Or maybe something was weighing on her that she needed to think through? "She must be feeling better."

Glancing distractedly around the room, Misty chose a chair in the corner. "What? Oh, Sonja? Yeah, she's doing better."

"Good. Okay, this should be plenty private, then."

As I settled onto the sofa Gran had shipped to the US from Ireland, I thought of all the times she read stories to me and Rosalyn on it. We had to have it reupholstered after vandals broke in and slashed the fabric. It used to be a gorgeous blue damask. Now it was covered in a floral tapestry that was very different but still beautiful. While Misty got comfortable in a cozy armchair across from me, I set up my voice recorder.

"Tell me about working for Wakefield's," I prompted.

"There's not a lot to tell. I told you before that this was just a temporary job. It's not like I have a secret desire to be a baker or anything like that. Heck, the fanciest thing I can make is spaghetti. And only then if the sauce comes from a jar."

"Did you see Ms. Wakefield very often?"

"Not really. I worked Monday, Wednesday, Friday, and

Saturday mornings, getting there early with the bakers, at four a.m., and leaving at eleven. Those hours worked out well with my classes. Sometimes Ms. Wakefield would come in early, as well, but most days she wouldn't get there until around seven. When she did, she'd walk through the kitchen and approve or reject everything being made that morning. Then she and the head bakers would have their morning meeting in her office."

"Did you have a relationship of any kind with Ms. Wakefield?"

"A relationship?" She blinked at me in surprise. "She'd say hi to me, if that's what you mean. She was friendly enough with the kitchen staff. She knew our names, usually, so it's not like we were faceless employees. There wasn't any chitchat, though. She never asked about our homelife or anything like that."

"You never 'talked shop,' so to speak, with her?"

She laughed at that. "No, never. I've learned a few things by listening to the other chefs, but I couldn't hold a conversation of any kind. I was shocked when she asked my opinion on the contest entry the other night." Misty fought with a sad smile at the memory. "The bakery is convenient to my school; that's why I applied there. I just need a paycheck and a job that preferably won't make me think too hard. That's all this is for me."

"Nothing hard about washing dishes. And I don't mean that as an insult to dishwashers. It's sort of meditative."

My mother made us clean up after dinner. Rosalyn always wanted to wash, but after breaking three plates in as many nights, Mom deemed me the only one who could touch the soap-slippery dishes. I preferred the repetitive scrubbing and rinsing, scrubbing and rinsing, to running all over the kitchen to put things away.

"Meditative," Misty echoed. "Exactly. People just bring me things to wash and otherwise leave me alone."

My turn to laugh. "Sorry, but you do seem to disappear into the background. I meant to talk to you when I was at The Inn earlier but completely forgot."

"That's always been my personality. I'm sort of a born wallflower."

"You overhear a lot, though, don't you?"

She shifted uncomfortably. "I do sometimes."

"I'll be honest with you, Misty. I got a sort of odd vibe when speaking with Latoya, Leif, and Kim earlier. Is there anything you may have overheard regarding Ms. Wakefield that could help me figure out what happened to her?"

Misty folded her hands in her lap, her thumbs twiddling. "You mean something to do with her death?" She looked up at me. "Do you think one of them might have done this to her?"

"Is there a reason you feel I should dig further into that possibility?" When thirty seconds had passed, and Misty hadn't responded, I pushed a little harder. "Misty? Is there something I should know about? Anything at all that might help me figure out what happened to Gin?"

"I don't know specifics," Misty blurted after another long silence. "I don't know for sure if any of them did anything to her. On the drive up here, they talked a lot about the contract she received. And they sounded really angry about it."

"Angry in what way?"

She shook her head. "I don't know. Kim drove the van and Latoya rode in the passenger seat next to him. Leif and I were in the middle row, Leif behind Latoya, me behind Kim. Sonja was in the third row only because I get really carsick if I sit back that far. Otherwise, I would've been in the back."

"They were all talking about this contract?"

"The other three were. Sonja must've been sleeping or something because she never said anything. Maybe it wasn't food poisoning, maybe something else was bothering her. She was quiet from the start." Misty poked at a little china bird figurine on the side table next to her, spinning it slowly as she spoke. "Anyway, I couldn't hear much of what Kim and Latoya were saying. They were speaking softly, and the radio was on, so between that and the road noise it was hard to hear. The bits and pieces I did pick up made me think they were talking about that contract. Something about some of the terms getting changed." She gave a little shrug. "That's all I know."

I sat with this information for a minute, Misty growing increasingly uncomfortable as the seconds ticked past.

"Did I do something wrong?" she asked.

"Did you know Gin's life was in danger?"

She shook her head hard. "No, I swear I didn't."

"Then there isn't anything you could have done to prevent her death. Many times, things aren't connectable until after the fact." She relaxed despite my gaze being locked on her. "You feel that it would be worth my time to check into this contract?"

"I think so." Misty sniffled, fighting back tears suddenly. "If I would've known—"

"I can't tell you how many people have said those exact words to me over the years. Thank you for your statement, Misty. I'll check into that contract. Please, don't speak to anyone else about this."

She barked out an ironic laugh. "Co-workers who ignore me? A village full of people who have no idea who I am? Who do you think I'm going to speak to?" She flung a hand down at Meeka who had entered the room earlier and sat at our side. "Your dog, maybe."

Meeka headbutted her leg, making Misty laugh.

"She's pretty good at keeping a secret if you need a sounding board." I scratched Meeka's ears and her tail swished across the floor. "You seem like a good person, Misty. Perhaps there's another job you'd be better suited for."

"I was thinking the same thing this morning. If we're done, I'd like to go back to my room. I was about to fill out some online applications."

I turned off the voice recorder and released Misty, thanking her again for her time, and went down the hall to the B&B office to make a phone call.

"Whispering Pines Sheriff's Station, Deputy Reed speaking."

"It's Jayne. Is Lupe there?"

"Yeah, she just got here with dinner. Do you need her?"

"Just for a minute. I've got a little assignment for her."

"That's good news. She'll like that."

This was something I could have done myself, but I was wiped out after this day. Besides, I was pretty sure Lupe could find information a lot faster than I could. She had sources.

"You have an assignment for me?" she asked hopefully.

"I do. As qualified as my deputy is to research things, he tends to get lost down rabbit holes. I need this information quickly."

"Tell me what you need."

Five minutes later, Lupe was digging into everything she could find on the Wakefield contract, and I was standing outside Sonja's room. I knocked twice, calling out to her the second time, but she didn't answer. Looked like she was still out walking. Our conversation would have to wait until morning.

Instead, I went up to my apartment and changed out of my uniform and then snuggled in Tripp's arms on the couch on the deck. The weather was definitely cooling off, but it wasn't so cold that we couldn't enjoy lounging outside with a fire going in the tabletop fire pit.

"Are you any closer to catching your bad guy?" he asked.

"I'm not even sure yet that there is a bad guy. I should hear from Dr. Bundy tomorrow, so I'll know if all this tracking down of Wakefield employees and questioning them today was worth my time or a waste of it."

"Can't ever hurt to be one step ahead of the game."

"Especially true when we're talking murder." I took a long pull off my Sprecher Octoberfest lager, keeping with the autumn theme of the week, and let out a happy sigh. "Perfect way to end a frustrating day."

"The beer?"

I snuggled further against his chest. "That too."

We snacked on Monterey Jack and Gruyère—turned out there were beer and cheese pairings as well as wine and cheese pairings, which I never knew—and thick slices of Tripp's homemade rustic bread while we discussed his day. I didn't want to talk about mine anymore but did mention the conference coming up in February in New Orleans.

"That's worth thinking about. Or, we could just go on vacation. If we close the B&B like we said we would, we can do anything we want. That deputy at the County Sheriff's Station can keep an eye on the villagers if Reed can't get away from school. Right?"

I yawned and mumbled that he was right but that we could think about it later. We sat, sometimes chatting sometimes not, beneath the nearly full moon. Next thing I knew, Meeka was interrupting our make-out session. Which, considering the other part of Lily Grace's vision, was a good thing. We were getting pretty involved.

"The furry one is right," Tripp said, his voice husky. "It's bedtime. I've got to make a full breakfast in the morning."

"Why?" I asked while straightening my shirt. "I thought everyone was happy with a continental spread."

He slid to the edge of the sofa. "The gluten-free people are checking out in the morning, and I want to send them off with a good final impression. Then we've got new people checking in tomorrow afternoon."

"We do like it when all rooms are booked."

Tripp paused at the top of the deck stairway and reached into his pocket. "Almost forgot to give you your keys back."

"I know where to find you." I kissed him goodnight and, as had become our routine, watched him walk across the yard to the house. There, he turned and waved goodnight.

Morgan's words from earlier echoed in my ear. "Don't you think it's a little bit silly for the two of you to live in separate buildings on the same property?"

Sometimes, I really did.

Chapter 24

TRIPP AND I HAD JUST finished breakfast when he turned on the small television hanging near the kitchen island. It took less than two minutes for me to know today wouldn't be any easier than yesterday. In fact, it would likely be worse.

"Every station is covering it," I murmured as I flipped through the channels.

"They're waiting for you." Tripp pointed at the image on the screen of a reporter standing in front of my station. He ran to the dining room to check the front yard. "No one here yet."

"Then I better get over there before someone tells them where the sheriff lives."

I'd just backed out of my spot and was about to leave when I saw someone emerge from the front of the house. I rolled down my window to greet her.

"Sonja?" She hesitated before coming over to me. "Good to see you out and about. I hear you're feeling better."

"I am. Thought I'd enjoy the morning air."

"Did the others find you yesterday?"

"If you mean did they tell me about Gin, they did." She turned up the collar of her charcoal-gray jacket and shoved her hands deep into the pockets. "It's awful."

She didn't seem very upset. Of course, she already knew. It's not like I just broke the news to her. I was itching to talk with her about Gin, but getting some sort of control over the journalists felt more urgent at the moment.

"If you were planning to walk toward the village," I began, "be aware that word of Gin's death has spread. I saw on television that a horde of reporters has descended on us."

She looked disappointed and then gave me a grateful smile. "Maybe I'll stick to walking in the woods here then. Don't know how many of them would know me, but I'm not prepared to talk about Gin yet."

Well, hopefully she would be ready when I got back later.

The bubble of safety that seemed to surround my home popped when I got to the end of my driveway. Vans from news stations, the kinds with big antennas and satellite dishes mounted on their roofs, lined the highway. They started at the west-side parking lot, which was crammed full of vehicles, and appeared to run clear over to hotel row which was just over the village limits border.

Damn. I knew that once word of Gin's death got out, it would get crazy here, but I hadn't expected this.

As I inched slowly along the highway, pausing for the occasional reporter or videographer who was climbing out of a van or blocking my lane with equipment, I thought of Sheriff Brighton's vehicle. It was a huge white Chevy Tahoe with "Sheriff" and "Whispering Pines, WI" emblazoned on both sides in bold gold and black letters. I'd thought a few times about asking Reeva if I could buy the truck from her, but at the moment, I was grateful to have my generic white Jeep Cherokee that the reporters didn't even notice. If they'd seen a "Sheriff" vehicle driving past, they would've been on me like a dog on a bone.

We made it to the station and found a group of journalists encircling the building. I had to tap my horn three times to get them to move so I could pull into my parking spot. When I got out, the questions started immediately.

"What can you tell us about Gin Wakefield's death?"

"Do you have any leads on whether this was an accident or murder?"

"I understand that she came up here with some of her employees. Do you know where they're staying?"

At least that much hadn't gotten out. Once they learned the crew was staying at Pine Time, there would be reporters camped out on my front lawn.

"I need to get my dog out of the back." I had to raise my voice over the buzz of questions. "Back up, please."

Rather than honoring my request, they kept lobbing questions at me.

"How did she die?"

"Where did you find her body?"

"Back up now." They still didn't respond, so instead of yelling I went silent. I stood there like I was about to make a statement. When they quieted, I said, "I'm not prepared to answer any questions at this time. I need to go inside and check in with my deputy. If you all go around to the front of the building, I'll come out in a few minutes."

Most scurried off, but a few eager videographers, filming my every move, stayed close. Too close.

"Look," my patience was fading rapidly, "I'm going to open the hatch now. If you don't get out of the way, I can't be responsible for any damage to your cameras."

That did it. They took a few steps back, leaving me just enough room to open the door. Meeka was shivering in her cage. She loved people but hated crowds, and mobs terrified her.

"Come on, girl." I gathered her into my arms, held her shivering little body close, and slammed the door shut. We made our way through the persistent reporters to the station's back door and found it locked. Great. I pounded with a closed fist, and a few seconds later, Reed opened it a crack.

"Sorry, had to lock it. They kept trying to get in." He opened the door far enough to let us in and then slammed it shut and locked it again. "This is nuts. They're like freaking zombies. I didn't think it would be a good idea to let them see Sugar sitting in a jail cell."

"Good plan." I gave Meeka an extra hug and ear scratch then set her down. In the main room, I found a woman sitting next to Reed's desk. Not Lupe as I expected, however. "What are you doing here?"

Reeva Long turned and gave me a big smile. "Good morning, Jayne. I came to help Martin with a special project."

"She's helping him design a cottage," Sugar tattled from her jail cell. She'd made herself at home in there with a patchwork quilt, some extra pillows, a thick sweater, slippers, and some magazines.

"Honey brought over a few things for her," Reed explained before I could ask.

"Wait until Flavia hears." Sugar chuckled while flipping the page of her magazine. "She's going to pop a cork."

"Hang on." I backed up to the previous statement. "Reeva's helping you do what?"

"You said something the other day about me getting my own place," Reed began. "I started thinking more about it, and I think it's time." He kicked his toe lightly against the leg of his desk. "Can't say that I'm ready for Lupe to move in, but she'd have a place to stay when she visits."

He turned pink when Sugar asked what exactly "visit" meant.

"And your aunt is helping you with this instead of your mother why?"

Reed just stared like I hadn't had enough coffee yet, and Reeva answered. "Do you honestly think that Flavia would help him move out of her house?"

Good point. "Can I just ask that neither of you gives me credit for this idea?"

"No problem," Reed replied.

I had to quit offering advice. First, Effie and Cybil thought I told Lily Grace to move in with Jola. All I did was suggest she talk with her newly discovered sister about frustrations Jola was likely to understand. Now, if Reed said anything, I'd suffer the wrath of Flavia. She already hated me, which had nothing to do with me. Flavia hated my grandmother and, therefore, me by relation.

"Where are you moving?" I asked. "You aren't leaving the village, are you?"

Reeva responded. "Karl signed an agreement with your grandparents thirty years ago to rent six acres. I certainly don't need that much property, so we're going to subdivide it."

I burst out laughing. "Are you telling me that he's going to move onto your property?"

"Told you," Sugar sang out gleefully again. "Can't you just hear that cork pushing to the surface?"

I hung Meeka's leash on a hook by the front door and shifted to work mode. "What's going on with all these reporters? When did they start showing up?"

"A couple got here in the middle of the night," Reed told me. "They must be from Milwaukee and Madison to have gotten here that fast. I had to pull the blinds on the windows because someone was shining lights inside. Most of them got here within the last hour or two. The Wakefield Corporation released a very brief statement about her death. People want answers."

"People aren't the only ones. I want answers too." I stared at the front door as though the words I should say to them might appear there. "Okay, I'm going to go out and talk to them. I can't say much, because I don't know much."

I opened the door, and instantly questions sprang from the crowd like popcorn out of a hot kettle.

"Everyone, quiet, please," I called out. The questions continued, so again I went silent, standing with my arms crossed until my off-the-cuff statement could be heard. "At approximately six thirty yesterday morning, a body was discovered by one of the village residents in the woods a short distance from here. For privacy reasons, I will not reveal the name of that person. I arrived at the scene at approximately six fifty and identified the victim as Ginger Wakefield. The medical examiner got here about an hour after that, confirmed that she was indeed deceased, and took her body to his lab to perform an autopsy. I have not gotten those results yet but expect to hear from him this morning. Until that time, I really can't answer any other questions. I don't want to speculate."

"You feel it an accident then?"

"Whispering Pines does have a reputation for being a hotspot for murder."

I knew our "reputation" was likely to come up and didn't react to the question. "As I just told you, I haven't seen the autopsy report so can't tell you if it was an accident or not."

"But you must think it's possible that she was murdered," a woman who reminded me of Lupe with her persistence called out. "You'd dismiss the idea outright otherwise."

The front door opened, and Reed stuck his head out. He whispered in my ear, "Dr. Bundy is on the phone."

"I know you all want answers. I know Ms. Wakefield had hundreds of thousands of fans. Her loss is a true tragedy and one that I take very seriously. I will say that her death has hit the Whispering Pines community especially hard. She grew up here, and many of our residents knew her personally. Out of respect for Ms. Wakefield and her family, I will not speculate on the manner of her death. I will tell you everything I can as I uncover more details."

It didn't matter what I said; the questions continued, so I went back inside the building and locked the door.

"How am I ever going to get out and investigate this without them following me?" I mumbled, mostly to myself.

"We'll figure it out," Reed assured. "Dr. Bundy is waiting."

Grateful to finally hear from the man, I went in my office and dropped into my chair, catching a glimpse of our whiteboard as I did. For a split second, I panicked, worried that one of the reporters may have seen the suspect board through the window. A glance at the drawn blinds assured me that my deputy had thought of everything. I picked up the phone.

"What do you know, Doc?"

"I know that a storm must be headed my way because my trick knee is being tricky."

Smiling, I responded, "Sorry to hear that. You should pick up one of Morgan's poultices the next time you're here." Then I realized, the only reason he came to the village was because someone had died. It's not like he stopped by for a shopping trip. Maybe Pine Time could gift him and his wife with a weekend sometime. "What do you know about our victim?"

"I know that bee stings result in localized pain and swelling for the victim. In someone who is allergic, stings can cause a more severe anaphylactic reaction."

"What does that mean?" I watched Meeka cross the room and flop down onto the cushion I'd brought in weeks ago. First time she'd used it. Guess the chatter in the main room was disturbing her nap.

"People can be sensitive to a variety of things," Dr. Bundy explained. "Plants cause seasonal allergies. A food allergy, obviously, is a reaction to a specific food. In both cases, the allergen enters the system, and the body fights the invader. Some reactions are minor and, while annoying, are not life-threatening—sneezing, headaches, itchy eyes, etc. Some reactions cause a stronger systemic reaction and result in anaphylaxis which can affect multiple organs at once. In Ms. Wakefield's case, death was caused by anaphylactic shock brought on by a Hymenoptera sting."

"A what?"

"Hymenoptera are winged insects—bees, wasps, hornets, and so on. In Ms. Wakefield's case, she suffered a severe reaction to envenomation. Venom is made up of various components. Half or better is melittin, a peptide which makes blood cells at the sting site burst and blood vessels expand. Then there's phospholipase which causes further pain and inflammation. Also, histamine, a protein that boosts blood flow to the area of the body being affected by allergens. Histamine also creates inflammation."

"Science was never my thing, Doc. Talk at the elementary level for me, would you?"

He chuckled softly. "Think of a scratch that has turned red and puffy. The red puffiness is inflammation, or a cluster of blood cells, preventing whatever is in the cut from entering your bloodstream."

"This is what happened to Wakefield?"

"Yes. Basically, her body went nuts trying to protect her from the invader, the venom. Her chest likely got tight. She was probably quite itchy, evidenced from the rash all over her body. Her lips and eyes swelled, and her airways narrowed making breathing very difficult. The melittin in the venom caused her blood vessels to expand which would have led to a drop in blood pressure. Her organs would have suffered from a lack of blood and oxygen. This would have ultimately led to her body going into anaphylactic shock."

The poor woman. What a horrifying thing to go through. "Are you saying that Gin Wakefield died from a bee sting?"

"Not just one, although, in her case, that might have been

enough. I found nine stings on her body—one on the back of her right hand, two on her abdomen, one on each ankle, one on her left thigh, one on her lower left hip, one at the base of her skull, and one on her throat in that dimple by the collarbone."

"Her suprasternal notch," I murmured.

He paused before saying, "I thought science wasn't your thing."

"A few things sank in." I sat back in my chair. "We found dead bees in her hotel room."

"Honey bees in a hotel room in late September." Dr. B's questioning tone matched the one in my head. "I don't know a lot about bees, but it seems to me it's a little chilly for them right now. I'd think they'd stick close to the hive."

"My thoughts exactly." So where was the closest hive? "What about an EpiPen? Did it appear she had injected herself?"

"An EpiPen is administered into the middle of the outer thigh. I did not find an injection mark."

"But she must've had a prescription."

"As I told you at the scene, anyone as allergic as Ms. Wakefield appeared to be would carry pens at all times. She wouldn't just keep them in her hotel room, she would have them on her person."

"Wakefield wore a small medical bag around her waist. She must've carried an EpiPen or two in there along with other supplies."

I brought up the pictures Reed had taken of her room as Dr. Bundy said, "She wasn't wearing the bag when we found her."

I stopped clicking when I reached a specific picture. "Nope; it was lying empty on the floor of her hotel room." That's what the items all over the floor by the lounge chair were, the contents of her medical bag. "We didn't find a pen in her room, and you didn't find one on her person. Why not?"

"Sorry, Sheriff. That's not my area of expertise. I can tell you what the facts are, I'm not so great at interpreting them. Unless we're talking medical facts, of course."

"She would've had a pen." I rubbed my fingers across my eyebrows, a stress-relieving massage technique. "I think I'm looking at another murder."

"Could be." He paused before adding, "On a side note, I know how much you enjoy the quirky details. It might interest you to know that I could rule this is a natural death."

"What? How?"

"The body sees an allergen as an invader and sends out antibodies to attack the allergen and protect the body from it. A natural response which, unfortunately, causes swelling that can result in death. Therefore, the state of Ms. Wakefield's body reacting to bee stings by surrounding the venom with antibodies, resulting in enough swelling to cause suffocation, could be considered death by natural response."

"You really know how to drop a mic, Doc." He was right, I did like the quirky details. "Interesting. I always thought a natural death was something that happened inside the body."

"An anaphylactic reaction does happen within the body."

"I meant like cancer or organ failure, but I see your point."

"It's a shame when our bodies don't do what we ask them to. Ms. Wakefield appeared to be in relatively good health overall. I found cirrhosis of the liver, likely brought on by alcohol consumption, and coronary atherosclerosis."

"Plaque in her arteries?"

"Yep. Just about everyone has some. She suffered from high cholesterol as well, not surprising considering her regular intake of full-fat sweets."

Suddenly, the full-fat chocolate chai didn't sound so good. It was scary to think about what might be going on beneath the skin. "I have a means of death. Now I have to figure out how those bees got into her room and what happened to her EpiPen."

"I have no doubt that you will catch your man. Or woman. Don't want you labeling me as a sexist. Male, female, or hermaphrodite are equally capable of killing another human being."

"Glad to hear you have such an open mind, Doc. Anything else you need to tell me?"

"One other thing." He paused for a second. "Pumpkin spice is out of control."

"I agree with you there," I said as I laughed.

"Saw a package of what appeared to be pumpkin spice meat at the grocery store yesterday. I pray that was a joke."

"That is disgusting. But I meant, is there anything else regarding our victim?"

"I know what you meant. And no, that's all I've got. As usual, I'll send over the report. Let me know if you have any questions."

"Will do. Thanks, Doc."

I hung up, and Reed immediately stepped into my office and asked, "What did he say?"

"We have definite death by bee sting." I gave him a recap quietly and off to the side, where Reeva and Sugar couldn't hear. "Any idea where the nearest beehive is?"

"There are plenty within village limits, but you're going to have to go for a bit of a hike. I suggest parking in the carnival lot and asking one of the carnies for directions to Beckett's place."

There was a name I hadn't heard before. "Who's Beckett?"

"As Sugar has said many times, he's the best beekeeper in all of Wisconsin."

Chapter 25

THE PLAN WAS, REED WOULD go out front to "make a statement" and lure the reporters away from the back door. Once the coast was clear, Meeka and I would scurry out to the SUV and drive away, hopefully unseen by the mob. But just as Reed stood from his desk, the phone rang.

"Whispering Pines Sheriff Station, Deputy Reed speaking." He listened and nodded his head. "She's here. One moment." He turned to me. "It's your mother."

Talk about timing. It was never a good idea to not take a phone call from my mother, though, no matter how busy I was.

"Hold on. This shouldn't take long." I went back into my office and picked up my extension. "I only have a few minutes, Mom. I've got a lot going on here."

"I can tell that from the television," she said. "It's all over the news. Gin Wakefield died in your village? Why didn't you call and let me know? You know I don't like to find things out this way."

Call her to let her know what was happening in Whispering Pines? She couldn't stand Whispering Pines. Was she seriously digging for gossip about a celebrity's death? As much as I was sickened by that, a tiny part of me felt stupidly important because there was a note of respect in her voice. She never thought of my job as being something to brag about, but here I was, responsible for the release of information most of the country, and many parts of the world, were dying to hear.

"It's an open investigation, Mom. I can't talk about it."

"I know there are reporters all over the village now. All the channels are covering this and speculating on what happened. Tell me whatever you told them."

I cleared my throat and echoed the voice I'd used with the reporters a few minutes ago. "Gin Wakefield was found dead yesterday morning. It's a terrible loss."

There was silence on the other end as she waited for more and then came a scolding, "Jayne."

"If I would have told them anything more than that, they would have reported it. That's why they're speculating." I didn't have time for this. "We don't know anything more at this point."

Could I have told her what Dr. Bundy found? Sure. Would I? Not a chance.

"You must know more than that," she objected. "You can tell me. I'm your mother."

I had to say, hearing the giddiness in her voice over something associated with me and my profession helped me understand why Rosalyn was always so eager to please her. Still, a woman had died.

"I really can't, Mom. I'm sorry." Then, just to give her a nugget, I added, "We should know more soon. As in, later today." She made a sound that indicated her satisfaction level was at mediocre. "Is that the only reason you called?"

"It was, but now that I have you on the phone, I might as well do a bed-and-breakfast check."

This meant she wanted an income and expense update. Since my parents were the financial backers on this B&B

venture, I had no choice but to reveal upon demand the state of the business. Even in the middle of what appeared to be a murder investigation.

"It's been great. We are completely booked for this entire week. With Gin Wakefield's crew staying with us—" I bit off my words.

"What? What did you say?" Mom pounced on my slip. "The Wakefield chefs are staying at Pine Time?"

Damn. I hadn't meant to say that. "You can't tell anyone."

"Who would I tell?"

"Oh, I don't know. How about any one of your employees or the customers who come into the spa."

"I would never tell the customers."

"Mom, I'm serious. It would make life really difficult if we had reporters camped out on the front yard. As it is, I'm not quite sure how to get home tonight without them following me."

"Very well. I cross my heart." Then she added, "Yes, I do have a heart."

I put my hand over my mouth, so she wouldn't hear me laughing. Occasionally, my mother was hilarious. Problem was, she usually didn't mean to be.

"I really need to get back to work on this investigation. Was there anything else you needed?"

"Nothing that I needed, per se, but you should know that Rosalyn has been talking about coming up to visit you."

I shot to my feet. "Rosalyn wants to come here? When?"

What did this mean? Was it simply a visit to the village she hadn't seen since she was eight years old, or was there something more to it? Was it a mission to poke through every nook and cranny of the house to report back to Mom? It would hardly be the first time she'd played stooge for her. Of course, she also liked to claim ownership of things that she had nothing to do with. I don't know how she did it, but she had this infuriating way of turning the spotlight on herself while explaining something wonderful about someone else.

"She mentions Halloween a lot," Mom said. "That is the favorite time of year for all those … Wiccans, isn't it?"

The word *Wiccans* stuck in her throat. Her distaste had nothing to do with the religion or Wiccan people. It was because Gran had been a practicing Wiccan, and Mom hated anything that had to do with my grandmother or Whispering Pines.

"It is their favorite time," I agreed. "This week is Mabon, their second favorite sabbat. We've got a week-long fest going on. It's fun. You should come with her if she does come."

"I don't think so. Will you have a room available for your sister?"

"Right now, we're fully booked. I'll call her if we have a cancellation and something opens up. That's not very likely, though. It will be Samhain."

A sharp hissing inhale of breath told me Mom had reached her limit on details regarding life in Whispering Pines. "I'm sure you'll figure out something for her. All right, I'll let you go. Keep me up-to-date on this Gin Wakefield thing."

"A woman died. This isn't something to gossip about."

"I'm aware of that. What kind of person do you think I am?" She paused for half a beat. "Don't answer that. I just feel that as your mother I should get a special privilege now and then."

And I'd now reached my limit on discussing this topic with her.

"I've gotta go, Mom. Talk to you later." I looked down at Meeka who appeared to be laughing at me, in her doggie way. Hard to tell through all that fur, though. She needed a trim. "Let's go, girl."

The plan to distract worked perfectly. Reed went out the front door while Meeka and I waited by the back. As soon as

Reed stepped outside, a roar of questions rose from the crowd. I counted to twenty, to give any lingering journalists in back time to run around to the front, then slipped out with Meeka tucked in my arm like a fuzzy white football and rushed out to the car. I didn't even take the time to put her in her cage, which she didn't like. Most dogs enjoyed being able to stick their heads out the window. After I'd hit the brakes too hard one time while driving in Madison rush-hour traffic, causing the little Westie to go flying to the floor of the Cherokee, Meeka preferred the security of her cage.

We'd barely gone a hundred yards when I spotted a news van following us. I caught a break when a crowd stepped out to cross the street, but the van would catch up in seconds if I didn't employ some evasive maneuvers. There were only two options when going east out of the village. One was to stay on the highway which led to Rhinelander, and the other was to go left at the fork and follow the road to the Whispering Pines circus' parking lot. On the west side of the lot was the entrance to a trail carved by the wheels of horse-drawn carriages. The circus used the wagons to transport both supplies to the circus grounds as well as circus goers to and from the village commons. The trail led into the woods and was labeled "Circus Wagons Only," but a sheriff's SUV could use it in an emergency.

Meeka scolded me with a sharp bark as she stood with her paws on the armrest of the passenger's door.

"This one time only. I promise." I needed to talk to this Beckett person without a team of journalists hovering around.

I crept along the bumpy path and ended up at the horse stables. Igor, the stable manager, came rushing over, ready to chew me out, until he realized who I was.

"Sheriff O'Shea," Igor said in his heavy European accent. "What are you doing driving on horse path?"

"Sorry, but it's sort of an emergency. I need to get up to

the honey farm, and I've got a crowd of journalists hot on my tail."

"Trying to be first to break Wakefield story, hey?"

"They are. Deputy Reed told me you could direct me to Beckett's farm."

Igor gestured north. "Is not far. There is path on far side of stable for Beckett's horse and wagon. Lead straight to farm."

"He uses a horse and wagon too?"

"Parks in lot." He pointed at a white cargo van with little honey bees all over it and "Beckett's Bees" on the side.

Got it. He used a wagon because motorized vehicles weren't allowed anywhere except on the roads, and there wasn't a road to the honey farm.

Igor motioned for me to follow him. "Come, I give you ride."

"Thanks. I'd love a ride."

Meeka loved it too. She snapped at low-hanging branches and hung her head over the side of the small horse-drawn wagon to watch the ground go past. Igor stopped in a small clearing by a barn. This was as far as the wagon could go. I thanked him for the ride, and he asked if I wanted him to stay.

"I'm not sure how long this will take. If you need to leave, we'll find our way back."

Igor pointed out a dirt footpath and told me to follow it through a dense section of foliage. The honey farm was at the other end of the path.

Chapter 26

AFTER WALKING ABOUT THIRTY YARDS through the woods, and batting away approximately thirty bazillion mosquitoes, we came to a small cottage. There was a shed to the left of the cottage. To the right, about the length of a football field away, was a circle of beehives.

Beckett had a large operation, or so it seemed to me, with at least thirty of these hives scattered across the field near his cottage. Meaning the tall white boxes, not the huge nests that hung in trees or ended up wedged in the eaves of roofs.

I started toward the field and was scolded a second later.

"First, no dogs. Second, you need protection if you don't want to get stung."

I turned and saw an older gentleman with gray hair and a large, bulbous nose. He was about five foot six, not much taller than me, and walked with a side-to-side sway like something was wrong with one of his legs or hips.

"Are you Beckett?" I asked.

"I am. And from your uniform, I assume you're Sheriff O'Shea." He held his hand out to me. "Pleasure to meet you."

"And you. I understand you make the best honey in all of Wisconsin."

He shrugged. A gesture that simultaneously brushed off any conceit while accepting the label as being the truth.

"I've got some questions about bees if you have a few minutes."

Beckett snapped to attention. "Always have time to talk bees. Even if I'm harvesting, I can talk while I do it. Let's get suited up, and I'll take you over to the bees."

"Oh, no, I just—"

"Can't discuss the critters without giving visuals. Trust me, it's interesting, you'll enjoy it. Your dog might upset them so should stay up on the porch."

Not only did Beckett provide me with a traditional beekeeper's white coverup, including a veiled hat and long elasticized gloves, he brought out a dish of water for Meeka as well.

"Each stack of boxes you see over there is its own colony or hive," he began as we crossed the field.

As we got close to the hives, I understood what he meant by "stack of boxes." Each hive was made up of individual white wooden boxes with handholds carved into the sides. Most of the hives were short, only three or four boxes tall, which equated to about three feet. A few were stacked to over six feet.

Beckett laid a hand on top of one of the short hives. "There's a lot going on inside there. Do you hear them?"

"How could I miss it?" The buzz coming from the boxes was a lot louder than I expected. "Are they making honey?"

"A little, but their biggest production is done for the year." He removed a bungee cord from around the hive and pulled off the cover. "This top box is called a super."

"Why is the super shorter than the boxes beneath it?" I was already interested in this lesson.

"The queen lives in the super."

I waved a hand across the field. "There's only one queen for all this?"

"No-no. Each colony has its own queen. See how the top box on all the hives is short?"

He was so patient with what should have been obvious to me. "Oh, yes, I see now."

"That's where the queen lays eggs and mates with the drones to create more worker bees."

"Is that it? The queen lives her entire life in that little box making baby bees? She doesn't even get to go down to the other boxes to supervise production?"

"That's what I'm saying. It's not necessarily great being queen. Just like the lady over in England, it's kind of a sheltered existence." He frowned, an expression both sad and respectful. "Besides mating with the queen, the drones also protect the colony. The worker bees are all infertile females and do just about everything else, including collecting nectar and pollen, tending to the queen and drones, feeding the larvae, and controlling the temperature in the hive."

"They can control the temperature?"

"Yep. They're quite ingenious, really. That buzzing sound is them flapping their wings. When the temperature starts to cool off, the worker bees flap their wings and keep the queen warm. When it gets too hot out, they flap and keep her cool. It's all about the queen."

I laughed, unable to hide how ironic I felt it was that the females did just about everything around the "house" while the males simply mated and fought off intruders.

Beckett grinned, understanding what I found funny. "Common reaction from women." He drew his finger across the line that indicated where the super stacked on top of the box below. "In between the super and the hive body is a screen called a queen excluder that keeps her in the super. The other bees are smaller than her and can pass through the excluder to the hive bodies where the honey is produced. I'll show you."

When I hesitated to step closer to the now wide-open hive, Beckett assured, "Don't worry, the outfit will protect you. They're not very active right now anyway since the temperature has cooled off. Tell you what, I'll use the smoker to ease your mind."

Beckett set down the super and grabbed something that resembled a watering can. He took the top off the can, scooped up a handful of dead needles from beneath a nearby pine tree, and dropped them in along with a lit match. He replaced the lid, and a few seconds later smoke billowed from the can's spout which he waved back-and-forth around the hive.

"The smoke keeps them mellow," Becket explained as the bees buzzed around but didn't seem overly interested in us. "Now, see all the little sticks?"

Inside the super was what appeared to be a row of flat wooden sticks, but I knew there had to be more beneath. "Is that where the honey is?"

"Gold star for the sheriff. Of course, you've already got one of those." He chuckled and demonstrated what to do with the smoker then handed it to me. With gentle movements, he pried loose one of the sticks, which had become stuck to the box with honey, and pulled out what looked like a picture frame covered with bees, wax, and a bit of dripping honey. "This is called a frame. The bees build a honeycomb structure from wax that gets produced in their bellies. Once the entire frame is filled with the honeycomb, they're ready to get to work. The worker bees go out and collect the nectar in their honey stomach."

"That's its actual name? A honey stomach?"

"It is. Once their honey stomach is full, they put the honey into one of the little honeycomb cells. When a cell is full, they seal it with a little cap of wax."

"Hang on. Are you saying the bee barfs up the honey into the cell?"

He let out a loud, hearty laugh. "That's pretty much exactly what they do. Once the frame is full, meaning every cell has a wax cap, I take it to my shed over there."

He pointed to the little shed on the other side of his cottage. "I'm happy to show you the extraction process if you want."

"As much as I honestly would love to see that, there is something specific I came here to ask you about."

"I figured. Go ahead and ask, I'm going to put the hive back together."

While he replaced the frame and the boxes, I explained, "I'm conducting an investigation into a death we had in the village yesterday."

"Gin Wakefield," he acknowledged as he put the super back on top. "I heard. Very sad. Since you're here to ask me questions, I assume she was allergic and died from either bee stings or honey."

"That's what the medical examiner concluded. He found numerous sting marks on her body. Would bees fly all the way from here over to the commons?"

"Bees will travel about two miles from their hive, so they could've been my bees. I'm the only keeper in these parts, which means if they're not mine, they're from natural hives. The thing is, it's getting colder at night, so they aren't nearly as active as they were even a month ago. Bees have a nicely defined comfort range. They don't fly when the temperature gets below fifty-five and they don't like temperatures above a hundred."

"It's surprising that you keep them so far north, then," I noted.

"These are Russian bees. They do very well in this area of Wisconsin because we're at about the same global parallel as they originate from in Russia. As long as I provide them with a food source in the winter, they're quite happy here." He described a flat piece of hardened sugar that the bees would feed off of until they could harvest nectar again in the spring. "Would my bees fly clear over to the commons this time of year? Not likely."

"That would mean that someone put them in her room."

His expression turned serious. "Are you wondering if someone stole some of my bees and used them as a weapon for murder?"

"That is what I'm thinking, yes."

He sighed, an unhappy sound. "I noticed yesterday morning that someone had been poking around one of the hives. I'm very particular with how I set them up. Bees don't like their world getting messed with, so I always put them back very precisely." He pointed to the farthest end of the field. "See how the hives start going around the bend out there?"

I squinted to the end where one hive was camouflaged slightly by foliage. "I see it."

"There are plenty more hives around the corner. If you go down there, you'll see that the hive just around the bend, the one next to the one you can see, had been moved. It was fine when I checked it at the end of the day, but I found it off its mark yesterday morning." Beckett rubbed his chin while he pondered the situation. "It was dusk when I went in for the night around six thirty, so the vandal struck after dark. They went down around the corner where I couldn't see them and did whatever they did. At first, I figured an animal was messing around with it, but then it seemed strange that just that one hive got messed with. After what you just said, it makes more sense that the intruder was human."

"You think they knew what they were doing?"

"Yep. I think someone shook that one to get the bees to come out and defend the colony ..."

"And then they captured a few."

If that was the case, if someone came up here with the specific plan to collect bees to put in Wakefield's room, that pushed this into the premeditated murder category.

"Could there be an explanation other than someone purposely putting them in the room?" I asked. "A way that the bees got in there on their own, I mean?"

"Bees are attracted to scents or colors," Beckett explained. "If there's something colorful hanging in a window, that might attract them over and then they could get in through a hole in a window screen or some other small opening. Obviously, the scent of nectar will summon them." He paused, sucking on a tooth as he thought. "There is one other thing. When a bee stings, it releases a pheromone. It's like a warning sign of danger to the others and they swarm to protect the colony. So, if one bee had gotten into the room and stung her, others nearby might've answered the call."

"Really?" I shook my head in admiration. "They are ingenious."

"The pheromone is called isoamyl acetate. Interestingly, it's the same chemical that gives bananas their distinctive smell."

I felt the blood drain from my face. "Bananas?"

"Yeah. Why?"

"We found over a dozen banana peels in Ms. Wakefield's room."

"Oh my. Was the heat turned up as well?"

I thought back and shook my head. "I don't recall that. Why do you ask?"

"Remember their fifty-five to one hundred comfort zone? The warmer the bee, the more active the bee. A warm room that smelled of bananas could make for some angry bees." He stared down toward the disturbed hive and then over at me. "Sounds like you've got a bigger problem than death by bee sting on your hands, Sheriff."

We started back for his cottage, walking in silence. After twenty or so yards, something with one of the hives caught his attention and Beckett swore softly. "Gonna have to take care of that."

"Take care of what?"

"Robber bees."

"Bees steal?"

"Follow me, I'll show you." We stopped at the closest hive where he pointed to an opening where a few bees were flying in and out. "See how they're just coming and going without really paying any attention to the other bees around them?"

"I see. Minding their own business."

"They are. Now come take a look over at this one." He indicated the opening of the offending hive. "What do you notice with these guys?"

Where the other bees at the first hive were flying around without even noticing each other, the bees at this opening appeared to be wrestling and fighting. "It's like some of the bees are trying to keep the others from going in."

"That's exactly what they're doing. The bees from another colony are trying to steal honey from this one. The flowers are nearly out of nectar this time of year, so bees will steal honey from another hive to keep their queen and hive alive."

A shudder ran through my body. "What happens if the queen dies?"

"Well, first I'll let the hive try to re-queen on its own, but that doesn't always work."

"They re-queen? What does that mean?"

"It means that they create their own leader. They raise one of the newly hatched bees as their queen. That won't be likely this time of year. Baby bees won't be born for a while. In this case, I'll need to buy a new queen and introduce her to the colony. Or, I simply let the bees move to a new hive on their own. As long as they don't try and steal the honey, an existing hive should let them in. To try and save this hive, I'll need to narrow the entrance to keep the robbers out. They'll tear off the wax caps and take all the honey otherwise."

"Then what would happen?"

"Well, the colony would die, of course." Beckett studied me for a minute. "Is that upsetting to you, Sheriff?"

I shook off the thoughts suddenly racing through my head. "No, I'm just amazed at the never-ending stream of ways to inflict death."

"I hear you. Humans are the worst species, though. Those in the animal kingdom act on instinct. The robber bees are simply trying to protect hearth and home. I'll have to get the sugar blocks installed sooner than I planned. They need food."

"This has been really helpful, Beckett. Not only was the lesson on bees and beekeeping interesting, you may have just helped crack this case open."

"Happy to be of service. Like I said, I'm always willing to talk about bees. Come on, I'll get you a little jar of honey to take home."

While Beckett was getting honey for me, I got Meeka from his front porch. By the time Beckett returned, I had another question. "I assume you supply honey to villagers?"

"I sure do. The gals over at Treat Me Sweetly buy quite a bit from me. I also sell to Maeve over at Grapes, Grains, and Grub, and Laurel buys for The Inn. I sell the beeswax to Shoppe Mystique. Briar makes candles, and Morgan uses it in her cosmetics." He held out a little jar to me but didn't let go of it. "You don't think one of them had anything to do with this."

"It would be irresponsible of me to not at least consider them. But no, I don't believe any of them are who I'm looking for."

He swiped his hand across his brow as though relieved. "That's good news. I sure wouldn't want to think one of our own was capable of murder. Stop back any time, Sheriff."

I thanked him and then Meeka and I headed back down the path toward the circus. We'd only gone a few yards when Reed contacted me over the walkie-talkie.

"I'm here. What do you need?"

"Lupe is at the station," Reed said. "She has information for you. How long until you're back? Over."

"Already on my way. I should be there in fifteen or twenty minutes. Over and out."

Igor wasn't waiting for us in the clearing anymore. That didn't surprise me, I'd been with Beckett for longer than I'd anticipated. The walk back to the circus wouldn't take long, but it would be long enough for me to mull over the thoughts racing around in my brain. Not just the information related to the investigation, but also the concepts of bees from one colony tearing apart another colony. And the fact that a hive could choose and raise their own queen fascinated me.

Gran had clearly been the queen of Whispering Pines while she was alive. The hive made up of the villagers had started to struggle as more and more negative things happened within the village. Guess that would be like robber bees invading. And then their queen died. Well, as far as I was concerned, their queen was murdered. Were the villagers now raising her replacement? I'd need to pay closer attention to this. Who were they grooming to be the new queen?

Chapter 27

WHEN WE GOT BACK TO the Cherokee, Igor was hanging out near the stable.

"Sorry I leave you," he said. "Must prepare for tourist transport."

"Don't worry about it. I enjoyed the walk." I really did. Not only did I mull the queen/hive quandary in my brain, I was alone in nature, except for Meeka, which was always peaceful. "I have a question for you. Did you see anyone go up to Beckett's farm a few nights ago?"

He thought about this as he checked a horse's hoof. "Few nights ago, horses very upset. Make much noise."

"Someone did go up there then."

"Is possible. Only thing that bother horses is people or predator."

"When was this?"

"Night of full moon. Very bright outside."

As we drove back to the station, it seemed impossible, but there were more reporters. To save time, I once again kept Meeka out of her cage.

"Be ready, girl. We'll have to race inside again."

She gave a sneeze of understanding, and as I pulled into

my parking spot, she jumped into the passenger's seat next to me. I only had to knock on the back door once, and Reed was there to let me in.

"Still crazy out there?" he asked.

"Good thing you were here and ready. Those reporters are like the creepy thing hiding in the mist, ready to pull me to my death."

"You're safe," he assured. "They haven't gotten answers from you yet. They might capture and torture you for it, though."

"Comforting." I found Lupe at his desk. "I hear you've got information for me. Come into my office and tell me all about it."

Lupe started talking before she was fully seated. "It turns out, the details for Wakefield's big contract first started being hashed out a long time ago."

"Right, I vaguely remember seeing ads about this time last year, and then the line of kitchenware hit stores in time for Christmas."

"That's when everything was made public. They were working on the details nearly a year before that. Gin and her crew spent months deciding what they wanted to include in their line. They went back and forth with the manufacturing company over which items to include. The Wakefield crew was given prototypes to test, and after lots of tweaking, retesting, and rejecting, they finally came up with the Wakefield line."

"Why would Misty want me to check into that?" I pulled a box of fruit and nut bars out of my desk drawer and offered one to Lupe. "That all sounds like standard business practices."

"That much is standard," Lupe agreed. "It's what happened afterward that I think caused the problems."

As I sat back and munched on my bar, Lupe explained

further.

"After researching online first, I made some phone calls and found out that Gin and Kim Robbins were joined at the hip on the details of this contract. The woman I spoke with said that Kim went over every word of the contract numerous times with their legal department. If something sounded even remotely off, he asked for a rewording for clarification."

"Again, sounds standard."

"One of the items that took the most time was a split on profits between Gin and her employees."

I sat up and took notice at that. "Profits? Between all of them?"

"Nope." She made me wait while she ate a bite of her bar. "Only between herself and Kim and the employees that are here this week. Not Misty."

"You're saying that the profits on this multimillion dollar kitchenware contract were to be divided between Gin, Kim, Leif, and Latoya."

"And Sonja Hall. The division wasn't equal, though. With every deal she has ever made, Gin always received a minimum of fifty-one percent. She insisted that no person or company would ever make more off her name than she did. The remaining forty-nine percent were split five ways."

"We only have four employees. Where did the other fifth go?"

"Back into the company. The employees weren't getting anywhere near as much as Gin, but almost half a million dollars apiece isn't bad."

"Kim Robbins has been with her every step of the way and only got what the others did?"

Lupe smiled. "That's where things got interesting. The terms that I told you, the fifty-one, forty-nine split, was the first draft. After lots of negotiation, the draft that was supposed to be signed would give Gin fifty-one percent, Kim twenty-five, and the rest equally split between the others."

"Supposed to be," I repeated.

"Right."

"But that's not what Wakefield signed, I take it."

The look of satisfaction on Lupe's face told me she thrived on this kind of investigative reporting. "My source told me that when the day finally came to sign the contract, Kim wasn't at the meeting. He had an emergency come up, so Gin went alone. She crossed out the line that gave her employees their shares."

I stared at her, not quite believing what I was hearing. "Are you saying that she kept all profits for herself?"

"No, she kept sixty percent for herself and split the remaining forty percent between a medical charity and her mother."

Her mother? Not what I expected to hear. "Both Laurel and Sugar told me that Gin's mom suffered from a neurological condition."

"So she stiffed her employees to help her mother?" Lupe's temper flared. "Gin Wakefield was worth millions. She could have easily taken care of her mother and still done the right thing for the others."

I went up to my whiteboard and circled the names Kim, Latoya, and Leif. I paused when I got to Sonja and tapped my marker on the board near her name.

"What are you thinking about?" Lupe asked, a little calmer now.

"Hot-pink running shoes."

"Um, why?"

"There's been a woman wandering around the fest dressed in all black except for hot-pink shoes."

"I remember her." Lupe leaned forward in her chair. "I tried to stop her to ask a few questions, but she kept walking. I wrote her off as being an eccentric. Is she important?"

"She might be, if she's Sonja Hall." I drew a line under her name. "Supposedly, Sonja got sick with a stomach bug on the way up here from Chicago. She's been in her room the entire time, but I saw her this morning going for a walk."

"And she was wearing pink shoes?"

I closed my eyes and tried to recall both this morning and the night I went to check on her. "I can't swear to it, but I think she might have been. Meeka became upset the other night when the curtains of Sonja's room were blowing outside the window. I went up and asked her about it, and she said she took off the screen so she could stick her head out to get fresh air."

"I can hear the 'but' in your voice."

"But there's a fire escape outside her window. What if she hasn't really been sick—"

"You think that she might have been sneaking around and did something to Ms. Wakefield?"

It would really help if I could tell Lupe about the bees. I needed to hold on to the method just a little longer. I still had too many unanswered questions to let that out yet.

"That's what I'm wondering." As I added *Really sick?* next to Sonja's name, my need to get back to Pine Time and interview Sonja grew stronger. "Great work, Lupe. This is good stuff."

Reed walked into the office. "She told you about the contract?"

"She did. We've got when, how, and why. Just need to figure out who."

"What did you find out from Beckett?" Reed asked.

Lupe, still in investigation mode, asked, "Beckett the beekeeper? His name came up quite often this week. People have been raving about his honey." Lupe stopped talking and narrowed her eyes at us. "Wait a minute. Gin Wakefield is allergic to honey. Is that why you went up to talk with

Beckett? Did someone slip her some?"

"Your girlfriend is really sharp," I told Reed.

"She is. That's why she's such a good reporter. She's so close; you have to tell her."

"Fine." I went to the board and next to *Method of Death* below Gin's name wrote *Bee Stings*. "The official cause of death is anaphylactic shock."

Lupe put a hand to her mouth, and Reed repeated, "What did Beckett tell you?"

I gave a quick recap as I checked my cargo pockets to be sure I had everything I needed. I added a couple fresh pairs of gloves and told them, "I need to get back over to The Inn."

Reed and Lupe followed me into the main room.

"Why are you going back there?" Reed asked.

"Someone put bees in Wakefield's room. If anyone knows who, it'll be Emery."

Reed went to a window and peeked through the blinds. "How are you going to do that with all those reporters? I think the crowd grew."

"Unless there are tunnels beneath the village that I don't know about, I'm just going to have to make a beeline." I paused and waited for a response. "Get it? Beeline?"

Lupe groaned, and Reed rolled his eyes.

"Since you pretty much know it's one of the Wakefield's," Sugar called out from her cell, "can I go home now?"

Reed and I gave each other simultaneous looks of *oh crap*.

"I completely forgot she was in there," Reed said.

"Me too." I walked over to the cell. "Not yet."

"What?" Sugar demanded. "Why not?"

"For starters, now you know too much. Secondly, I haven't ruled you out yet. Maybe I'll find out you put the bees in the room."

Sugar flopped onto her cot and grumbled about unjust imprisonment.

"Anything you need from me?" Reed asked. "Other than keeping our prisoner from trying to bust free?"

"Keep an eye on our K-9. I'm going to leave her here. She can't deal with all those people." Loud enough for Sugar to hear, I said, "I think we're about to get an answer soon."

"Thank the Goddess!" Sugar replied.

I gave Meeka some water and an ear scratch then left the building. I repeated "no comment" every few seconds as the reporters surrounded and followed me down the Fairy Path. When a few of them followed me into The Inn's lobby, I went straight to Emery behind the desk.

"Come into the boardroom with me, please. I need to talk with you."

He pointed at himself and took on the wide-eyed look of a little boy about to get chewed out by his principal.

"You're not in trouble," I promised, and he wilted with relief.

"Okay. Someone needs to watch the desk. Let me get Wesley."

"Wesley knows how to run the front desk?"

"No, but he's big enough that no one will mess with him."

"Good plan." I waited only two minutes before Emery appeared, smiling.

"Wesley's standing in front of the door in a Superman pose. No one's getting past him." Emery took a seat. "What's up, Sheriff?"

"I need you to help me with Ms. Wakefield's death. Take a minute and try to recall the details of that night."

Before I'd finished speaking, Emery had his eyes closed, legs pulled up into full lotus, and his hands in his lap with his thumbs and index fingers pressed together. A minute later, he opened his eyes. "Okay, I'm ready. What do you want to know?"

"Did anyone try to get into Ms. Wakefield's room that

night before she died?"

"Oh, sure." He seemed happy to be able to provide this information, and then his smile faded. "I probably should've mentioned that before."

My frustration level ticked up a notch. "Probably. It's okay, though. This is why I always tell people that I might return with more questions. Who wanted to get into her room?"

"The guy and the girl."

This time he didn't supply any more. "I'm going to need more detail than that, Emery. Which guy and which girl?"

"Her employees. The younger guy with the ponytail and the girl with the spiky black hair. The big guy was out by the Pentacle Garden with Ms. Wakefield. They were going over their contest plans or something."

"This is good." This was really good. "Latoya and Leif went up to her room. What time was this?"

"Around eight maybe. It was after the fest closed down."

"Okay, tell me exactly what you remember them saying."

"The girl ... Latoya, is that her name?" I nodded. "Latoya told me that they were going up to use Ms. Wakefield's bathroom."

"And you let them up there?"

"Didn't have to let them. They had her key."

That had to be when they put the bees in there. The timing was right.

"Did they have anything with them?"

Emery closed his eyes again. "Latoya had a cloth bag. One of those just big enough for a few books." He peeked an eye open at me. "Did I do something wrong?"

"They may have done something when they went up, but they had a key. There was no reason for you to stop them. How long were they upstairs?"

He shrugged. "Not long. Five minutes, maybe."

My mind went through the timeline. Thirty seconds to get to her room. That left four and a half minutes to plant bees and banana peels and get back down here. Plenty of time.

"Oh, geez," Emery moaned. "They did it, didn't they? They did something to Ms. Wakefield."

"What makes you think that?"

"She was here in the lobby with her employees from about nine o'clock until ten and then she and Laurel sat here talking until almost eleven. Then Ms. Wakefield went up to her room, and Laurel went to her apartment. If I ever step away from the desk, it's for no more than three minutes. That's the longest it takes me to pee, I timed it." He laughed, embarrassed. "You didn't need to know that. Anyway, I probably should've gone while Laurel was sitting here to watch the desk, but it was kind of fun listening to their conversation. They talked about growing up in the village, and Laurel told Ms. Wakefield how jealous she was of her abilities as a kitchen witch. Maybe ten minutes after they left, I ran to do my thing and heard the stairs creaking, you know the way they do. When I got back here, the front door was open."

"Why is that pertinent to this?" I asked, confused.

"If you've heard people on those stairs as often as I have, you can tell if someone's going up or coming down by the creaks and pops. Whoever it was that night, they were coming down. When I do the night shift, I keep track of who comes and goes. I have a little sheet and I jot down when each guest goes upstairs for the night. If they come back down I note it and then re-note when they go up again. It's a dumb thing, but if there was ever a fire or whatever and we needed to evacuate, we'd know for sure who's in the building and who wasn't."

If Laurel didn't promote him to assistant manager soon, I'd start a petition. "That's actually a very wise practice,

Emery. What does this have to do with Ms. Wakefield?"

"Everyone else had been up in their rooms for at least an hour when Ms. Wakefield went upstairs. Because it had only been a few minutes since she had gone up, I assumed it was her coming back down for some reason. After an hour or so, folks don't usually come back down. Unless someone is just 'visiting,' if you know what I mean." He blushed and then became emotional. "I should have gone outside to see who it was."

"Why? Is that something you normally do?"

"No, but this time, whoever it was, they were having problems. They stumbled down the stairs like they were drunk or something."

"You don't know for sure that it was her."

"No, but it would've been a safe guess. And now, knowing that she had probably been out on the Fairy Path for a long time, I'm sure it was her."

"You're probably right, but if it eases your mind, I don't think there's anything you could've done for her even if you had gone out immediately."

After swearing him to secrecy, I told him about the autopsy results.

"Oh, man. You think Leif and Latoya put bees in the room when they went up there?"

"That's my guess. Unless you had an EpiPen in hand, I don't think you would've been able to save Ms. Wakefield."

Ignoring the journalists' plea for answers, I rushed back to the station. Once at the building's front door, I told them, "I believe I will have answers for you soon. I need you all to give me space to finish this investigation, though. By circling around me and bombarding me with questions I don't have answers for, you're not helping. In fact, you could be delaying justice and potentially allowing suspects to go free."

"Sounds like you're looking for a killer."

"Are you saying Gin Wakefield was murdered? Can you at least confirm that for us?"

I blew out a sigh of frustration and went into the station. I stood with my back against the door trying to figure out how I was going to bring the Wakefield crew in with all those reporters around. There was no way I could get them into the station without their pictures hitting social media seconds later. Cell phones may not work in Whispering Pines, but most of the news vans had satellite connections.

We could cover their heads and make them unidentifiable. All that fuss would compromise the element of surprise that always helped with questioning a suspect, though.

"What's going on?" Reed appeared at my side.

The answer came to me then. I didn't know if it would work, but it was the best option I could think of. "Lupe, I need you to stay with Sugar. Reed, follow me in the van."

"Okay." His face brightened, anxious to do something active to help. "Where are we going?"

"To the bed-and-breakfast. Bring extra zip strip cuffs."

Chapter 28

I INSTRUCTED REED TO PARK the van lengthwise at the start of the driveway near the campground. If the reporters wanted to get on my property, they'd have to hoof it more than a quarter mile. Far from a perfect barrier, but at least they wouldn't be able to get their vans up close.

As I pulled up to my spot next to Tripp's truck, I saw Misty and Sonja sitting on the front porch, deep in conversation. When I opened my door, Meeka burst free and ran over to stand in front of the two as though trying to keep them from getting away. She had good instincts, my K-9. Unfortunately, she was so small, her only weapon would be to trip them if they decided to bolt.

Tripp waved to me from the office window as I went up to the porch. I waved back and held up a finger, indicating I'd be there in a moment.

"Just the two I wanted to speak with," I told them as Misty shrunk into her chair and Sonja went pale. "I need to take care of one thing inside and will be right back. Please, stay right here." I slipped in the front door and hurried over to the office. "I need your help."

"With what?" Tripp got to his feet, ready to assist.

"Kim, Leif, and Latoya are here, right?"

"Far as I know."

"Good. Make sure they don't leave the house."

He was about to ask why, but then understood. "I'll hang out in the hallway. I can see the front and back doors from there."

"Perfect. Thanks."

When I got back outside, Reed was crossing the yard toward us. I motioned for him to stop about thirty feet away.

"Sonja, would you stand over by Deputy Reed, please?"

Without hesitation, she went over to him, hands shoved in her jacket pockets, eyes focused on the ground.

I took the chair Sonja had just vacated, turned on my recorder, and asked, "You know more than you told me last night, don't you?"

Misty hesitated, her hands clasping, unclasping, and then rubbing up and down her thighs. "I didn't know for sure what they were going to do. It really was hard to hear what they were saying in the van that day, and I didn't want to accuse anyone of something they didn't do. I knew they were talking about Gin and that whatever they were planning, it wasn't anything good. They mentioned 'the contract' a few times. I figured it was the kitchenware contract and thought they were planning some sort of financial attack on Gin. Whenever she stepped out of the kitchen or away from the planning meetings these last couple days, they would gather in a huddle and talk quietly so I couldn't hear them. Or someone would make a comment about how things needed to happen like they'd planned. It was like code talk, so I had no idea they were planning to kill her." Tears filled her eyes then, and she put her hands to her face. "I swear I didn't know. I feel absolutely sick about this." She pulled her hands away, her expression desperate. "I keep thinking I should have said something to you."

"I believe that you didn't know Ms. Wakefield's life was in danger and believe you would have said something if you did. Should you have told me what you knew? There wouldn't be much I could have done with the information. On the other hand, it would have moved things along more quickly over the last day or two. Is there anything else you haven't told me that I should know?"

She wiped the tears from beneath her eyes and exhaled a shaky breath. "I don't think Sonja did anything. I doubt she was really sick these last few days. At least not physically. Guilt might have been doing some nasty things to her, but I truly don't believe she was involved." She paused and blurted, "I don't mean to make this about me, but did you mean it when you said it wouldn't have mattered if I would've told you what I heard?"

"I meant it. All I could have done at that point was note your statement as a possible problem to be aware of."

"Okay." Her head bobbed up and down as she tried to come to grips with her role. "Okay. Will I be charged with anything?"

"That's not up to me to decide. Go on over by Deputy Reed now and tell Sonja to come back."

When I'd seen Sonja this morning, she was a little pale, but now I saw deep, dark circles around her eyes. Had they been there this morning? Probably. I was in a hurry to corral the journalists, so I might have missed it. I agreed with Misty; Sonja hadn't been sick. She could be suffering from a severe attack of guilty conscience, though.

I hit start on the voice recorder and set it on the arm of my Adirondack chair. "Please state your name and position with the Wakefield Corporation for the recording and then tell me what's been going on since you left Chicago."

"My name," Sonja began and had to clear her throat. "My name is Sonja Hall, and I'm the cake designer for the

Wakefield Corporation. About a week before coming here to Whispering Pines, the others in the group started plotting revenge on Gin Wakefield."

Her words came easily; she was eager to purge her guilt.

"The 'others' being who exactly?" I asked.

She swallowed and kept her gaze fixed on the patio floor in front of her. "Kim Robbins, Latoya Craig, and Leif Forsberg."

"Were you in on this revenge plot, or did one of them tell you about it?"

"I was with them during the initial discussions."

"Then you were in on this plan."

"I knew what they were planning, yes, ma'am. I didn't actually take part in anything, though."

I made a note in my notebook about her refusal to look at me. "What sort of revenge had they planned? For what reason?"

"The company CFO, Kim Robbins, found out that Chef Wakefield had changed the terms in a contract that affected the rest of us badly. As the head chefs of the corporation, we were supposed to get a percentage of this deal, but Gin changed those terms at the last minute."

"Do you know how she changed the contract? Meaning, what the payout structure was changed from and to?"

Sonja finally looked at me, her expression a mixture of sorrow and anger. "I do. We were each supposed to get close to half a million dollars, and she changed it so none of us were to get any sort of payout. Not a cent. I don't know what the final contract actually stated, other than that we were to get nothing."

"Was the plan, then, to murder Ms. Wakefield?"

"Not right away. When Kim found out, he invited us all over to his place after work one night and told us what she had done. Everyone was immediately and justifiably angry.

Latoya was ready to charge over to Gin's condo to confront her and demand she honor the original terms. Bakers don't make a lot of money. The four of us earn a living, but we don't live extravagantly. Kim does all right, but that's because he's a partner in this business. Latoya is starting to earn a little off her YouTube videos with product endorsements. I guess in order to publish her cookbook, she has to quit or she'll get nailed for violating that non-compete agreement we all had to sign with Wakefield's.

"Not even Kim was going to get this payout after the terms were changed?"

"Nope. He was furious."

Understandably. He uprooted his life for her. What a betrayal.

"What happened by the end of that night when you all were over at his house?"

She slid the zipper pull of her jacket up and down. "It started out as a simple plan to confront her. Many bottles of booze ended up on the table in front of us, and we were all drinking. There was talk of exposing her to her adoring public. That wouldn't get us our money, though. Kim tossed around the idea of embezzling. None of us were comfortable with that."

"But you all were comfortable with murder?"

She scowled at me. "I don't remember if it was Kim or Latoya who first said that. It was a joke, one of those sick things you say when you mix too much alcohol with a lot of anger. Well, Leif and I were angry, but nowhere near as much as Latoya and Kim were. Toy turned down an amazing package from that casino in Vegas. Immediately, her work would have been on display in front of tens of thousands of people every day. She would have made a name for herself within months. Gin convinced her to work for Wakefield's, though."

"In Latoya's mind," I guessed, "this payout was compensation for not accepting the Las Vegas deal?"

"Right. And it would've been more than enough to start her off on her own. She was ready to leave, just holding out for that paycheck." Sonja sat straight in her chair, pushed her chest forward and her shoulders back, then inhaled like she couldn't get a deep enough breath. "I'm not a bad person, Sheriff. When I figured out where the conversation was heading that night at Kim's, I left."

"Did you tell them you didn't want to be involved with this."

"Not in so many words. I didn't join in anymore of their discussions, though. I even tried to get out of coming here this weekend, but Gin wouldn't hear of it. She said nothing was more important than celebrating our success. I think she felt guilty about what she'd done." Sonja laughed at the thought. "Like a week away from the bakery would compensate for taking all that money from us."

A thought occurred to me then. "Wait, let's back up for a minute. This kitchenware line came out almost nine months ago, and Kim learned the truth only a few weeks ago. Why the delay?"

Sonja shrugged. "I don't understand it all exactly. There was an initial payout to Gin, but the rest of us wouldn't see any money until a certain sales threshold was met, and then it would only be quarterly payments. I don't recall the terms Kim had negotiated for us."

"At what point did you decide to pretend you were sick?"

"On the way up here. We stopped for lunch at some little diner, and I overheard one of the customers there complaining about not feeling well and that she was worried it might have been something she ate. I saw that as my out. The others didn't let me off that easily. Gin believed me, but Latoya was at my door two or three times a day, demanding that I quit faking."

"She knew you weren't sick?"

"She knew. Honestly, I was getting a little worried about my own safety. If I didn't help them with their plan, I mean." She looked toward Misty. "Can I ask you something, Sheriff?"

"Go ahead."

"At what point did you figure out it was us?"

"It was a number of things," I told her. "An investigation of Ms. Wakefield's hotel room was standard procedure. We found dead honey bees there, and I remembered her reaction when Misty suggested using honey as a sweetener the other night. Then Latoya made an off-color joke about giving Gin just enough honey to put her in bed for a while."

Sonja nodded as though this made sense. "Latoya, being a specialty baker, knows a lot about honey. She even mentioned talking to her landlord about setting up a hive on the roof of her apartment building and harvesting her own. This was a fight she and Gin had all the time. Toy wanted to make products with honey, and Gin wouldn't allow it in the building."

Latoya knows about beekeeping. I jotted this down in my notebook as a question to raise with Latoya later. "Did she know about the beekeeper here in Whispering Pines?"

She shook her head. "No clue."

"Misty suggested that I dig into the details of that contract. You just confirmed what my assistant found out about that. And then there was you yourself, another piece in this rather large puzzle."

She blinked, surprised, and looked away. "Me? I just sat in my room for the last four days."

"Except you were working out in your room when I came up to check on you the other night, weren't you? Or had you just climbed up the fire escape?"

Maybe that's what had upset Meeka. Not the curtain but Sonja climbing the escape.

She flushed, from embarrassment this time instead of physical exertion. "I had plenty of books I could read on my e-reader and television shows to watch. I sketched out design ideas for cakes. I was getting bored after a day and a half, though. I'm also used to running around the bakery all day, not sitting still. So, yes, I climbed down the fire escape."

"And Mabon Fest was in full swing just a little way away. All that food and so many different chefs, it was too much for you to stay away from. Wasn't it?"

She averted her gaze again. "I'm not sure I know what you mean."

"There was a woman dressed all in black wandering the crowd who caught my attention a couple times. The disguise was good, except for one thing."

"What?" Sonja leaned forward as though taking notes for the next time she wanted to go incognito.

"If you're going to go all black, then go all black. If you can't do that, wear something that doesn't stand out as instantly recognizable." I pointed at her feet. "Not many people wear hot-pink running shoes."

"They're all I brought." There was a touch of righteousness in her voice as she asked, "Am I in trouble for this? I mean, I didn't actually do anything."

"In Misty's case, she only had a suspicion. In your case, you had actual knowledge that the people you worked with were planning to kill your employer."

"I didn't know about the bees."

"Sonja, you had direct knowledge of this. You could be charged with being a party to a crime." I Mirandized her as I attached zip cuffs to her wrists and motioned for Reed to come over. "The dining room is just inside the front door to the left. Please hold Ms. Hall in there until I've spoken with the others."

Chapter 29

LATOYA AND KIM WERE TALKING in the great room.

"Any idea where Leif is?" I asked Tripp who was still at his post in the hallway.

"Upstairs, I think. At least that's where he was going the last time I saw him."

"Great. Thanks for helping. Reed can take over now."

Tripp pressed a quick kiss to my temple and disappeared into the B&B office down the hall.

"Forsberg first?" Reed asked.

"He'll be the easiest to get to talk. Craig and Robbins will both be tough. Already having Forsberg's confession might help pry them loose."

Reed gave a little salute and positioned himself in the hallway where he could keep an eye on both the dining room and great room at the same time. I went upstairs to Leif's room, right next to Sonja's on the front side of the house.

He opened the door and froze when he saw me standing there. He looked awful, twitchy and agitated like a crack addict needing a hit. "Sheriff O'Shea."

"I need to speak with you, Mr. Forsberg. We can chat here in your room or in the sitting area near the top of the stairs."

He swallowed and pointed down the hallway. "Over there sounds good."

The sitting area wasn't large, only wide enough for a lounge chair and small table, and deep enough to hold a matching set of both as well as a two-foot-wide bookcase along the side.

With the voice recorder running, I stated, "Tell me about the night Gin Wakefield died."

"I already—"

"In particular, I'd like to know what you and Latoya Craig did in her room at approximately eight o'clock that evening."

Leif stammered a few incoherent words.

I pushed on. "During our investigation of her room, we found numerous dead honey bees and an unusual number of banana peels."

Leif slumped like he was going to fold in on himself.

"By your reaction, I'm guessing you know something about that. So, I'll ask again, what did you and Latoya Craig do in Gin's room at approximately eight o'clock that evening?"

He shook his head. "Nothing. I don't know what you're talking about. We were with Gin and Kim outside at one of the picnic tables near the sweet shop at that time. We were making plans for the next day's entry."

His voice rose slightly in pitch as he spoke. Subtle but distinct enough that I caught it.

"All right." I kept my own voice even. "What can you tell me about the kitchenware contract? I heard from a few people that Ms. Wakefield changed some of the conditions."

He crossed his legs at the ankles and his arms over his slim chest. "She did. Sonja, Toy, Kim, and I were supposed to get some of the profits. Then she changed it, and we got nothing."

"Some of the profits? I heard half a million dollars each."

Leif shrugged in response.

"And what about the night you all got together at Kim's house about a week ago and formulated a plan to kill her?"

"That wasn't how it started." He must've realized the implied admission of guilt in the statement; his left foot started shaking like a metronome set on triple time. "Kim asked us over to tell us what happened. We were just trying to come up with a way to convince her to change it back."

"The conversation turned dark, though, didn't it?"

He tugged at the collar of his T-shirt. "Kim was so angry his whole body was trembling. Latoya went from zero to a hundred in a blink and started ranting about revenge."

"When did it turn from an angry discussion to one plotting murder?"

Leif paused, sniffed, and finally admitted, "That same night. They started talking about how she deserved to die for this."

"*They* did. You and Sonja weren't involved?"

He agonized for a long moment. "Sonja left after a while. She said she didn't want anything to do with this. She almost didn't come on the trip here."

"And you?"

"I listened to all their ranting. I didn't contribute to the discussion, though."

Innocence via silence. Was that his defense? "At what point did you all decide to put the bees in her room? That was Latoya's idea, right? She has knowledge of beekeeping."

"How do you know—?" His brow furrowed with confusion. "Not until after the cake planning session here that second night."

He broke down then and put his hands to his face. I froze and barely breathed, doing nothing that would disrupt his confession.

"Misty made that comment about using honey," he finally continued, "and Latoya ran with it. She and Kim came to my room that night to talk about her plan. Honestly, I was horrified."

"But not horrified enough to stop them."

"I guess I didn't want to believe they'd go through with it. Toy started asking around about the local bee guy. Pretty soon she had directions to the beeyard."

"When did you go up and get the bees?"

He closed his eyes and exhaled a defeated sigh. "That night. Kim and Gin had dinner together; he told her they needed to discuss business. Toy and I went up after the fest shut down. It was a little tricky to find, but the full moon helped. We went to a hive way at the back, and Toy showed me where the bees went in and out. We put them in a jar with a smear of honey inside."

"The morning before Gin died, Latoya was collecting banana peels. You already had made the plan to collect bees at that point?"

He nodded, both legs bouncing now.

"Please respond verbally for the recording."

"Yes. We already had the plan." He stared at me as though waiting for the next question. When I didn't ask one, he continued on his own. "When we got back from the beeyard, we found Kim and Gin at the picnic table. Latoya made up an excuse about needing a bathroom. We were right outside The Inn, so she asked Gin if she could use hers." He shook his head in disbelief. "It was too easy. We went up to her room, and I put the banana peelings in her garbage cans while Latoya put the bees at the foot of her bed beneath the covers. As we left the room, Toy turned the temperature way up."

The fifty-five to one hundred comfort zone. Latoya knew heat and the chemical from the banana peels would aggravate the bees. Putting them beneath the sheets explained why there were so many stings over the lower half of Gin's body. Finally, I could see the scene.

I open my hotel door and am assaulted by the smell of bananas. Why? And why is it so ungodly hot in here? Incompetent housekeeper must've turned the temperature up instead of down.

I set the temperature to sixty-three where I like it and get ready for bed. I put on my trusty old Maldives T-shirt — the memories it sparks gives me the confidence boost I need in this village — then wash my face and brush my teeth. It will be a while before the room cools off enough that I'll be able to sleep. I'll watch TV for a while.

I grab the remote and shove my feet beneath the covers. A sharp pain in my foot jolts me a second later. And then another and another. I throw the covers back and jump out of bed. Oh, God. Bees! I've been stung. And again! How did they get into my bed?

My EpiPen. I need to inject now. I can already feel my tongue starting to swell. I grab my medical bag and ... where are my pens? I drop to the floor, swat at a bee buzzing near my head, and it stings my hand and another jabs my throat. I empty the bag's contents onto the floor. The pens have to be here. I never take them from my bag. I check the dresser even though I know they're not in there. Nothing. I have to get to the healing center. Goddess, help me get there in time.

Leif appeared catatonic and couldn't speak anymore. I told him I was arresting him for the murder of Gin Wakefield, read him his rights, and brought him down to join Sonja in the dining room.

"Now who?" Reed asked, handing me another pair of zip cuffs.

"Latoya, I think. Would you call Deputy Atkins and tell him we've got a gang for him to bring in?"

We weren't equipped at our station to process these kinds of crimes. The County Sheriff's Office had become like a satellite office for us. We called them so often, we had Atkins on speed dial at the station. I stopped in the B&B office and asked Tripp to look up the number for Reed. Then I went to get my next suspect.

Kim eyed me as I entered the great room and asked Latoya to come with me. I eyed him back and warned, "Don't go anywhere. You're next."

I took Latoya out on the patio and sat so I could see both her and Kim inside. He never took his eyes off us.

"I have almost identical statements from Sonja and Leif," I began once the recorder was running. "I understand that the collective anger over Gin denying you all your payouts turned ugly quickly."

Latoya seethed. I wasn't sure if it was over what Gin had done or that they'd been caught. Probably a combination of the two. She didn't respond, just leaned back and stared out at the lake with her tattooed arms draped over the back of the loveseat.

"The problem," I continued, "was that you left too much evidence behind. Twelve banana peels and ten bees?" I paused long enough that she glanced at me. "Emery at The Inn told me you asked to get into the room the next morning. Let me guess, the plan was to wait long enough that it would be safe to announce something must be wrong with Gin. You couldn't find her, you'd say, and ask to get into her room so you could check on her. Then you'd remove all the evidence, race back downstairs, and declare she was dead."

Latoya rolled her eyes and otherwise ignored me.

"Was that pretty much how it went? But she didn't die in the room like you figured she would. Geez, that had to put a wrinkle in your carefully planned murder plot."

At that point, I matched Latoya's silence. It took a while, nearly five minutes, until she finally spoke.

"You're good, Sheriff. There's not much I can add to that. I was with her once when she almost ate something made with honey. She got a forkful to her mouth and actually touched it to her lips before she smelled it. Just the contact made her swell up like a blowfish. The woman was so damn allergic, yes, I expected she'd drop dead in her room."

"The will to live can make people do incredible things. Did you know that adrenaline and epinephrine, the ingredient in her EpiPen, are the same thing? The amount of adrenaline rushing through her system must've given her the strength to make it as far down the Fairy Path as she did." Invoking the spirit of Columbo, one of the greatest fictional detectives ever, I said, "Speaking of the EpiPen, there's one thing I'm not clear on. How did you get them? She carried that bag with her everywhere."

At this, Latoya smiled, triumphant. "You helped with that, Sheriff. That night we were here, discussing cakes, and the two of you sat out on the dock." She jerked a thumb over her shoulder toward the great room. "She left her precious bag on the coffee table." Latoya chuckled at that. "She always had two pens in the bag along with a supply of Benadryl, hand sanitizer, hand wipes … other things too; I didn't look at it all. I slid out the pens while the two of you bonded over wine, red I assume, and Kim put them in his jacket pocket."

"Risky move. What if she noticed they were gone?"

She shrugged. "We'd deal with that if we needed to."

I asked about the contract change and the meeting at Kim's house. She repeated everything Sonja and Leif had said.

"If she would've just stayed in her room …" Her tone clearly indicated that Latoya blamed Gin for them getting caught. "The plan would've gone perfectly if we could've gone back up the next morning."

"You're underestimating me, Ms. Craig. It's been too chilly for bees to fly. People saw you go up to the room. I would've put it all together eventually."

She seemed to be sidetracked with working through the errors rather than listening to me. I waited for her to come to grips with the flaws in her genius and announced, "Latoya Craig—"

"You going to arrest me now?"

"Yes, I am, for the death of Gin Wakefield."

She stood and held her hands out for the cuffs. "I should've taken the Vegas job."

Inside, Kim watched as Reed took Latoya to the dining room and then turned to stare me down as I approached him. Since no one else was in the great room, I sat in a chair next to him and placed the recorder on the coffee table. Right in the approximate spot Gin's bag had lain that fateful night.

Meeka sat on the floor between us, licking her little chops as if to show off how sharp her tiny teeth were. Reed returned to the hallway between the great room and dining room to listen to the interview as I hit the start button on the recorder.

Chapter 30

THE LIGHT ON THE VOICE recorder had barely turned on, indicating it was in fact recording, when Kim started speaking.

"I didn't do anything." As though that was all I needed to hear to let him go.

"I have statements from three of your co-workers indicating that you did do something."

"What do they say I did?" he challenged, puffing out his wide chest.

I took my time flipping forward and back through my notebook. "All of them state that you invited them to your house to discuss the fact that Gin changed the payout details on the contract."

I paused there to see his reaction.

"And? It's a crime for me to have people over to my house?"

"They say that you initiated a discussion about getting revenge on Gin."

"Again, having a discussion isn't against the law. Last I knew, it isn't a crime to have a gathering. What kind of a country do we live in if either is illegal?"

The more boisterous he became, the guiltier he seemed.

He wanted to talk, so I sat back and let him.

"What Ginger did, changing the contract, was plain cruel. She and I had agonized for months over the details. She wouldn't budge on the fifty-one percent for herself, and I knew she never would so didn't fight that. She'd insisted on maintaining fifty-one percent of everything with her name on it from the start, which made good business sense. Something I, as her Chief Financial Officer, initially suggested."

He was doing the same thing Rosalyn always did. He was praising Gin for being a good businesswoman while taking credit for her business sense.

"How to divide that remaining forty-nine percent took forever to work out." He made an angry *tsk* sound. "Five equal shares."

"What had you wanted for yourself? Somehow, I have a hard time believing you'd be happy with an amount equal to the others."

"I've been with her from the beginning," he said instantly. "Since her business was nothing but a hopes-and-dreams discussion over Mai Tais on the beach." He clenched his jaw. "I gave up everything for her dream. Not that it hasn't worked out well for me. Initially, I wanted the fifty-one/forty-nine deal to apply to all monies that came from the sale of kitchenware. She flat out refused. We finally agreed on the five-way split applying only to the initial payment, which was worth multiple millions. Future royalties would be divided between herself at fifty-one percent, twenty-five to me since I brokered the deal, and the rest back into the business."

"I take it you weren't happy with that."

"I could accept the future royalties split, but I wanted twenty-five on the initial payout too. I might not be responsible for the end product, but I made sure she stayed profitable from day one and made sure her marketing was topnotch. I won't apologize for wanting what I'm worth."

"Are you aware that instead the money will be divided between her mother and various neurological research institutes?"

He gave a derisive snort. "I'm sure the press will play up how generous she was. If that was true, why hadn't she been donating all along?"

"Couldn't say. And now we'll never know, will we?"

He clenched his jaw and pursed his lips. In a more subdued voice, he replied, "I guess we won't."

"All of this must've made you quite angry."

He grunted and looked away. "Of course it did."

"Angry enough to initiate a murder plot against her."

"That wasn't me. Latoya is the one who brought up that option." Kim sat forward and removed his suit coat. Behind him, Reed put his hand to his Glock, ready to act if necessary. "I shot that down the moment she said it. Yes, I wanted Ginger to suffer a consequence for what she'd done to us, but I didn't want her dead."

"You wanted to ruin her financially?"

A smug expression came over his face. "I admit to considering that. I could have made it happen."

"But somehow, between the night of that initial conversation and your arrival here four days ago, financial ruin turned into murder."

"You can't prove anything."

Confidence oozed off the man like pus from a festering wound.

"I have statements," I repeated, "from three of your co-workers stating that you were in on the murder."

"But I didn't do anything. Leif and Latoya collected the bees and placed them in Ginger's room along with the banana peels."

"You kept Gin distracted while they collected those bees. You kept her busy and away from her room while they were up there. You were an active participant."

"You have no proof." He spoke each word slowly, placing special emphasis on *proof*. "It's all hearsay. My word against theirs."

"Actually, I have banana peels."

He frowned at me. "What is that supposed to mean?"

I cleared my throat. "Did you know that it's possible to lift fingerprints from a banana peel?" The smug look started to fade. "I understand you took the EpiPens from Latoya and put them in your pocket. We'll be able to get prints off them as well. It may not be a lot but combining your prints with their statements should be enough to, at minimum, sway a jury to charge you as an accessory."

Still sitting on the floor next to me, Meeka placed a paw on my leg. Her version of a high-five.

I said nothing while letting Kim stew in this information.

After a few minutes, he said, "Ginger hurt me deeply. I'd never been anything but loyal to her. During all those years of supporting her dream, it slowly became my dream as well. I was as proud of the product we put out as she was. Every step of the way, I analyzed the market and talked to customers to be sure we were giving them exactly what they wanted." A watered-down version of the smugness returned. "Producing the product is only part of running a business, you know. It doesn't matter how amazing your cookies and cakes are; if you can't get them to the right customer, it's not a business. I played a large role in the company's success."

He stopped speaking, and I remained mute, waiting for the statement I knew was coming.

"Yes, I knew about the plan to murder Ginger. It was only a thought, though, everything fell into place, so to speak, as soon as we got here. First that Sugar woman, then the beekeeper. It's almost like this place ripens ill intent." He gazed down at his large hands. Expecting to see Gin's blood there? "No, I didn't do anything to prevent it. Yes, I was involved."

I got stuck for a minute on his ill intent comment. Bad things had happened here that had changed the village's personality. It almost felt like all that nastiness had seeped into the very ground we lived on and was alive and growing. Like the village itself was now attracting and creating more negativity. But that was impossible.

Outside, a gust of wind blew in off the lake. I could see the trees blowing back and forth, around and around, but I couldn't hear their whispers. Were they agreeing or disagreeing with me? Or warning me?

Kim's barrel chest and huge arms made it impossible for one pair of zip strips to span the distance. It took one around each wrist and two zipped together between them to restrain him. Reed and I debated about bringing the group to the station and having Deputy Atkins pick them up there. Neither of us wanted to deal with the media in that capacity, though, so we waited for him at the B&B.

"I have to ask something," Reed said as we waited in the sitting room with a clear view of our detainees in the dining room. "That thing you said about fingerprints off a banana peel, is that true?"

"True statement," I confirmed. "It's possible to lift prints off other fruit with a smooth skin too."

"But we didn't test the peels for prints."

"Getting prints off any surface is never a guarantee, but we can and probably should recommend that Deputy Atkins have his lab try."

Reed stared, disapproving. "You bluffed."

"The 'bluff' can be one of the best tools at our disposal. And I never said we had his prints. I simply asked him if he was aware of the possibility."

His disapproving look turned into a grin. "I'll go wait by

the van for Atkins. I'll do what I can to keep the reporters away."

"Tell them I'll have a statement for them later in front of the station."

"Oh, that reminds me," he said halfway to the front door, "we need to let Sugar out of the cell."

Poor Sugar. What kind of lasting effect would this have on her? Not just psychologically but socially as well. Even when I made a public statement declaring her innocent of wrongdoing, there would be villagers who would always insist she was involved somehow. Maybe, if there was a silver lining on this dark cloud, it would help soften her oftentimes gruff attitude.

Fortunately, Atkins arrived quickly with a second squad car and deputy in tow. They loaded the four up as reporters swarmed to get pictures and ask questions.

"The reporters are insane out there," Atkins told me as he came back inside Pine Time before leaving. "We're going to hit the road with them before something bad happens. You'll send over copies of their statements and everything else you've got on this?"

"We will. The rest of the evidence is in our lockup. Deputy Reed will deliver it later today." I checked my watch. It was nearly six o'clock. "Or maybe tomorrow."

"Sounds good." Atkins shook his head. "Murder by bee sting. Guess they get points for creativity."

"Any word on Donovan?" I asked before he left.

"I told you, no news means no updates. They're still hunting, and I expanded the BOLO to neighboring jurisdictions as well. Don't worry. We're on it."

I had no other choice than to let my fellow officers take care of this.

Atkins put his hand on the doorknob and looked over his shoulder at me. "Nice place, by the way."

"Thanks. I told you before, you're welcome anytime."

I watched through the dining room windows as they pulled away. A few minutes later, the crowd of journalists thinned and then vanished except for a few stubborn ones. Probably hoping to get a statement from me here before the formal one I'd give over at the station.

"Meet you in the village for dinner?" Tripp asked.

"If you think we can find someplace quiet."

"Maybe if you're out of uniform you won't be so recognizable. The villagers will respect your space. At least until the tourists leave."

I blinked up at him with faux innocence. "Wouldn't me being out of uniform make me stand out even more?"

It took him a second and then he pulled me in close and nuzzled my ear. "I didn't mean naked. But if that's what you want—"

I laughed, kissed him, and whistled for Meeka. "Don't distract me. I have to make a statement to the press."

Chapter 31

OUTSIDE THE STATION, REPORTERS, TOURISTS, and villagers alike gathered to hear my official statement on Ginger "Gin" Wakefield's death. I stood there for an hour answering all their questions without going too deeply into the details. Those things would come out after Kim, Leif, and Latoya had been formally charged. When they started repeating questions, I decided Q&A time with me was done.

"How did it go?" Reed asked when I stepped inside.

"As well as could be expected. Hopefully they'll move along now. Nothing more to see, nothing more to learn." I glanced at the jail cell where Sugar had been for the last couple days. She wasn't there but her belongings were. "Sugar didn't take her stuff?"

"She's in your office." Reed spoke with a hushed voice, "She's suddenly not doing so well."

I made two cups of tea, brought them into my office, and handed one to Sugar. Instead of going around and sitting in my desk chair, I took the seat next to her.

"Thanks." Sugar wrapped her hands around the cup to warm them and took a little sip. Staring vacantly at the cup, she said, "I never wanted this to happen."

"I know. I also know you didn't do anything. We'll make a point of spreading word of your innocence around the village."

She turned to me, a look of hurt in her eyes so deep it almost pained me. "You thought I did, though, didn't you? You thought I killed Gin."

This woman and I had a strange relationship. It's not that we disliked each other, but there was a barrier of some kind between us that kept us from really connecting.

"When the council voted me in as sheriff, you said you voted against me because you didn't want me getting involved with the 'muck' around here. Then not too long ago, you told me you thought my purpose here was to deal with the dark cloud that seems to have settled over Whispering Pines. Remember that?"

She replied with a single nod.

"I never know if you're on my side or not, Sugar. So I understand how you must be feeling." I sipped my tea before continuing. "No, I didn't believe you killed Gin, but things were stacking up against you. My job requires that I follow the evidence, not my heart. That's what I was doing. Following the evidence."

Sugar blinked repeatedly as she lifted the cup to her lips and then wiped away a tear trailing down her cheek. "I didn't hate Gin. Things got so out of control." Another tear fell. "She was my best friend. I've been missing her for twenty years, and now we'll never be able to fix what happened."

Her shoulders started to shake as her tears turned into sobs. I took her cup and set it on the desk with mine. Then I wrapped my arms around her and let her cry it out. When she pulled away minutes later, her eyes were puffy and red.

"Will you be okay?" I handed her some tissues.

She blew her nose, shrugged her shoulders, and shook her head all at the same time. "I don't know."

"Why don't I give you a ride home? Talk to Honey. Get

some sleep. Maybe things will be a little better in the morning. If not, go over and talk to someone at Unity. They'll help you get through this."

"Okay." She sat, fighting off another round of tears, and finally said, "I'd like that ride. I'm not ready to deal with anyone I might cross on the way home."

~~~

The last two days of the fest concluded with no further drama. Except for the fact that an unexpected wave of new tourists arrived wanting to see where Gin had died. They were quiet and respectful, though. They gathered next to the drum circle and talked about their favorite Wakefield Sweets and Treats snacks and products. A makeshift memorial appeared on the Fairy Path; I suspected that Ruby had started it by marking the spot with the crocheted chef's hat at the center of the ever-growing display. Villagers who had lived here when Gin had mourned her passing silently. Laurel was quietly planning a village memorial service for her which we'd hold once the tourists were gone.

Until then, there were Mabon-related tasks to perform. Morgan and Briar invited Tripp and me over to help them harvest their huge garden. Tripp's job was to collect seeds from nearly dead flowers. Mine was to cut down the still living plants and tie them into bundles so Morgan could hang some to dry in Shoppe Mystique and some in the amazing conservatory here at their cottage.

"This is kind of meditative," Tripp said as he dropped seeds into an envelope.

"Don't say that too loudly," I cautioned. "Briar will hire you."

"How's the binding coming?" he asked. "Are you doing it mindfully?"

"Of course. I don't want to be responsible for a charm bag going off the rails."

Morgan instructed me to think positively while I performed my task, thereby infusing my own good will into another person's life through the spell she would cast for them using these plants. I had to admit, I liked that.

"Are you at a stopping point?" Morgan asked, appearing on the pea-gravel path that wound through the garden.

"We could be." I finished wrapping twine around the base of a flower bundle. As I snipped the twine, I thought *do good work* as I had every time.

"I'm just finishing here," Tripp said. "What's up?"

"Dinner's ready," Morgan announced as she removed her pocketed gardening apron from her waist. The apron was so full of tools, she rattled when she walked. "Mama made pulled pork."

My mouth started watering. "Tell me she got the jester's recipe."

"The very one." Morgan smiled. "She had to turn on her charm to get it and then had to promise to never share it with anyone."

I gasped. "Briar flirted with a carny? Your mother is such a trollop."

I was joking, but Morgan winked and said, "You have no idea."

"Don't think I want to know what that means," I told Tripp as we headed for the vine-covered patio at the back of their cottage.

Not only had Briar made pulled pork but also baked beans, green beans, macaroni-and-cheese, homemade pickles, and cornbread.

Tripp stared at the spread like a starving man then turned to Briar. "Will you adopt me?"

Briar and Morgan laughed, but if they knew how painful

the topic of family could be for Tripp, they'd realize just how sweet a sentiment that was. In his mind, growing up with his aunt and uncle meant he never had a "real" home. That was the one thing he wanted most, a home full of family.

"And apple cake for dessert," Briar teased.

"Forget adoption," Tripp said after swallowing his first bite of pork, "marry me, Briar."

"Jayne has dibs on that." Briar winked at me and giggled when I blushed.

"So, how about Reeva winning the baking competition?" I blurted, changing the topic. With the Wakefield crew gone, and Sugar sequestered in her home—Honey swore she was okay, just needed time to herself—Reeva had won handily.

"I say it was well deserved." Briar raised her glass of iced Mabon tea in a toast. "I don't care what others have said about Gin Wakefield, Reeva was always the most skilled kitchen witch in the village. I don't know why she never opened a bakery or restaurant."

Morgan leveled a pointed look on her. "You mean beside the fact that Flavia forced her to leave twenty years ago?"

Briar considered that. "Fair argument."

With a forkful of mac-and-cheese poised near my mouth, I said, "Reeva told me that she's thinking about opening a diner."

"Someplace else for breakfast?" Morgan asked. "A little competition for Wesley? I'd vote yes for that proposal."

I stared as Morgan loaded her plate with a generous serving of everything. "You can take seconds, you know."

"I will," she assured.

And she was serious too. Lately, she was either eating half her body weight or a nibble and was done. What was going on with that witch?

We all ate our fill and then sat back to talk about Samhain, which was only four short weeks from now. I could hardly wait to see Whispering Pines decked out in its spooky Halloween finest. When our stomachs had settled a little, Briar brought out the apple cake and two mooncakes. When she split the mooncakes open to reveal the deep orange salted egg moon in the middle of the black sesame paste sky, Tripp gasped.

"I packed up one of each flavor for you to take home," Briar told us.

"Oh good. I never got to try them the other day." I popped a bite of apple cake in my mouth and my eyes rolled back.

After dessert, we stayed, chatting and laughing until Briar started drifting off in her chair. We had just stood to leave when Meeka came racing down the pathway, Morgan's all-black rooster Pitch closing in fast. Meeka hid behind Tripp as Pitch tried to nip her tail.

"We can come back to help more with the garden if you'd like," I told Morgan.

"There's still quite a bit to do, so if you have time, we'll gladly accept the help. And Pitch loves having a playmate." She walked us through the cottage to the front door and gave us both hugs good night. "Blessed be, both of you."

We rode the short distance home from the Barlow's in comfortable silence. My thoughts drifted to Gin and how fragile life could be. It made me appreciative of all that I had. Despite some rather minor frustrations, my life was indeed blessed.

"What are you so deep in thought about?" Tripp asked as he walked me up to my apartment.

I glanced over my shoulder at the B&B, up at my boathouse apartment, and then out at the waning moonlight reflecting off the lake. My life was good and would get even better if I'd quit fighting some things. One big thing in particular.

"I have something for you." I reached into my jeans

pocket and pulled out a key I'd been carrying around all day. While drying my hair that morning, I realized Lily Grace's visions could sometimes be nudges as well as predictors. Now was the time to act on it. "Doesn't seem fair that I can get into your house whenever I want, but you can't get into mine."

Tripp stared at the key in his palm. "Wow. This is a pretty big step. Are you sure?"

"It's just a key." I tried to sound casual as my heart started racing double-time. What did he think it meant? "It's not that big of a deal."

But it kind of was.

"I know," he said, but his tone was playful. He wasn't taking my not a big deal claim seriously.

"I mean it. Not a big—"

He took a half step forward, standing close enough now that I could feel his body heat. Then he gazed down at me in that way that not only made me forget what I was saying, my insides went gooey. That gaze made me feel wanted, loved, and secure all at the same time. It made me know for certain that there was no place else in the world I'd rather be than right here with him.

"Best present ever." He kissed me with tender passion, one hand cupping the back of my head, and then pulled away and headed for the stairs. "See you tomorrow." Just before descending, he stopped and held out the key between his thumb and index finger then gave me that smirk that brought out a dimple on his left cheek. "Or maybe sooner. Sleep well, Jayne."

Suspense and fantasy author Shawn McGuire loves creating characters and places her fans want to return to again and again. She started writing after seeing the first Star Wars movie (that's episode IV) as a kid. She couldn't wait for the next installment to come out so wrote her own. Sadly, those notebooks are long lost, but her desire to tell a tale is as strong now as it was then. She lives in Wisconsin near the beautiful Mississippi River and when not writing or reading, she might be baking, crafting, going for a long walk, or nibbling really dark chocolate.

Made in the USA
Coppell, TX
25 April 2025

48688874R00163